CHOOSE YOUR
PARENTS WISELY

A novel by
TOM TROTT

<u>Brighton's No.1 Private Detective</u>

You Can't Make Old Friends
Choose Your Parents Wisely
It Never Goes Away

<u>Other books by Tom Trott</u>

The Benevolent Dictator

for my parents,
but don't take it personally

PROLOGUE

THE MOST TERRIFYING moment of childhood is when you discover your parents are only human. They are fallible. They make mistakes. The moment is always the same: some minor catastrophe, and they don't know what to do. Panic simmers beneath the surface. It is terrifying because it's their job to protect you. But the situation is resolved, somehow. The moment ends.

Beyond the moment, a greater horror dawns. It used to be reassuring to know that you would grow up. Grow up to be sure of things, like they were. But now you know that maybe you won't ever grow out of being the terrified, tired, desperate person that you are...

Sparks crackled from his lighter. He knew the truth was here somewhere, in the darkness. Hidden amongst the broken windows, and the dirt, and the rats.

He crunched his way through the place, stepping over

jagged steel, ducking through collapsed frames, up and down stairs, rusty bolts screaming in agony.

The feeble orange glow of the lighter gave him a dancing bubble of light, revealing straight steel, curved steel, bolts, glass, the word "DANGER" painted in black; details without context, until he was lost in darkness. But he was not alone.

In the middle of the void was a steel trapdoor. The chill wind played a tune across it. He tried to wrench it open but it wouldn't move.

Fumbling in the swaying light he could see a padlock. He grabbed one of the iron bars that were rusting away on the floor, making sure not to let iron splinters through his gloves, and swung as hard as he could. It pinged off without resistance and flew away into the darkness as though it wanted to give up its secrets. To be absolved of its sins. It was just an innocent padlock, it hadn't asked to be part of this.

It took everything he had left to lift the rusted door. The little flame flickered in the air that escaped. Or was it the breeze? Cold night rain was dripping through the obliterated roof, plummeting seven storeys down. All he could see in the flickering glow was bricks, and steel steps leading down into the crypt. His hand was shaking, but he convinced himself it was only the cold, and stepped down into the darkness…

I

Tell Me About This Fucking Girl

MR VOGELI had said eight o'clock. He had said eight, and I had waited around till then because he was Swiss and in my warped mind that meant that he might have money. He had definitely said eight o'clock. He couldn't do any other time, it had to be eight o'clock. I had waited until nine, and then some time after that I fell asleep. Now it was ten o'clock, time to give up and go home.

I was stuck to the chair. A heatwave had struck the south coast, and Brighton was bearing the brunt of it. This was the hottest year on record, maybe the environmentalists had a point. It was ten o'clock at night and it was too damn hot. When I got home I had an idea to run a cold bath and sleep in it. Or maybe a shower, that way I wouldn't drown.

I swivelled round lazily and looked out through the blinds, into the Lanes. They were still bursting with tourists who only wore clothes because they had to, packed tight, like fatty deposits in the city's arteries. Being the height of summer the sky was still pale blue, and people hadn't yet been reminded they had to go to work tomorrow. Or maybe they didn't, what day was it again? Maybe it was Friday actually, in which case I couldn't blame them. Who could sleep in this heat anyway?

I could hear small, distant voices from the outer office so I peeled myself off the chair and staggered through the door. It was Thalia, she had dutifully waited too and was watching something on the laptop.

'Are we calling it a day?' she asked.

'You didn't need to stay.'

'Neither did you.'

'Except it's my job.'

'And my job is to assist you. How would you feel if Mr Vogeli arrived and your assistant wasn't here to greet him?'

'Secretary.'

'That's not what it says on the stationery.'

'Yeah, but you order the stationery.'

'Of course: I'm your assistant.'

This argument would keep for tomorrow.

'They still haven't found her,' she mused, talking

4

about what she was watching.

'Really?' I responded automatically, still thinking about Mr Vogeli.

'Is there nothing you can do to help, Joe?'

'Help who?'

'The girl.'

'What girl?'

'What do you mean, "what girl?"' she asked incredulously, 'Haven't you been watching the news?'

'No.'

'I leave the paper on your desk every day, have you looked at it at all?'

'No.'

There was a loud knocking on the downstairs door, the one onto the street. More like a loud thumping. *Mr Vogeli at last!* I opened the door to the landing, the one with the rippled glass that reads 'J. GRABARZ, No.1 Private Detective', and called down.

'It's open!' I yelled. Then I retreated back into the reception room.

A worrying number of footsteps thundered up the stairs. His message had suggested it was just him coming, not the entire Swiss Guard.

'I thought the Swiss were known for their punctuality,' I said loudly enough for him to hear me.

Then the door opened and four men around my age, or maybe older, marched into the room. They were wearing polo shirts with vomit-inducing combinations

5

of stripes; pink and blue, peppermint and white; you probably *could* throw up on them and no one would be able to tell.

They were unmistakably local, with their shorn heads and their gold-effect watches. They had the smell of those pathetic types with the vain fantasy that they're good at golf. And the even bigger fantasy that if they *were* good at golf someone somewhere would give a shit.

Most obviously of all, they were not Mr Vogeli.

'Who the fuck are you?' I asked politely.

The one who seemed to be the ringleader squared up to me, getting incredibly close and trying to make much more of the extra half-an-inch he had on me.

'We're looking for joy. We're going to search this place.'

I was confused, and I looked it too. 'You're looking for joy?'

'If she's not here there'll be no problem.'

A woman. Judging by the look of them, I hoped they didn't find her. 'You won't find any Joy here.'

'Sorry if I don't take your word for it,' he sneered.

'Somehow I don't believe you are. Who the fuck is Joy, and, I repeat, who the fuck are you?'

'Joy Tothova, who the fuck else!?'

'Lovely name, what's it got to do with me?'

'That council bloke on the radio said if everyone just searches the house next door, we'll be able to find her

6

straight away. That's what we're doing.'

'You live next door, really? I thought it was a sweet shop.'

'We work round here.' Before I could interrupt: 'Not at the sweet shop.'

He gave me and the office a thorough examination. 'You're the bloke no one knows. Who exactly are you? We hardly see you come in and out, you're here late, and we've no idea what the fuck you do.'

I looked toward my door, the one that answers those questions. What more was there to do? Still, their ignorance was insulting even in people as stupid as them. I wasn't famous, I never got stopped in the street, but in a town this size some people at least used to know my name.

'And who are you?' I asked.

'Just good citizens.'

I took a moment to look at them, one of them was raising his eyebrows at Thalia in a suggestive way. That really pissed me off.

'Get out of my office.'

They weren't threatened by me at all. The leader nodded to the others and they jumped on me. I elbowed one of them in the stomach, trying to get free, but they were holding me down. I managed to make enough of a fuss to lose my dignity, but not enough to get free. After less than twenty seconds they relaxed and I jumped back up. It had only taken him that long to search the place. After all, where was there to look?

'She's not here,' he barked.

'What a shame,' I added caustically, 'you could have been heroes.'

He looked at Thalia with his best impression of charm. 'Why do you work for this arsehole, darling?'

She didn't say anything, she didn't react at all.

'Come on,' he said to his bunch of bastards, and they sauntered out of the room, taking sarcastic glee in carefully closing the door behind them.

I felt ruffled. And I felt humiliated. And I don't like either of those feelings. Which meant I had to know what was going on. I glared at Thalia, who was trying not to feel bad for me.

'Tell me about this fucking girl.'

I had wanted her to give me a brief summary, but apparently she wasn't going to sit there and explain the damn thing. She dusted off the papers from the bin and told me to read them for once.

Inside my flat at last, I stripped completely naked and opened both windows. That's right, *both* windows, that's how tragic my life is. I was giving the air the chance to cool me down but it didn't want to know. It only came inside to find somewhere to die, and sat there going stale like a marsh.

I seriously considered my shower idea but instead I

just laid on the bed sheet. It wasn't enough but it was all I could manage so I went about reading the rags.

The headline on Wednesday's evening edition was 'GIRL MISSING', which was at least to the point. There was a photo of her on the front page: white, blonde, smiling, rosy cheeks and freckles. It had been done in a studio, one of those smug-shots that always hang on people's stairs. Only it wasn't irritating in this case. She looked like a lovely girl. The caption underneath read "Joy Tothova, missing since this morning".

The actual article was a surprisingly scant one for a front page story, and read more like a police report: "Joy Tothova went missing today, in the Fiveways area of Brighton. Eight years old, Joy is around 4ft 1in (124cm), athletic, with long blonde hair. She has blue eyes and freckles. She was wearing a blue t-shirt and black ¾ length leggings with white trainers."

And that was it, pretty much. It looked like the paper had picked up a press release just before their deadline. It was odd, disappearances are almost never reported until the next day. I mean, how do you know it's a disappearance until then? They might just be out late. Not at eight years old, obviously, but still you'd have to work hard to get the police to give a shit before it gets dark. In this case, I couldn't help being suspicious that the girl wouldn't be on the front page if she wasn't so photogenic.

I folded the paper and aimed it at the bin just beyond my feet. It went in but knocked it over. I would clean it up tomorrow, I was too tired, and I was probably stuck to the bed already.

The next day the hacks had mobilised. The headline screamed: "FIND OUR BEAUTFUL GIRL" and slightly smaller, "PLEAD PARENTS OF MISSING 8-YEAR-OLD". Now they had plenty of pictures, and they ran a profile of the girl over the inside two pages, even before the usual contents and weather and whatever other crap they pad out the adverts with.

Apparently, Joy was not only a medal-winning school athlete but an A* pupil too. The article interviewed the poor parents, who apparently "struggled through stories of their cherished little girl with an admirably British stiff upper lip". I checked the byline, that kind of snivelling, faux-Romantic, inappropriately patriotic drivel had to be written by Bill Harker. It was. If there was one person who didn't give a shit about shoving his tape recorder in your face, it is was Bill Harker. I called him "Hacker", it seemed appropriate.

I skipped the rest of his piece, which was the majority of the coverage, only catching the end of it: "with no news of Joy, thoughts naturally turn to uncomfortable nightmare scenarios, such as paedophile sex rings." *Your thoughts, Bill. Your thoughts.*

Hacker was a scaremonger, and it always irritated me that this was how you had to get the news. I tossed the rag near the toppled bin and picked up Thursday's evening edition. It was the same, so I tossed that too.

Finally, I picked up today's morning edition. We didn't have an evening edition for some reason. Maybe they had sold out; those thugs had bought them all.

"KIDNAP MUM SLAMS 'LAZY' POLICE" it said in big letters, above the same photogenic picture of Joy they had run on Wednesday, and underneath, "MOTHER SAYS PLOD WASTING TIME IN HUNT FOR MISSING DAUGHTER".

The story had taken a nasty turn. Joy's mother, Maria Tothova, claimed "the police are refusing to investigate Joy's abduction" and instead "insist that she is likely to have run away". She told of how Joy's friends' families had been questioned, their houses searched, rather than questioning "known criminals" and "known paedophiles".

The Senior Investigating Officer, one DI Richard Daye, was quoted as saying that "no rock would be left unturned" in the search for Joy, which made her sound worryingly like lost car keys.

The thing that really upset the parents though, and that Hacker mocked with glee, was Daye's professional opinion that "there are no signs Joy has been abducted". How, Bill was keen to ask, could there be no signs? Surely the fact that she was missing was a big one!

I knew Daye, and had a lot of respect for him; he was all detective. But you can't be all detective anymore, you have to be part politician. He didn't play well under scrutiny, on camera, he was much better left alone to do his job, and that was never going to happen. This world was now for the media savvy, not dinosaurs like Daye.

He should have been a shamus like me, I'm under nobody's microscope. But no, he was too straight for that. Too decent. He had dedicated himself to police work, made a dent in the evil of the world, and for that they would prise his fingers off the doorframe like they did with all retirees. They ought to give him a medal or something, but they wouldn't. Maybe I should institute my own: The Joe Grabarz Medal For Lifetime Service; he started good and he ended good. It sounds easy, but how many manage it?

That was the last of it for now, I couldn't believe it was enough to whip people up into a frenzy. And who was this councillor encouraging people to search their neighbours' houses? I bet the police loved him, even more than they loved me. Maybe it was the heat that had done it.

It was smothering me now, so I peeled myself up off the bed, stood the bin back up, and then threw some water at my face. I patted some more water all over my neck, chest, and back and stood by the window again. The night had finally managed to summon a breeze and I let what little air there was blast chill me. Damn, that felt good, it was the first time I had been cool all day.

I could hear a low whistling from the flat rooves that my hovel and all the others looked onto. It sounded like a chew toy, but plaintive. A baby seagull. He kept whistling, again and again. It took effort every time and they became cracked and faint. He was calling to his parents, but he didn't seem to be getting any answer. I could just about see his silhouette near a chimney. The silhouette never moved, but the whistling carried on.

I wandered to the other window and looked out onto Preston Circus, to the Fire Station and the cinema. Taxis were still humming along the road, drunk people still stumbling around, wailing sirens drifting from the centre on the hot air. The sky was black now but the city was awash with twinkling lights, from Kemptown to the pier to West Street, Brighton in the summer never closes. The party never ends.

2

Professional Curiosity

THE OLD MAN'S FACE slipped away from me. Falling in slow motion. Down into the water. Then under the waves, shimmering, until it faded into the darkness...

I woke up in a cold sweat. It had been the same dream again. But what concerned me more was how on earth my sweat managed to be cold in this heat. I could feel it behind the blinds, waiting to break in with the new day.

I pushed myself up off the mattress and stumbled into the shower. I made it as cold as possible, I figured that I could top up on cold now and then maybe it would last me some of the day.

Once dressed I opened my door and walked down one flight of stairs to the black plastic box where the first person up is obliged to put the post.

The front page of the weekend edition was a bit different from the last three days: "BUS FARES TO RISE <u>AGAIN</u>".

Back upstairs, with avocado toast and orange juice already on the go, I made an espresso in the little one-person macchinetta I had bought from the Open Market. I had recently been converted to making proper coffee at home by having too many posh ones out. After that, anything you make cheaply at home looks and tastes like charcoal.

Once I had let the sharp, dark nectar, slap me round the mouth a few times, I took my first proper look at the rag. There was nothing on the front about the girl. I guess there was nothing new to print. No scandal yet. Perfect parents, perfect daughter; brilliant for a breaking story, but terrible for follow-up.

All the way on page five was an article headed "MISSING GIRL: POLICE AND PARENTS TO HOLD PRESS CONFERENCE". The article said the press conference would be held at their house on York Avenue, Hove, at eleven o'clock.

I went back to the bedroom and looked out at the flat rooves. The baby seagull was still there. Still alone. In the morning light I could see how fluffy he was, how comical. How innocent. *Poor thing*. I grabbed a slice of bread and threw it onto the rooves. He'd find it eventually.

York Avenue, Hove? I ummed and ahhed. It was only just over the train line, twenty minutes' walk. What was the time now? 10:35. I could always take a look…

It was another sunny Saturday, and it was no surprise that the Circus was already clogged to a standstill with tourists desperate for their square foot of beach space. If they weren't honking they were blaring the radio out of their open windows, or trying to keep their kids well behaved for just a few more minutes. They didn't know it would take them another hour to reach the sea. And then there wouldn't be anywhere to park. *Turn around now*, I felt like telling them all as I breezed past on the pavement. But they wouldn't listen. Tourists in Brighton are the maddest creatures in the world.

York Avenue is in Hove, and as a result is incredibly civilised. It sums up the city perfectly that the road is a mixture of 1930s half-rendered palaces and ugly blocks of social housing. Of course, many of the houses are now carved up into two or three flats, but if, like the Tothovas, you were lucky enough to own a whole one, you had something really special. A black and white tiled walk to a central stained glass door, and only marginally less rooms than the Pavilion.

It was in front of this palace that a long table had

been placed on the pavement, chairs behind, with Sussex Police backboards behind them. No one was at the table yet except a technician setting up the microphones. There were television cameras trained on him, and behind them a gaggle of journalists variously preparing notepads, laptops, and all manner of recording devices. Pushing in on them from all sides were concerned neighbours, panicked residents desperate to help, and anyone else getting off on the excitement and the misery of it all. Together, there must have been at least a hundred people. They had shut the road for it.

Some way to the side, leaning on a junction box and looking almost painfully relaxed was Clarence Alderney, in his cream suit and with his ivory topped cane as always. Clarence was the private dick the rich went to, because he dressed smartly and spoke clearly, unlike me. He was second-generation Sri Lankan Tamil, and I always thought he dressed like a member of the Raj to reassure any older, institutionally racist clients who, despite their bigotry, paid the best.

Standing next to him, as relaxed as a coiled spring, was Perry Clyde, a big bald bastard of a private eye, the other end of the spectrum because he didn't mind working for criminals. In fact, I think he probably preferred it. I was the middle of that spectrum, we were it.

'Hello,' Clarence said with some surprise as I wandered toward them.

'Morning, Clarence,' I replied, 'Perry.'

Perry just nodded back.

'I'm surprised to see you here,' mused Clarence, 'I didn't think you'd be interested.'

'They're not clients of yours, are they? I know they're not Perry's.'

'No.'

I shrugged. 'If you're interested and Perry's interested, what made you think I wouldn't be?'

'I don't know, the time of day?' he said with a smile.

Clarence was a nice person, I could always see why the rich liked him. But it was also the reason he couldn't handle my cases. That was a good thing, I suppose, it meant we were never in competition. Heaven forbid, a fourth detective would turn up in Brighton, then there might be some rivalries.

I leaned on the junction box, scanning the crowd like the other two. Us cool kids at the back of the bus.

Half of the crowd had sunglasses on, protecting them from our detective's analysis. We three had sunglasses on too, protecting ourselves, and giving us the opportunity to scan as much as we wanted.

The people milling around were of one type, they seemed to know each other. People would regularly spot someone, wave, and then scooch through gaps to air kiss and conspire quietly. Was attendance here organised? Was Facebook and Twitter abuzz with civilian action, and theories about who did it? I was buggered if I knew, I barely knew what a Facebook was.

Thalia would know.

It almost made me sick to see how much attention this was getting. Not because people shouldn't care, but because it was so selective. People didn't always give a shit about a missing girl, I could testify to that.

'Look at this!' a voice half shouted over the bustle. It was Hacker, with his pallid face, red drunk's-nose, stained suit, and vomit inducing teeth. And breath, my god, you could smell him a mile away the second he opened his mouth. He looked like a corpse that had been found bloated in a whisky barrel.

'All three of you together,' he screeched, 'I've got a headline for this: BRIGHTON BOTTOM FEEDERS UNITE TO CATCH KIDNAPPER.'

'Fuck off, Bill,' was all Perry needed to say, and with a cackle to himself Hacker headed through the crowd.

'Right,' Perry announced out of nowhere, 'I'll be back in a bit,' and he disappeared.

'Where's he going?' I asked.

'No idea, maybe he's going to buff his head in case Bill snaps a photo.'

I laughed quietly, more out of politeness than anything else. Then a thought struck me. I snapped up his wooden cane and before he could stop me, broke it over my knee into two clean pieces.

Clarence jumped up and frowned as though he would hit me if he was anyone else. But he doesn't do those kind of things.

'That's for sending my financials to that bastard lawyer,' I told him.

A few months ago Clarence had turned over my bank statements for a client of his. He was lucky he had a broken cane and not a broken nose.

He nodded gently, and after he had taken the two halves, held out a hand for me to shake. Which I did. We understood each other, I think.

Suddenly the crowd hummed into life, like an orchestra tuning up. Flashes popped, despite the day being about as bright as it could ever be, and the cameras rolled. Journalists, like sharks, can sense blood in the water from a mile away. It was 11:07.

First out of the door were two uniformed officers; followed by Roy Parker, the Chief Superintendent, who hates me; and then by DCI Noël "Penny" Price, who hates me about as much as it is possible for one human to hate another.

Following them as they headed swiftly to the table, I got my first glimpse of the Tothovas. Mummy Tothova was a very healthy looking woman in her early forties. She had fantastic skin, and was very slim, with long blonde hair, and an oversized poncho made of some rough, unprocessed material, giving her the overall impression of one of those middle class vegetarian, or possibly vegan, charity-volunteering angels, who you just know wouldn't be so angelic if they'd been raised in Whitehawk and not Hove.

Daddy Tothova was also forty-something, but a little older than her, with glasses and a half-balding scalp. His shirt was white with blue lines making a grid like maths paper. The type worn by those boring people who desperately think they should have an imagination and so are not confident enough to wear a plain white shirt. The sort of shirt you only have to add some variety to your wardrobe. Your second, third, or fourth choice shirt. Your Thursday shirt. Except today was Saturday.

They all shuffled along behind the tables, into shot, with the chief in the middle, and Price at his side. There was no sign of Daye anywhere, they'd given him the push.

The chief begged everyone to be quiet, and then he began the conference by stating exactly what everyone had already deduced: that DI Daye had 'chosen to step aside' and that 'DCI Price was now in charge of the investigation.'

I doubted intensely that Daye had "chosen" to step aside, I was sure that he had been shoved aside, but it didn't make any difference now.

Then Parker handed over to Price, whose preamble was most notable for her use of the word 'abductor', making it plain to us all that she was taking this seriously, unlike Daye. I mean, she didn't say that, but she *was* saying it, if you get what I mean.

The world's only reluctant blonde bombshell had

just joined the Sussex force this year. Having made a name for herself in London, she had been drafted in to shake up the city. They all had big plans for her. Taking over this investigation, and doing it right, in the full exposure of the media, would be a great step forward in those plans.

As she continued, Clarence whispered in my ear, 'So what are you doing here, really?'

I gave him a sideways look, 'professional curiosity, same as you.'

'Sure. I believe you.'

His eyes were still on the press conference.

'Detective!' Hacker interrupted Price's flow, 'Do *you* believe that Joy has been abducted?'

Good question, Bill! At least he wasn't completely useless. And I guess I didn't mind his powers of evil being directed onto someone who deserved it. I enjoyed watching her squirm. Not that she really squirmed externally, but I could tell what was happening behind those solid slate eyes.

'Yes,' she said definitively, 'yes, I do.'

The print hacks, including Bill, all scratched this down into their pads. It was good for her to learn this early how valuable a commodity her words were. They were the word of God, heaven help her if they lost faith.

She continued, but again Clarence was whispering in my ear: 'Look at this.'

I didn't do anything.

He paused for a moment, and then his voice was lower, 'Look at it all.'

'What?'

'This is the biggest case of the year, even bigger than those legal highs.'

'All those deaths are worth less than this girl?'

'To these lot standing here, yes. Look around, how many of these were out on the streets when it was drug dealers and junkies getting killed? But one little girl and they're mobilised. Mark my words, twenty-sixteen is going to be the year that Joy Tothova disappeared.'

'I think that depends on whether we find her or not.'

'It's not good.'

'You'd rather they didn't care?'

'Maybe. It would be simpler.'

'True.'

He was overreacting. He was used to lost pearls and paying ex-wives to stay quiet.

'It's not good,' he whispered again, more to himself this time.

'Detective!' a young television journalist shouted, interrupting what had become an overlong diatribe about the police wanting the public's help, but warning that they should not take matters into their own hands, 'Do you have any new leads?' she pleaded.

'I will get to that in a minute,' Price said sternly, 'but as I was saying, Sussex Police does not endorse civilian house-searches, and any unlawful activity of this kind will be treated without sympathy.'

'What do you think about councillor McCready's statements on the radio yesterday?' Hacker shouted.

'Sussex Police does not comment about what councillors say on local radio.'

'What about you? What do you think?' another asked. This was getting a little rowdy.

She paused for a moment, before falling back on a tried and tested non-statement: 'I think his choice of words were unwise.'

The crowd bubbled up again like a saucepan on the boil, but she spoke over the top of them.

'However, we are very interested in the public's help in locating a vehicle seen in the Fiveways area Wednesday morning.'

She had cast a silencing spell on them. They were listening now, rapt, all eyes on her.

'A dark blue Ford Transit-style van. It was seen parked on Hythe Road at around eleven hundred hours.'

'Is this van believed to have been used in the abduction?' a journo shouted.

'It is one of many lines of enquiry we are pursuing.'

The hacks kept on with more questions, but they weren't very interesting. Clarence leaned in yet again.

'You don't own a blue van, do you?'

I tilted my head in his general direction.

'Just doing my bit. How about a bet?' he asked.

'A bet?'

'You do know what a bet is.'

'I'm trying to listen.'

'No you're not.'

'What are the terms?' I sighed.

'Terms?'

'The bet.'

'Well, I find the girl, or at least find the lead, and you have to replace my stick.'

'That terrible thing? I did you a favour.'

'The top of that "terrible thing", is Sri Lankan ivory.'

'Ivory is evil.'

'It's pre-1947.'

'Because it wasn't evil back then, was it?'

'This is a piece of my history. It's a reminder of what your ancestors did to mine.'

'I don't even know who my ancestors were.'

'You're white, aren't you?'

'Probably.'

'Well, you are compared to me.'

I couldn't help smiling at that. I had a bit more respect for Clarence, I always thought he dressed like he did to look, frankly, less Asian. But instead it was the opposite, it was part of his proud heritage. Good for him. I wish I had some of that.

'No deal,' I said.

'Chicken.'

'I'm not looking for the girl. Like I said, I'm just here out of professional curiosity.'

'Yeah, yeah, I heard you the first time.'

By this point Price had passed over to the father, and he began an emotional appeal to anyone who had information about their daughter.

As the mother wept silently, some in the crowd looked at their feet, ashamed at having turned up to this circus of exploitation. Others were drawn in closer. Camerapersons were fiddling; they had to be changing either the framing or the focus to make sure they got her in. *Cry for the camera, dear.*

Then she did something unscripted: 'Someone has our little girl,' she said rather more loudly than anyone was expecting, 'please,' she looked into the cameras, 'if you have Joy, let her go.' Then she buried her head into her husband's chest. Cameras flashed madly.

'We won't be taking any more questions at this time,' the chief said in an effort to control the situation. Time to shut this down.

'We have a signed legal document,' the dad said out of nowhere as he pulled an envelope from his pocket. No one, least of all Parker and Price, appeared to have any idea what he was doing.

Both dad and mum stood up in front of the cameras as dad pulled a piece of paper from the envelope. I was too far away to get any sense of what it was.

'This document,' he continued, 'offers a monetary

reward to whoever finds Joy,' the crowd began to simmer, 'of one hundred thousand pounds.'

Then the crowd exploded.

It was chaos. The chief was saying something, trying to take control, but you couldn't hear a word of it. And all you could see was the parents, the document held out between them, being snapped by every camera and smartphone within a hundred metres. Then they were surrounded, hidden from view.

After some valiant moments trying to stop the frenzy, Chief Parker managed to usher both parents away from the cameras, back inside the house.

That moment was like a gunshot going off and suddenly the journalists were scattering like frightened birds. Only they weren't frightened, they were all rushing to their offices or their cars or their whatever. They were excited. They had to get on this now.

Standing next to me was a quizzical smirk. And attached to it, Clarence Alderney:

'Still just here out of professional curiosity?'

3

The Red Mark

ELEVEN YEARS AGO, I was a dickhead. After leaving school, or being thrown out, depending on how you look at it, I survived by doing the only thing I was good at. I'd learnt to pick locks at school, and in care, so I could get out of places. It was only when I needed somewhere to sleep off the streets that it became handy to get *into* places.

Back then the only things I had in my possession were clothes, cigarettes, one lighter, one beard, and my moped; and any money I ever managed to have was spent on the thimble of petrol it used. If there was a world championship for couch-surfing I would have won every discipline. I would squeeze anyone I vaguely knew for a bed, just for a few nights, but then I would stretch it out and out until I used up every last morsel of their patience and hospitality. When I think about myself then, I get a violent twitch in my stomach.

I would cycle through the list of kind people I knew, and when I couldn't get anywhere I would squat. This is where the lock picking came in. It could be a shut-up pub, or a flat above a shop, anything vacant, often secured with a padlock. I would pick my way in and bed-up for the night.

But the problem with squatting is you have to buy your own food. In care, and with a million foster families I had always been catered for. But now I had to pay for it myself, so I decided to sell some of the stuff that was lying around in the squats. No one would miss it. And it was never much, but it could be some copper or something else. This would be enough to keep me in hamburgers for a few more days.

For some people it's a lifestyle choice, but I never wanted to squat for more than a few days. The problem was that as soon as the lock was gone you were joined by a million other lowlifes. I was offered a lot of interesting substances.

The problem with money is that you can never survive with less. And although I was soon back in the cycle of couch-surfing, I needed money for... well, I don't know what for, I just needed it.

And so I started stealing from the people who were kind enough to offer me a bed. Now, if you're looking for tips, this is a really good way to lose all your friends.

To be clear, they didn't ever tell me they knew, they were just keen to get me out of their place, and then they never let me stay there again. They were always busy.

So soon I needed my own place to live, and the only skill I had to pay the rent with was housebreaking. So I started in proper, and I sold my haul to a bloke known as Big Dave; because he was called Dave and he was a fat son of a bitch. I really got good at it; soon I was one of his regulars.

But one day a policeman came knocking. One of my victims had a very nosey neighbour who had seen me turn up on my moped and disappear round the back of the house. The sharp old crone had taken down the plate, and by chance a PCSO had spotted it round the back of my flat. The neighbour identified me. They fingerprinted me, and it was a match for prints found on the gate and window frame, from before I had put my gloves on. Call me stupid, but I didn't think they'd bother to check the outside.

So I was charged, and it went to court. But at that point my legal aid lawyer managed to convince the magistrate that because my prints were only found on the *outside* of the house, there was really no evidence to support a charge of breaking and entering, and therefore nothing to demonstrate that I was the one who had nicked all their stuff. I had already fenced it, thank god.

Once she had painted a picture of the long and costly trial this would precipitate, I was let off. I remember flinching in anticipation of the charging DI's protestations, but he said nothing. As I was marched out of the court I watched him watching me. He was as calm as ever, his marble face regarding me as placidly as the statues in the lobby.

I had got away with my tail burnt, and I made a solemn vow to never return to that world. Never. I tried for three whole weeks to find myself a job, an honest job, but no one wanted to hire me. And I was lazy. And I didn't really know how to do anything else.

Since having it searched by police, I had lost my flat. The landlord, who I'm pretty sure was running rent boys, didn't want that kind of attention. I was squatting in a boarded-up shop, and I had to dig a little deeper every night to survive the creeping cold of an autumn that was far too eager to be winter. So when I heard from Juliet Camfield that her parents were spending a fortnight at their Spanish villa, I found myself riding over to theirs.

The Camfields had been one of my many foster parents, and as you can guess from anyone with a daughter named Juliet, they were quite well off. They had a house on Osborne Road, and the place looked like a fairy tale to me as the cold November rain made it through my charity shop clothes. My lazy beard was tighter knit than my scarf, and both were drenched, icy droplets clinging to my neck, making me shiver so violently I almost lost control of the bike. I really wanted to use their shower once I'd broken in, but that would leave prints everywhere, and I couldn't do that again. Although, at least in prison they would clothe me and feed me. I would even have a mattress.

I parked my moped at the end of the road this time and ran as fast as I could to the house, soaking my thin shoes in deep puddles. The living room curtains were drawn, which I thought was odd if they were away, so I kept quiet and careful as I tiptoed down the side alley.

Peering in through the kitchen window, I could hardly see anything, but there didn't appear to be anyone home. Everything was tidy and put away. No crumbs on the side.

Standing at the back door I pulled off my sodden fingerless gloves and pulled on a pair of cheap latex ones, then I slipped the fingerless ones back over the top. That's how horribly affected I was. The door was just a flimsy wooden one, I could bow the frame enough to pop the bolt out just by slipping my flick knife into the gap and twisting it. There was a click, and the door popped open an inch. But I froze.

The rain pattered on the tin lid of a compost bin. The occasional car sluiced down the road. But the only sound I could hear was my better instincts echoing at the back of my skull: *I shouldn't be doing this.*

Something jingled behind me. I turned and

watched a ginger cat shoot out of next door's fence, dart across the garden, and disappear again. It was so damn middle class here. Nothing bad could ever happen in this neighbourhood. I had a lot of happy memories here. Happy for me, at least, maybe not for the Camfields.

When I turned back to the house, two wide green eyes were staring at me! It was Poppy, the Camfields' cat, her black body hidden in the reflection on the glass. Her face disappeared, then reappeared poking out the gap of the open door, cautiously studying the rain.

My better instincts were still there, but I was able to shout them down, I'd had a lot of experience at that. So I pushed Poppy back with my leg as I slipped in and shut the door behind me.

The door rattled. It probably did that before but it leant the empty house an eerie atmosphere. *Still, what I wouldn't give for a house like this.* It almost made me want to cry, that longing for domesticity, for something I could never have. Not my own longing, but a longing that had been planted there by a thousand adverts and a thousand happy families. At least, happy in the windows that face the street.

Poppy curled her way between my legs, I wondered if she remembered me. I hadn't been here since I was eight, or nine-ish, I think. *Wait a minute…* Poppy was ten back then, that would make her twenty-two or twenty-three? That's not impossible for a cat, but this one didn't look that old.

She jumped up onto the kitchen surface to try and claw at my face for attention. Then she sniffed at the butter dish on the side. She pawed at the glass lid, trying to get it off, so I picked up whatever new cat this was and put her back on the floor.

I kneeled down and stroked her. She was fussing over me like mad, I wondered who was feeding her whilst the Camfields were away. And whether they would suddenly come in the door.

As it was at the moment, the cat didn't have any food, so I asked it, 'Where's your food?'

It meowed.

'Where is it?' I cooed in a voice that was fast becoming silly.

Amazingly it seemed to understand me and scratched at the cupboard under the sink.

I found sachets inside and squeezed one into a bowl. A thick slab of jelly and meat slopped out and the cat went to town. She tried to get her head in front of my hands whilst I was still squeezing out the last chunks, which meant she ended up with some on her head, but she didn't seem to care.

I stood up and in the process spotted the butter again. It should really be in a cupboard at least. *It should be, shouldn't it?*

I instinctively washed my fingers, which just reminded me I was wearing the latex gloves. I was here to rob the place, not feed the cat. So, I headed into the living room to see what the situation was.

I stepped into the dark, curtains-drawn living room half thinking about the butter, about why it was left on the side, but I stopped thinking the second I switched the lights on.

'Thanks for feeding Mishka.'

The house certainly wasn't empty. Not by a long shot. Sitting in the living room, in a semi-circle, all staring at me, were women I recognised. And one I didn't. It was like a dream. It was difficult to place them out of context, who were these women that I knew so well? Then after what seemed like ages, but was probably only a couple of seconds, my memory dredged up the names Elaine Sweet, Shalini Navaratnam, Debra Steinicke, and the list went on. Every foster mum I had ever had. Practically. And the one other woman I didn't recognise. This all flashed through my head in about five seconds, and then I turned back by instinct, but Rita Tiernan had shut the door behind me.

I looked to the middle of them, where Theresa Camfield was sitting on a sofa that was effectively the head of the table. It was her who had spoken.

'There's no need to be scared, Joe. Take a seat.'

There didn't seem anything else to do, so I did what she suggested, sinking into a corner armchair, but all the time desperately trying to think of another way to escape. *What the fuck is going on?*

The living room was as tasteful as ever. A deep blue feature wall, and the rest neutral tones. A white painted fireplace, with a pile of logs ready to be lit. On the mantelpiece various ethnic-knacks collected from travels to poorer parts of the world in a form of postmodern colonialism. And there was art on the walls. Not photographs, art. That's how you knew they were posh.

Theresa was a stocky woman, very outdoorsy. They owned a horse that was stabled up near Steyning. That sort of family. City jobs, but if you met them on holiday you'd think they lived in a country village somewhere. She was the sort of woman who could break a finger, strap it up, and not visit the doctor for three days. She had a ruddy complexion, and a big hearty laugh. But she wasn't laughing now. Everyone was very serious.

'Would you like a drink?' she asked.

'A beer would great,' I said.

She was momentarily motionless, she hadn't been offering alcohol. She didn't approve of alcohol outside of a special occasion. Not even on a wet evening like this. But then she nodded to Rita who headed into the kitchen.

My earliest memory is Rita picking me up under my arms and carrying me to the toilet. I had shit my pants, which was all I was wearing, and she calmly carried me to the loo. I was about three or four. When I remember it, I remember seeing myself, seeing her carry me, as though I was someone else. Maybe I didn't remember it, maybe it was just my imagined version of something I was told. But in my imagined memory she was always lovely. She was my first mother, everything that had defined a mother for me, and therefore perfect. I think I loved her. But then her husband developed Parkinson's, and she had made a vow to look after him first, so I was jettisoned. He died a few years later. It was a traumatic time, but I was lucky to learn at five something that a lot of people only learn when it's too late: when things get tough, the only person who puts me first is me.

I heard the sound of a bottle being opened, and then it arrived in my left hand. I kept my eyes on Theresa even whilst I took a swig.

'I guess you're wondering what all this is about?' she asked.

I didn't answer. I don't like games.

'We have obviously set this up.'

'You mean this isn't your book club?' I joked.

They weren't amused, they were too tense. Plus it wasn't that witty, but I was younger then and I hadn't developed my best material yet.

'I told Juliet to tell you we were going away,' she continued. I had figured that out already.

'Did you tell her to fuck me?' All their eyes shot open. 'Or was that just a perk.' It was a horrible thing to say, I know that. But like I said: eleven years ago I was a dickhead.

Theresa bit her lip, thrown off by my vulgarity, so I decided to move us on myself:

'This is about her.' I nodded my head in the direction of the one I didn't recognise.

'What makes you think that?' Theresa asked.

'The only thing that connects you all is me, and I don't know who she is.'

The other mothers shared an impressed look.

Theresa just nodded. 'I said you were the man for the job.'

The woman I didn't recognise was middle-aged and South Asian, and she had her hair and neck covered. I had lived with the Navaratnams, but they were Sri Lankan, and were Christian, so I didn't have much to go on, but I guessed she was Muslim, and to my very untrained eye she looked Pakistani. Brighton has an even higher proportion of white people than the country as a whole, so unfortunately she rather stuck out in the room, despite Mrs Navaratnam being there; after all, as one of my foster mums she had become part of life's furniture.

I addressed her directly: 'I don't remember burgling you.'

They were less impressed now. The woman just looked to Theresa.

She shifted in her seat. 'Funny you should mention that. You went to court a few weeks ago, didn't you? How did that go?'

I raised my arms in some sort of shrug. 'I'm a free man, aren't I?'

'I'm glad to see that. Where are you living at the moment?'

I didn't answer, and just took a swig of my beer instead. It was generic. The sort that comes in big crates for dads and husbands who aren't allowed off down the pub anymore.

Theresa had taken off her watch and was slapping her hand with it. Out of frustration, I guess.

'Fine, let's get the point, shall we? You've always been a bit too smart for your own good, Joe.'

'Thank you.'

'I don't mean clever. I don't mean intelligent either, or knowledgeable. Just smart.'

'Cheers,' I drawled.

'Add to that, breaking into places. Asking awkward questions. Saying awkward things. Knowing all the wrong people. That makes you the person we need right now. Believe me, I wish it wasn't true.'

'I believe you.'

I took out a cigarette, one of my thin roll-ups, and lit it. I kept a Zippo lighter rather than using the cheap disposable ones. I guess I thought it was cool. It was a *bit* cool.

'I don't like people smoking in my house,' Theresa blurted.

'It's my very subtle way of telling you to hurry up. If

you're quick your house won't smell of smoke and I won't drop ash on your cream carpet.'

'Fine. There's not a subtle way of putting this—'

'Good,' I interrupted.

'Krishma here, helps with Juliet and me in the Children's Parade—'

'Lovely.'

'Her daughter's been kidnapped!' she shouted. Then she calmed down a bit.

I just took a drag on my cigarette.

'Ok?' She brandished her eyebrows at me. 'Do you understand what we want you to do?'

I took a moment to look at them all. What did they think I was, a P.I.?

'I thought you were going to ask me to break in somewhere.'

'What would we want with that?' she asked witheringly.

'I wouldn't want to know.'

I took in some more carcinogens and then I looked between them all. What *did* they want? This woman's daughter had been abducted. So call the police. I didn't remember reading about a missing girl, and I saw a lot of newspapers. Often they were my bed linen.

I studied Theresa, her tough face like an overcooked ham. She was the only mother who had ever smacked me. And only once. I was sitting at the bottom of the stairs, just outside this room, refusing to put my shoes on. She was stressed, I was insufferable. And she smacked me. It was wrong, but I put my shoes on. It took all my strength not to cry as I laced them up. Good practice. Another lesson learnt. I saw this one from outside as well, I could watch it happen, no longer happening to me.

Apart from that, Theresa had always been lovely. She became even more lovely after that, because of the guilt no doubt. But it was no good. I was trapped in that moment, the split second after the slap. As the red mark spread on my skin and my nerves fired. The shock. The pain. The betrayal. It was permanent.

This was a dream. My mothers sitting in judgement of me, of the things I had done. As though it was my fault! I was everything they had made me.

What the hell was going on? I could get by without being thrown random errands by this lot.

'I'll pass, thanks.'

'We'll pay you,' Theresa said.

'I should hope so. But I'll still pass, thanks.'

I downed the end of the bottle and stood up, cigarette stuck to my lip. 'Thanks for the beer,' then I nodded to them all, 'mothers.'

'If you leave I'll call the police.'

They seemed as shocked as I was. I stared at Theresa with a patronising expression, but it slowly faded. She wasn't bluffing. I *had* come here to rob her. I *had* broken in. Second time, how lucky could I be?

I slumped back down into the chair.

She didn't say anything, she just raised her eyebrows at me. At the stuck cigarette.

I posted the lit rollup into the empty bottle where it hissed and died, and locked onto her gaze.

'Tell me about this fucking girl.'

4

Good People, Bad Habits

AFTER THE PRESS CONFERENCE I headed back to my flat. Half of my mind was trying to figure out what angle to take, the other half was writing cheques I couldn't cash. About a hundred thousand pounds worth.

The money would be great, there was no point in denying it, but I had better reasons. Clarence was right: the whole situation was bad. And now her parents had turned their little girl into a golden ticket.

I re-read the papers to try and pick out the facts beneath the noise, but no one gets their news from the newspapers anymore so they've stopped printing it. They're nothing but speculation and provocative opinions, which not even the writer believes. It was all offal when I needed meat.

The only lead I had was the one everyone had: a blue van. If that was the way she was going to be found, it would be the police that found her. They had the manpower, ranks of men at their command. I had one tired, grouchy one, who didn't want to wear out his shoes or spend all his petrol money traipsing from address to address checking every blue van in the city.

No, if fate wanted me to find her, I would find her a different way.

There were still a couple of panda cars sitting outside, if pandas are silver with blue and yellow checks now. I guessed there would be a permanent presence inside the house, some sympathetic female officer to reassure them that everything would be ok. Or if things looked bad, just that they were doing everything they could. There were also a couple of other cars loitering, I guessed they were hacks. In some ways I was surprised there weren't more, but that said there was nowhere to park, and the places you could park were extortion.

Their house was opposite a block of flats and it had a little bit of tarmac out the front. I planted my Honda there and sat down next to it. Occasionally I would kneel down to make it look like I was servicing it, or cleaning it, or something, keeping my helmet on.

I studied their house, now I could see it without a crowd in front. There was nothing on the outside to say what kind of family they were; no "beware of the dog", no pile of wellies in the porch, no scummy tricycle in the front garden. Nothing in the front garden but shingle and a few smart, well behaved plants. It looked like a set, a studio backlot. Everything except the "#VoteRemain" poster forgotten about, or not forgotten about, in an upstairs window.

The house itself looked like a 1930s build, or thereabouts. Nothing too ostentatious, not one of the mock-Tudor monstrosities that, like all the richest suburbs, make up much of York Avenue. Instead, theirs was a house you could be proud of without boasting. A modest red brick, first floor rendered, tasteful stained glass panels above the windows and on the pastel-blue wooden door. I say blue, it was blue and green at the same time. The colour of a mermaid's tail.

The eight-storey flats I was parked under were ugly to the point where I was glad the reflections off the windows blinded me if I was foolish enough to look. When the sun slipped behind a cloud I could see "Vote Leave" posters, and ratty blinds behind all the windows but one. That other one was net curtains, narrowly parted, and behind them a pair of beady eyes that whipped away. A nosey neighbour. Every detective loves a nosey neighbour.

I waited for someone to exit and caught the door before it latched, then wandered up the three flights of stairs to what I thought was the right door. After I knocked, I heard some shuffling and then the door opened just an inch, the chain still on.

'Who's there?' squawked a jittery voice.

There were those beady eyes, moustache, and a screwed-up face to match. She must have been a hundred if she was a day.

'Hello, ma'am. I was wondering if I could speak to you.' I showed her a card that read "George Webster, Brighton & Hove City Council".

'What could you want to speak to me about?'

'It's about crime prevention madam, I just want to ask you a few questions.'

Those eyes of hers took me in. My clothes, my shoes, my attempted smile.

'Crime prevention!?' she shrieked, 'I wasn't born yesterday.'

I believed her.

'You're nosing around about those two over the road.'

I couldn't deny it, so I just stared at her.

'I'll make you a cup of tea.'

She took the chain off and shuffled out of sight. I followed inside, into her chintzy grotto. Where other people have photos of family, she had photos of the Royals. It was that cliché. Everything was pink and beige like rhubarb and custard. Antimacassars. Nest of tables. And dusty boiled sweets waiting in glass bowls for the fingers of children who never visit.

From the living room I could see down to the Tothovas' house, in fact it would give you an incredible vantage point into the front bedrooms. But at the moment those curtains were closed, just like every other room in the house. If you didn't know better you would think the place was empty.

'You don't take sugar, do you?' asked a voice over my shoulder. The crone had returned.

'Just as it comes,' I lied. 'Which room is that?'

She shuffled over quickly and glanced down for less than a second, 'Study on the left, girl's on the right.' Then she handed me my thimble of tea and shuffled to her chair with barely disguised agony.

The girl's bedroom. I wondered what I could see if those curtains were open. Price? Parker? PCs bagging teddy bears and clothes for the dogs?

'Do you know them?' I asked her.

'No. Seen plenty of 'em though.'

'Oh?'

I was leading her, and she picked up on it: "ere, what is it you do anyway? You're not from the paper are you? I don't want my name in there.'

'You haven't told me your name.'

She frowned, but in a way that made her look more satisfied. I sat in the chair nearest the window and smiled, doing my best to appear harmless.

'You see a lot of them, you said?'

'I'm not nosey,' she reassured me.

47

'Of course not. I understand, you're just looking out for your neighbourhood—'

'I'm not looking out for anyone,' she snapped. She tried to adjust the antimacassar behind her head but it was too far for her to twist so she gave up. 'It's all repeats on the telly, and my grandson won't visit anymore, so I spend a lot of my time just staring out there for something to do.'

She should buy a book, I thought. But then again, at her age she might have read them all.

'You can't look out that window without seeing them,' she added, just to make it even clearer that she was not a snooper.

'The papers make them sound like great people.'

She snorted in derision. She hadn't meant to do it. But she had, so I just stared at her with my eyebrows raised.

'They're not so special,' was her only explanation.

'How exactly?'

'Nothing important.'

'Like what?'

'That girl is too young to be going to bed at nine o'clock.'

'What time would you put her to bed?'

'I don't know, but definitely no later than half eight.'

This was a waste of time. The only thing she could tell me was when they put the bins out.

'I'd better be going, thank you for the tea,' I said as

I stood up.

'You haven't touched it.'

I pulled from my pocket a business card with the office number and address.

'This is my card. My *real* card. If you see anything suspicious, anything at all, call me.'

I offered it to her talons but they didn't take it, so I placed it on top of the boiled sweets instead.

Nothing much happened over the next three hours, but the process of sitting by my bike and watching anyway took me back to the days when I used to do things properly. Whenever that was.

For old time's sake I took a dusty notebook and pen out of a saddlebag and logged the little that happened:

3:37pm — Uniform leaves house, (female, black, short dark hair, attractive). Nickname: Bunny Rabbit. Makes phone call in police car #1

3:43pm — Bunny Rabbit returns to house

3:57pm — Loitering car (susp. journo) leaves as traffic warden arrives

3:58pm — 2nd loitering car has residents parking permit. Suspicious, may be fake. Traffic warden not suspicious, leaves

4:17pm — Bunny Rabbit exits house and leaves in p/c #1

4:43pm — 1st journo car returns, has to park further down

road. Man waits leaning on car, smoking. (35-ish, white, black coat, ginger hair). Nickname: Carrot Top

Occasionally the curtains would twitch. If Parker or Price were in there they'd recognise me. Anyone else, I wasn't so sure. But there was no way Parker or Price could be in there for that long, they would be too busy trying to get on the News at Ten. It was only me who was sitting here like a mug.

Nothing else happened until half six. Being July the sun was blazing, tricking everyone into thinking it was still the afternoon. It shouldn't be allowed.

By now I could hear the sounds of car horns and buses drifting from Dyke Road, the cram of families now attempting to leave the city. Tired, scrappy kids sitting in sweaty backseats, with chips in their stomachs, salt on their skin, and sand in their underpants. Well, not sand in Brighton. Pebbles in their underpants, maybe. That would be uncomfortable.

I almost missed the front door opening. I kept my head down and watched through my visor as a uniformed officer trotted down the steps, into the panda car, and got it running. Carrot Top had noticed him too, one foot in his car now.

Two minutes later Mr and Mrs Tothova were escorted down the steps and into the back seat. She had changed her clothes. The black & white pulled out into the road, Carrot Top jumped behind the wheel of his battered Volvo and was off after them in a second. I straddled my bike, summoning it to life and letting it roar as loud as it wanted to, getting it out of its system. This was a covert operation, after all. Then I chased after them.

After the Seven Dials, down the side of the station, we all had to wait at the lights onto Queens Road. I stayed behind Carrot Top, both keeping our distance to stay unnoticed, and with me doing something I never do: not skipping the traffic and just waiting my turn in the queue. Pretending I was a car.

The lights went green and the black & white made it through, but as the drivers in front of us slowly woke up it was clear we weren't going to make it through this cycle. So tough love to Carrot Top, I did what I always do: shot down the side of the queue, and through the lights on amber.

Once we had emerged from North Road onto the Steine, they pulled up in front of a church. It was obviously there, and had obviously been there for over a hundred years, but I had never noticed it. It didn't seem that anyone else could see it either. It was lost amongst the Sturm und Drang of a hot Saturday evening, like a shy virgin in the corner of a party. Being in the shadow of both St Peters and St Bart's, this little nonconformist church was never going to get noticed, even with its doors open, inviting, golden light spilling suggestively down the steps. The police escort seemed pointless here, even pretentious. The cider swilling teenagers, the stag dos, the hen parties, they didn't give a shit who these people were. Or what had happened to their daughter.

The uniformed officers waited in the car, engine off, as the Tothovas trudged up the steps and disappeared. I had to keep moving so I cruised on to the next left and zipped round the back of the block. Behind the church was a quiet car park, belonging to one of the strange blocks of flats that dot the town centre; the zoning laws refusing their removal like Chinese nail houses. I found a suitable dark corner to hide my bike from traffic wardens and thieves.

To approach the side door I pushed through a crowd of people that were lingering in the alley, but as I got closer I could see they were queueing to get in. Queueing for what, I had no idea. Wanting to keep a low profile I marched to the back of the queue and took my place like a good little boy.

Most of the people making up the line looked on the cusp of homelessness, with a few earthy, arty, hippy types sticking out like salad at a barbecue. I kept my head down and listened to their conversations.

'I wonder what we've got tonight?'

'Smells like curry.'

'Lovely, I could do with a curry.'

'I saw them carrying crates in earlier. Looked like sweet potatoes to me.'

'They might be doing two things.'

'Might be curried sweet potato soup.'

'Might be sweet potato curry.'

'Can you do sweet potato curry?'

'Of course you can. Chuck some lentils in, lovely job.'

Was this a pop up kitchen? One of the many things popping up in bohemian parts of the city: pop up markets, pop up cafés, pop up theatres, pop up artisan cheesemakers, pop up breweries. It was the fashion to pop up at the moment. I might set up a pop up detective agency, no rent would be a plus.

Apart from the arty types though, most of the people in the queue didn't look like they could pay seven pounds for organic falafel, so I guessed it was free. It was here for those who needed it. And for the hippies abusing the system. The stuff was probably past its date, given away by supermarkets, and the tree-huggers would feel a self-righteous warmth in their breast for eating it. I might come here regularly.

After what seemed like half an hour the side doors to the hall swang open and the line began to shuffle in. Now I could smell the curry, and it smelt good. I even began to salivate, I hadn't realised how hungry I had got waiting outside their house all afternoon. All I had eaten today was avocado toast.

As we approached I could see the row of tables set up for serving. Diners picked up a plate canteen-style, then stopped at each person to get their bits. I could see the Tothovas already, they were right in the middle of it, dolloping rice and something else on people's plates. He was still in his Thursday shirt but she was dressed all in white. Every second person said a few extra words to them and they nodded in thanks, gave a feeble "we're all right" smile and scooped more rice. They must have felt like shit, but they gave good face.

I shuffled along the line and picked up my plate. Then some forgettable posh do-gooder offered me a poppadom and I said yes. Then I was onto mummy Tothova, who offered me wholegrain rice of course, this is Brighton, after all. It might even have been wild rice: the rice for people who want something even more self-righteous to trump their wholegrain friends.

I studied her face for the two seconds I had. From a distance she had looked like a damp flannel, wrung out and hung up here to dry. But up close she was radiant. There's no other word for it. She wasn't young, not girl-ish at all, it wasn't youth that she radiated, but life. Beauty. Light. I don't know, it was impossible to quan-tify. She looked like a creature from another time. Another world. From the sky. From a woodland glade. An elf maiden. Her hair as golden as Botticelli's Ve-nus', her dark blue eyes deep ocean pools. Her white skin looked as cold as porcelain and you wanted to place your warm hands on her cheeks but were afraid of what would happen if you touched an angel. Stop me if this is becoming too much for you.

I felt a sudden swell of sympathy for her, and I wanted to say something like all the others. But it wouldn't help. And what she needed was for me to nod, say thank you, and leave all the rest unsaid. So that's what I did.

Next, Mr Tothova offered me some dark daal of some kind, and I love daal so I said yes. He slopped it onto my plate and I studied him now. He looked hollowed out, like he might have been slopping himself onto the plate, serving himself up to me like they served themselves up to the media. Everything on the surface was fine, but the inside was empty. A stiff breeze would topple him.

I moved onto the next volunteer, not registering them, just looking at the steaming vat of sweet potato curry. It looked nice. I mean, I wanted something more substantial than sweet potato, but that's not why you have a curry, is it? It's all about the spices that were tickling my nostrils.

'Hello, chief,' the man said in surprise.

I looked up. It was Lenny. Lenny was a homeless guy whose spot used to be outside my office. He used to do the occasional errand for me, but I hadn't seen him in months and had been wondering what happened to him.

I didn't say anything, giving him a little wink to let him know I was incognito. He nodded, and I said my thanks and took my plate toward the tables.

It was ok, after all that. Not great. It smelt nice, but the taste was the sort of thing that wouldn't offend anyone's taste buds. It filled the hole in my stomach.

Once they had walked round the tables offering seconds, Lenny came and sat at my table.

'Evening, boss.'

'Good to see you again,' I told him.

He looked well, his grey stubble was clean and glistening, and he had some colour to him that suggested he had been sleeping under a roof. I couldn't tell if he had a new camo coat or the old one clean, but I was glad to see he was doing well, and I told him as much.

'Like you care,' he said with a smile.

'Do you work here?' I asked.

'I volunteer once a week. These guys helped me a lot. Got me somewhere to live, work.'

'What work?'

'What I used to do: construction. It's not at the level I used to do it, but it's still good.'

I nodded, glancing over his shoulder at the other volunteers who were milling around. 'You said these guys helped you, who are these guys?'

'The charity: Firstlights.'

'First lights?'

'No, Firstlights.'

'What's the difference?'

'It's one word: Firstlights.'

'Fine, whatever. The Tothovas, they volunteer here too?'

'They run the thing. It's their charity.'

'They started it?'

'Right.'

Maybe they *were* saints. 'Did they ever bring the girl here?'

'Joy? One time. Sweet girl, very smart.' He took a big gulp from a mug of tea. 'How about you, boss?'

'How about me-what?'

'How's the search going for your nemesis?'

I smiled mirthlessly. 'He's not *my* anything, I'm *his* nemesis.'

'Hello!'

I looked up. The posh guy who had served the poppadoms had dragged a chair from the next table and was muscling in between me and Lenny. Late twenties, with floppy black hair, thick eyebrows, white designer shirt, designer jeans, and polished black shoes. He was one of those people right at the topmost tier of upper middle class, and as a result even his volunteering clothes looked too nice to drop curry on. He was born in formal wear. Spot him out of context and you would think he was on his way to a wedding.

'Are you a friend of Lenny's?' he asked.

I gave Lenny a quick look but he was ahead of me: 'No, we was just chatting. This is John.'

'Nice to meet you, John,' he held out a hand, 'I'm

Tab.' I didn't know if that was a name or what.

I just nodded. He took the hand back and didn't look insulted.

'So what are you chatting about over here, it looked quite intense, I thought you must know each other.'

Lenny kept up the act, 'I was just telling John about Firstlights, he's not been getting much work at the moment.'

'Oh really, what's your trade?' he asked.

'Whaling,' I answered.

'Oh really?'

God, he thinks I'm serious. 'No, I was joking.'

'Oh, I see.' He looked forlorn, as though he had grown up with the hope that one day he would understand jokes.

'I'm a taxidermist,' I explained.

'Oh really?'

'Yes.'

'What do you specialise in?'

'Whales.'

'Oh really?'

I just nodded. 'Yes, really.'

Lenny cut in: 'He was just asking about Firstlights.'

'Why is it called Firstlights?' I asked Tab.

'I don't know,' he mused, 'I guess it's because of that saying, you know: the night is always darkest before the dawn. And for a lot of people, the help they get from Firstlights is the dawn of a new day.'

'*Is* the night always darkest before the dawn?' I pressed him.

'Yes, I think so. Dawn is when it starts to get light again.'

'Well, I suppose so. But surely it's the same level of darkness for most of the night, not just the bit before dawn.'

'I don't think so.'

'Well, if not, surely you'd think the night would be darkest right in the middle, when the sun is on the other side of the Earth.'

'I don't know, maybe.'

'Still, it's a nice name.'

'It doesn't matter about the name,' Tab shot with a bit more weight, 'the work Maria and Graham do here is incredible.'

'Do you know them well?'

Just as suddenly as he had flared up he closed into his shell again. 'No, hardly at all. I've only been helping here for a couple of months. And I only do Saturdays.'

'Still, you must know them.'

'They don't serve every week.'

'They don't?'

He didn't answer.

'Tab,' Lenny said, glancing over his shoulder, 'I think they want you to help wash up.'

'Oh really?' he looked up eagerly, 'Nice meeting you,' then he bounded off on all fours like a puppy.

'What was that about?' I asked.

'He was just being friendly.'

'Oh really?' I mocked.

'You don't like anyone, do you, Joe.'

'Like them? Sure. Trust them? No way.'

Some people were starting to leave now, the unlimited tea and coffee had run out. I rubbed my eyes and stood up.

'Are you off?' Lenny asked.

I looked toward the Tothovas. I could spot at least two patrons snapping stealthy photos of them.

'I've seen enough,' I told him.

Everyone had.

I plucked my bike from its dark corner. It must have been nearly ten o'clock, the sky a shade of purple now. It would be dark in ten minutes.

Normally I wouldn't hesitate to fire up the Honda and listen to its roar, but these streets behind the Steine were strangely tranquil, and so I found myself wheeling my bike along them, not wishing to break the fragile quiet that was held in the air like a sheet of glass.

I pushed it along Tidy Street, where the basements' glow through glass tiles lent the place a festive atmosphere. Then down Gloucester Road and onto Cheltenham place, past The Basketmakers Arms, a pub barely the size of two living rooms, with its own merry glow. Then eventually to New Road, past the Theatre Royal with its spilling crowd of middle-aged middle class punters, and its row of taxis idling.

But there was far more on New Road this Saturday night. The wide pedestrianised road was as packed as during the Festival, but instead of performance poets, artists, and actors desperately leafletting for their shows, the place was a sea of floating faces, each illuminated by the candle in their hands. Flowers were stacked against the wooden barrier at the border of Pavilion Gardens, with tea lights and cards. The crowd were laying more and more.

I must have made some expression of shock, or disbelief, because a forty-something man wearing socks with sandals leant in to me and said in a low voice: 'You should see in there,' gesturing toward the gardens.

I wheeled my bike onto the path and past the trees. The gardens are not enormous, but they are big enough. Open to the public, the main section is crisscrossed by two curving paths, across bordered lawn.

There was not a single blade of grass visible. The entire lawn was covered in flowers, candles, teddy bears, cards, notes. People stood at the railings, staring over this sea of sympathy. They all seemed to have brought their own children, despite the late hour, what the point of that was I couldn't understand. It was all to show how much they cared. But the parents didn't want flowers, they wanted their little girl back.

I exited onto Princes Place.

'T-shirts, twenty pounds!'

I couldn't help looking, there aren't normally market stalls on Princes Place. The T-shirts were white, across the chest was the slogan "FIND JOY", and across the stomach was the same picture of the girl from the front page of the newspaper.

'T-shirt, twenty pounds,' the unwashed vendor was accosting me now.

'That's a bit steep,' I told him.

'What?'

'Expensive. Twenty quid for a screen printed T-shirt?'

'It's to help find the girl.'

Of course it is. 'What's the money going to?'

'What?' He pretended not to hear me, even putting his hand to his ear.

'The money, what is it going to, the twenty pounds?'

'It's to help find the girl.'

You said that already. 'I'll pass.'

I kept walking, past the other vultures.

'Cards, one pound!'

'Teddy bears, ten pounds!'

'Candles, two pounds! Four for five pounds.'

They were no different to the newspapers, I supposed, making money from tragedy. No different to me. Everyone has to pay rent.

* * *

After I had locked up my bike, I finally made it into Meeting House Lane, through the street door, and into my domain.

There was a glow on the stairs.

'You're here late,' I said, pushing open the door with my name on it.

Thalia was putting back an earring that must have come loose. She looked especially buxom tonight, in a bra and dress that were doing everything they could for her, and they had a lot to work with. She had her legs out too, I guess it was too darn hot for modesty. Some people are sniffy about thick legs, but I liked her thick legs. I say people are sniffy, men aren't that picky in my experience. Sure, they'll talk fussy, say they don't find some woman attractive, but the truth is they'd do it with a fish if you could get it in high heels.

'I was just doing some filing,' she said.

'I've got an assignment for you.'

'Now?'

'No, no, you can start tomorrow.'

'Ok good, what is it?' She started tidying up the desk in the outer office, putting away the laptop. I begged her to bend over a bit more.

'I want to know everything there is to know about Joy Tothova and her parents.'

'Like what?'

'Everything. School, friends, church, jobs, spirit animals, past lives. If I need to know something, I want to be able to look in the file and find it.'

'That sounds like real detective work.'

'It's not fun.'

She gestured around at the filing. *It's more fun than this*, she was saying.

'Keep it in the office and just update it whenever you can.'

'You know, if I did it on the computer you could look at it wherever you were.'

'On my phone?'

'Well, obviously not on *your* phone.' She changed subject to the receipt she was holding, 'Mrs X paid up, so that's it unless our Mr Vogeli turns up.'

'Good. I want to focus on this.'

She nodded as though she was pleased I was finally turning my attention to it. She thought I was being a good citizen. God, did she look good right now.

'Hey, do you want to come back to mine tonight?'

Occasionally, when were lonely, or more honestly, when we were horny, we would hook up. It didn't mean anything, but we were developing quite a good language in bed. But this time, instead of giving a cheeky smile, she looked a little embarrassed.

'I've got a date,' she said.

'I see.' I froze for a moment, before deciding that wasn't the way to look like I didn't care. 'Have fun,' was all I said as I shut the inner door behind me.

I sulked behind my desk. After a few minutes I heard her tiptoe out and the door shutting softly. After that I swivelled my chair listlessly and stared down into the Lanes, watching the happy, horny lads chasing barely clothed women across the cobbles.

Maybe I should cut the Tothovas some slack, I thought. Sure, their particular brand of righteousness grated on me, but they were doing a damn sight more than me to make this city a better place. They were serving food to those in need. I was sulking like a toddler.

My phone vibrated. I dredged it from my pocket. A text. A text from Monica Todman! *When God closes a door, he opens a smoking-hot, 51-year-old nymphomaniac window.*

"*Be at mine in 17 minutes,*" it said.

I was out of my office in less than one. Had started my bike in another one. And was outside her Hove mansion in twelve more. I had to wait on the doorstep for the other three.

It was always the same. Every. Single. Time. Her butler answered when the time was up, and showed me in with unconcealed disdain. Then he showed me up to the bedroom, closing the door behind me.

Ever since she had been a client six months ago, she had been my greatest weakness. She had texted me the rules the first time. There was no talking allowed. No eye contact. No pulling, scratching, or biting. I was to file my nails between times. Only soft things were allowed in the room. And I had to leave the second it was over.

This evening was no different. Her soft, plush bedroom was lit by a hundred candles. Her four-poster bed was made up with silk. On a side table next to it was a brandy Old Fashioned made with brown sugar. And on the bed was Monica Todman. Blindfolded. Naked. On all fours, with her arse in the air.

5

The Angry Corner

I LISTENED IN SILENCE as Krishma Jilani whispered her story. The mothers watched her with wet eyes, all except Theresa, who watched me.

It had been ninety-one days. On the ninth of August she had arrived home from her work as a hospital cleaner to find their flat empty. It was a Tuesday, and Mahnoor always came home after school, always. She called the school there and then. They said Mahnoor left the gates on time, same as always. So she called the other parents. She wasn't anywhere. Her husband came home. She wasn't with him either. They called 999. Then sat up the whole night staring at the front door. The next day two detectives came and spoke to them. They gave them the only photos they had. And then, in

67

the three months that had passed, they found precisely nothing.

They got excuses, of course. And assurances that they were doing everything they could. But in ninety-one days they hadn't found a single piece of evidence. The girl had vanished.

The mum told her story in broken English, I was told the dad spoke it better, and the girl better than both of them. Probably better than me. The girl had teachers and friends to learn it from, the parents not so much. She just had the other parents, and he had a few other Pakistani mates at their mosque. I say *their* mosque as though they had much choice in Brighton.

With absolutely no idea what I could do I told the mothers I would do what I could. They told me they would pay me if I did. I told them I would need money now, in case I had to buy information. They emptied their purses and I ended up with a hundred and seventy-five quid, and a lot of change. I told them I needed somewhere to sleep, and Debra said she had a caravan in her drive. I was more than welcome to it, on the condition that I never came in the house. I felt a warm glow inside to be so trusted.

The only condition they gave me about my investigation was that I was not, under any circumstances, to speak to the father. He didn't know about this little idea of theirs to get me involved, and he was not going to know. He was 'very traditional', whatever that meant. I

68

told them I understood.

Afterwards, Debra gave me a lift to hers like I was still a little boy. My moped scuffed the boot of her pointless people carrier (she didn't have any people to carry). When I was fourteen she had lived near Queen's Park, but since then she had divorced and moved. Now she lived in a small square house in Hollingdean, round from the estates. At least it came with a drive. I had to wait on the doorstep whilst she got the key to the caravan, and then she gave me the briefest possible tour. I don't think she liked being in the tight space with me.

Despite being only fifty-something she had the coiffured helmet of hair you expect to see on a pensioner. Hairsprayed to the point where it could be removed in one piece and swapped for something different. Except that it couldn't, of course, because if it could there was no way you would choose that one. I could see why her husband had left her, I couldn't live with that hair either.

The first thing I did was use the shower, which because the caravan wasn't hooked up, was cold. And the water was scummy. But it was more than I usually had. Then I climbed into the bed, which to you I'm sure would be lumpy and thin, and make you miss home, but to me was heaven.

It was then, lying there, listening to the rain pinging on the roof, that I finally thought about what they were asking. They wanted me to do something. Just *something*. I didn't know what. I don't think they did either.

Michael Greene, a male, sixty-three, had just got back from walking Bessie, a black labradoodle, four, along the Eastbourne seafront when he returned to his flat, and stepped into the living room. As he let the dog off its lead and took off his flat cap, he looked pretty bloody surprised to see me sitting there, casually smoking a cigarette, in his favourite arm chair.

For a moment he looked around, as though there might be an innocent reason for this stranger being in his house. But then it died. Bessie half ruined the moment by trying to lick my face.

'Bessie!' he barked, and she came back to him. Then he tried his best to sound intimidating. Or at least less intimidated. 'I'll call the police.'

'I wouldn't do that if I were you, Mr Greene.'

He lurched. I knew his name. The doorbell said "K. Black".

'Why not?' he whispered.

'If you try to call anyone I'll strangle you with the cord.'

'It's a handset, you prat.'

'Then I'll make you eat it.'

He stared at me.

'Sit down,' I commanded.

He didn't.

'You're going to answer some questions, or I'm going to beat the answers out of you.'

We could hear Bessie scratching at the cupboards in the kitchen. 'She wants food,' he cheeped, 'she always gets fed after her walk.'

'Then feed her.'

He shuffled into the kitchen. A foil tray was opened, biscuits tinkled into a bowl, a tap ran, then silence. I fingered the flick knife in my pocket. But then he sidled back in and leant on the wall facing me.

He had curly grey hair, and a beard that hid his face. What was visible beneath was a mass of wrinkles and sadness. Tight, thin skin, was stretched over his cheeks until I felt I could see the bones themselves.

The flat was small and cramped, and filled with the smell of an old person. Textured wallpaper was peeling away, a green granny chair filled each corner, and the carpet was nylon, pink, and you could probably lose a shoe in it.

From some other room a clock struck seven, and we could hear Bessie munching away.

'You don't abuse the dog, do you?'

His eyes opened a fraction more than the squint he was giving me. Then he hissed, 'What do you want?'

'You served ten months for making and possessing indecent images of children.'

He didn't deny it.

'You're going to give me a list of names—'

He scoffed at that, his arms folded, looking down at me over them.

'Aren't you?' I asked.

'You want a list of names?' he barely asked, 'of whom, the kids?'

'No,' I spat.

'Who then?'

'Other sick bastards like yourself.'

'Oh sure, I'll go get my Filofax, shall I?'

I launched out of my chair and grabbed him by his fleece. Then I threw him down where I'd been sitting.

'This isn't a joke.'

'Yes,' he said defiantly, 'it is. You want me to give you a list of other people who have served their time so you can go and intimidate them too?'

I swished the blade out of my flick knife.

'I can't tell you any names!' he screamed.

'I don't believe you.'

'Honestly, I only looked at stuff, I never met anyone or spoke to anyone. Not even online.'

'You were charged with making illegal images.'

'That just means I copied them!'

'What?'

'I downloaded a few of them onto my hard drive, that's all that means.'

'I don't believe you.'

'Please, please, it's the truth. Technically I made another copy, that's all that means. It dates back to copying printed photographs, please, you have to believe me, it's the truth...'

He collapsed into a pile of blubbering noises. He was weeping. Bessie came in and sniffed at him, trying to cheer him up.

I put my knife away and sat back in a chair, finishing my cigarette.

Slowly, he stopped sniffling, and after a while he sat up slightly, watching me smoke.

'What is this about?' he breathed.

I explained the situation in broad details.

'That's different.'

'How?'

'What I did, that was just pictures.'

'But who takes the pictures?'

He looked down at the pink nylon. 'I don't know.' He picked dog hairs out of the chair. 'People like me, we're cowards. That's why we're sitting alone at our computers. This girl, if that's what you think this is—'

'I don't know what this is.'

'—there's no way they would break into the house. Or even abduct her at the door. They would lure her somewhere—'

'How would you know?'

'Would you just listen to me?'

I shut up.

'They would be speaking to her online,' he said.

'I'm pretty sure they don't have a computer.'

'How sure?'

'*Pretty* sure.'

'Fine, then maybe someone at the school. A teacher, maybe.'

'You would know.'

We stared at each other.

'I never hurt anyone,' he stated definitively.

'No, you just wanked off to it.'

He was silent again. His beady, squinty eyes were studying me like bugs from underneath a rock.

'I know you, don't I?'

It was my turn to be silent.

'You were one of my pupils. I don't remember your name.'

'I don't know what you're talking about.'

'Now who's being dishonest?'

I fished for my knife again.

'Fine,' he held up his hand, 'let's forget it.'

I wished I could.

'So you think it's someone at her school?' I asked.

'I don't know. If it's a sex thing, maybe. But I don't know why you think it's a sex thing.'

'Isn't everything?'

'Maybe for you.'

I smirked, 'You mean it isn't for you?'

'You don't get it. For me, nothing is about sex.

Nothing *can* be about sex, ever again. I just have to pad around this flat until I die.'

'Poor you.'

'The funny thing is I wanted to be caught.'

'Really? Why didn't you turn yourself in then?'

'You may learn this one day,' he looked me up and down, 'one day soon, probably. That when you do something really bad it sticks to the inside of you. And until everyone knows, every knock on the door scares you stiff, and you don't ever get to rest. My first night in prison was the best sleep I've ever had.'

He was right, he was a coward. I didn't care what his excuses were. And I didn't know why I was sitting here listening to them.

The irony was that as a teacher, we all loved him. He was great. He never made us do any work, and when he got upset with us talking too much he would just sulk over to his 'angry corner'. Then he would flap his hands at us and squeal that he could never stay angry at us. It used to make us feel so loved. So safe and warm. Now it made me feel sick.

No it didn't, that was how I wanted it to make me feel. Instead it made me want to cry. It made me want to hug the young me tight, and keep him safe. But he would always be alone.

'Why don't they just go to the police?' he asked.

Why didn't they? They should ask Bessie to do something, it was a better idea than asking me. My plan had been threatening a pensioner.

6

Holier Than Thou

THE OLD MAN'S FACE rose from the deep. Breaking through the waves. Up, up, toward my hand. An inch away from my grip, and then…

I was in my own bed. I say bed, on my mattress I mean. What had happed last night? That was right: Monica Todman had happened.

The first time I had thought it was every man's dream. Dominance. Now it was weird. I tried not to think about it. It's what she wanted. We wanted the same thing, didn't we? God, what was I still thinking about it for? It meant nothing, it was just a bit of fun. That was the whole damn point. Fun.

It was Sunday, and it was nine o'clock, and I had a

text from Thalia. I cheered up a bit; her date can't have gone that well if she was awake already. I opened it. It was just the name of a church.

Standing at the bedroom window I poked my head out onto the flat rooves. The bread was still there, sitting limply in a puddle. The baby seagull was still on a higher roof a few metres away. Still alone. Still fluffy. Still hungry. I convinced myself there was nothing more I could do.

After an espresso and more avocado smashed onto burnt bread, I put on the least creased shirt I could find and a jacket that made me look vaguely less like a scumbag, then wandered out into the heat.

Today wasn't as unbearable as yesterday, but any drop in temperature was defeated by the clothes I was wearing. By the time I reached the church my smartness was undone, and I had to use sweat to smooth down my hair.

The building looked like a bigger brother to the church they ran the charity in. It had the same red brick and flint construction, the same geometric stained glass windows, and just like the other one it wasn't old enough yet to be attractive. But I'm one of those people who thinks the only attractive churches are made of stone and take a hundred years to build. A philistine, I guess. At least both of these places had Gothic arches: Roman arches look terrible. At least on English churches.

I followed a few feet behind a young couple pushing a pram through the large double doors. An old woman in a made-to-last suit jacket was standing in the atrium and insisted on shaking my hand. I guess it was her job to welcome me. I'd much rather have been able to slink in unseen, and I had the horrible feeling that at some point in the service, or afterwards, people would advance on me like zombies, desperately seeking to sink their teeth in me as though I was one stale biscuit away from indoctrination.

Luckily for me I was one of the last people to arrive and I could take up an empty pew in the back row. I say pew, it was a row of clipped together blue faux leather cushioned pine chairs with a box attached to the back where the person behind could put their hymn sheets. It wasn't just the pews that were missing either, the place looked like it had been gutted.

I hadn't been in a church, not for a service at least, since I was a kid. In care, and with school, I had been to a Methodist service, and heard a C of E vicar talk about Jesus, that was it. I had never been to a service as part of a job, and to be honest I didn't feel any magic as I glanced around at the interior. It seemed to me that every new iteration of Protestantism was more boring than the last, removing anything beautiful until you're worshipping in an empty building. First they removed the Icons of the Catholics and the Orthodox, and hung banners instead. Then they got rid of pictures in the windows. Then they got rid of the banners too, because they were just too damn colourful, and they plastered everything white. Because if your idea of faith is inspired by a painting, or by music, or by anything that isn't the pure, undiluted, full-fat love of God, straight from the source, then it's not really faith, it's just a love of pretty pictures. Jesus didn't need gold, he didn't even need a temple. That at least was true. But this place was heading toward demolishing the building and sitting in an empty field on cardboard boxes because 'the church is not a building, it is us.'

And so the service got underway in that vein, and I scanned the crowd row by row for the Tothovas, but I needn't have bothered because they were right at the front, and one of the first things the priest did was pray for them. People corrected me later that he was not a priest, or indeed a vicar, he was a minister. Minister of what, I didn't ask.

This place was practically round the corner from me, over on the posh side of the train tracks, less than ten minutes' walk from Fiveways, where the girl had disappeared. I had expected their church to be in Hove, like their house. I mean sure, which church you attend is a personal choice, and if you're not Church of England or Catholic then you might not choose your local, but for them to be shopping at Fiveways too? They must have moved recently.

As the bearded minister, who wore flip-flops and

looked like a tech guru, said a prayer, the Tothovas held hands and bowed their heads. Everyone had done the same, and most had closed their eyes. Occasionally one of them would grunt in audible agreement with something he said, which seemed to be the strange middle class version of shouting 'Amen!' or 'Hallelujah!'. Instead people mumbled 'Amen' when the prayer ended and it was the loudest they ever got when they weren't singing.

When the time did come for songs they came all in one bunch. We must have sung three or four in one go, transitioning from hymns that sounded like nineties rock ballads to hymns that sounded like nineties country hits, all accompanied by a band that consisted of around seven men who could half-play the guitar, an out of place oboe, and two primary school teachers on microphones who seemed to be singing completely different harmonies to the ones we were encouraged to aim for. When singing, about half the people in the congregation reached out a hand above them, as though God was just beyond their fingertips. To me they looked like the aliens in *Toy Story* that reach for 'the claaaaw'. I just mouthed along.

We were almost an hour in before the actual sermon started. It was vaguely interesting, he seemed to know his stuff.

The Tothovas attention seemed less engaged and every five minutes the man sitting next to Mrs Tothova would whisper something in her ear. She would nod, and then occasionally their shoulders would shift as though hands were being held or un-held.

I couldn't see who he was. He had a suit on, unlike anyone else, and black hair. He was white, he looked like he was in his late thirties or early forties, and he was bearded. That was about all I could tell.

After the lecture we sang some more and then the whole thing ended without a bang. The minister informed us that there were coffees, smoothies, and gluten-free brownies available in the vestibule, and that we should help ourselves. And then, as the atmosphere began to hum with quiet conversation and the most eager to get a drink or take a piss jumped out into the aisle, several heads in front meerkat-ed up and Exorcist-ed round to stare at me with horrific smiles. One jumped right up at me and tried to lick my face.

'Hello!' he almost shouted with an outstretched hand. 'I haven't seen you here before.'

'No,' I replied, 'I used to be a Satanist but it turns out I'm allergic to pentagrams.'

'I'm just going to get a cup of tea,' he chirped. He hadn't registered a word I'd said.

I moved out into the aisle.

'Hello again,' a deep voice said behind me. I turned around but there was no one there. No one above shoulder height, that is. It was the old woman in the suit jacket who had "welcomed" me at the door. 'Chris.

Nice to meet you.'

'Thank you,' I said, shaking her hand, 'Jake.'

'Nick,' said a man I hadn't noticed was standing right next to me. He was in a fleece with his arms folded and leaning so close that I could tell what he'd had for breakfast. 'What do you do, Jake?' he asked.

Don't be sarcastic, don't be sarcastic, don't be sarcastic! 'I'm a taxi driver,' I replied.

They asked me some questions, confirming this was my first time. Then they wanted to know what I thought. I was very complimentary. Through my teeth, I told them it had made me look at Our Lord in a whole new way. There's an inherent lack of dignity in pretending to be someone you're not, and I hate that. But in my business dignity costs.

'Do you want a coffee?' Nick asked.

'That would be great, thanks. One sugar.'

'Chris?'

'No thanks,' she told him, 'I don't do caffeine.'

He disappeared. At the front, the Tothovas were talking with the minister, who was nodding sympathetically.

'That couple at the front,' I asked, 'who are they? I recognise them.'

'Oh,' she muttered gravely, and lowered her voice. 'You might have seen them on the television. Graham and Maria are the ones whose little girl has been taken.'

'Oh, yes. I think I heard about that.'

She made a kind of rumbling noise in her throat.

'Did the girl come here then?'

'Yes. I used to teach her in Sunday School, actually. Lovely girl. Good Christian girl, if you know what I mean.'

Good Christian? Yes, I know the phrase. These people would cum in their pants when they thought how good they were.

I took another glance at them. 'They seem so nice. How terrible.'

'They're lovely people. Good Christians.'

There it was again. People who bake a cake for Malawi, volunteer at a charity, all whilst planning their next Venice minibreak. If you drive a BMW to church, you've missed the point.

'Is it true they give all their money to charity?'

'Well, I don't think so…' she spluttered.

'Sorry, I thought, when you said they were good Christians…'

'Well, I don't think—'

'Isn't that what Jesus said,' I interrupted, 'that it's easier for a rich man to enter—'

'Yes,' she cut me off, 'but I don't think he meant we should give up everything we—'

'That's what his disciples did.'

'Yes, but—'

'Here you go,' Nick had returned with my coffee.

I glanced over at the Tothovas again. The bearded

man was hanging around them, he looked as much a stranger here as I did.

'Who's that man with the Tothovas, I recognise him too, I think?'

'Really?' Chris drawled.

I had slipped up.

'I have no idea,' she continued, 'if you'll excuse me…'

She marched off with purpose. I was on borrowed time.

Nick frowned slightly, noticing her irritation without understanding. 'That's Ben McCready,' he said, 'he's a councillor. Hove somewhere, I think.'

McCready. I didn't recognise him with the beard. He'd been a city councillor for some time now, this was his third term. When he was elected he had been one of the youngest. *The* youngest if you didn't count those smug students parties sometimes place in their safest wards.

He was the future once. Then he was caught sending dick pics to an underage girl. He had managed to hold his seat though. People believed her parents when they said she said she was eighteen.

Hove, somewhere. I tried to remember which ward and which flavour he was, councillors in Brighton only come in three flavours. I peered over his shoulder again. McCready was staring straight at me. *Shit.* He whispered something in Maria's ear and then he started to approach.

'Oh look, he's coming this way,' Nick announced helpfully.

He was with us in a flash.

'Hello,' he smarmed, holding out his hand to each of us.

'Hello. I'm Nick,' said Nick.

I took a mouthful of my coffee, and then made a face. 'Oh, Nick, did you put sugar in this?'

'Yes,' he answered, confused.

'I'm trying to cut down, can you get me another one?'

There was a moment of inaction, but the action of me passing him the cardboard cup sent him drifting on his way.

McCready was wearing a three piece suit, without a tie but with a blue display handkerchief, and his beard was just the right amount of kempt to look clean but not try-hard. He was born stylish. I didn't like him already.

'I didn't get your name,' he asked.

'George,' I shook his hand again, 'and yours?'

'Ben,' he said with a practised smile.

'I recognise you, Ben, you're on the council aren't you?'

'Yes, that's right.'

'Which ward is it again?'

'Hove Park.'

'Hove Park, really? What made you come to a church over this way?'

'I don't go to church, although I respect the role faith plays in people's lives,' he pandered, 'I just came to show my support for Maria and Graham.'

'Good friends of yours, are they?'

'Can't a councillor support his constituents?'

'Of course he can. But they're not in your ward.'

The practised smile became an unpractised frown. York Avenue is in Goldsmid, we both knew that.

'Yes,' he hissed, 'they're very good friends of mine, but that doesn't matter.' He never broke eye contact. 'They're very important people.'

'Yes, I know.'

'I don't want them bothered.'

'How come you know them so well?'

He held up a hand to stop me. 'I'm not interested in having a conversation with you.' He counted the next three points on his fingers: 'They're very important people. I don't want them bothered. I think you should leave.'

'Excuse me?'

Who the hell did he think he was? It wasn't him these people worshipped.

'I don't want them bothered, Mr Grabarz.'

Oh I see. So he recognised me. I guess I should've been flattered. Instead I bit my lip.

He raised his eyebrows. *Do you understand?* he was

asking.

'It does explain a lot,' I said.

He sighed. He had to engage with me, he was too curious by nature. 'What?'

'Here I was, wondering why the police went against the rulebook and put out a missing persons report soon enough to actually find someone. I was also wondering why the newspapers ran it the very same day. But now I know it's because they're very important people, and nothing at all to do with them being very good friends of yours.'

'You're a shit, Grabarz.'

I couldn't help a grin. 'You see, that's the difference between you and me, councillor: we're both shits, I just don't pretend otherwise.'

Nick hadn't returned with my coffee. McCready wanted to slap me round the face. Everybody wants to these days.

'A bunch of hooligans searched my office because of what you said on the radio.'

'I didn't tell anybody to do anything.'

'Really.' I rolled my eyes.

'Did you even hear the interview?'

'Of course not.'

'Don't believe everything people tell you.'

He pointed with his eyes to the exit. I didn't want to hang amongst these hypocrites anyway.

I walked through the vestibule and back to the big

wooden doors.

'There you are,' Nick was standing in the way with my coffee, I took it from his hands a little too quickly and spilt some on his hand, 'Ouch!'

Chris was a few steps to the right, whispering to someone, and wearing the frown she should have used when they showed her that suit. She tried to burn a hole in my back with her glower.

Outside, I sipped the coffee, realised it didn't have sugar in it, and threw it on a plant.

The centre was still packed with idiots, and the tarty shops were selling themselves, all smiles and willing staff. The sun was beating down on the cobbles by one o'clock and I was glad to get into the shadows of the Lanes. A different man had taken Lenny's spot in the last months, it was prime real estate after all, and despite looking homeless he was selling those wind-up toys that do a backflip, and for the first time ever I saw someone buy one.

Brighton in the summer is great for businesses. So many people crammed into tiny streets, all needing somewhere to eat and drink and get out of the heat. Great for all businesses except mine. In the last few months I had attracted enough clients to keep Thalia employed, pay the rent on the office and flat, eat food, and even buy the occasional thing. But my customers are Brightonians, or people looking for Brightonians, and in the summer everyone is a tourist. The residents are on holiday, the students have gone home, and I'm left sitting in my office on a Sunday afternoon with nothing to do and no money to do it with.

I was enjoying the Joy Tothova case. Not in a sick way. Since the winter I had surveilled some husbands, some wives, found a missing dog, acted as a chaperone to a man who owed money to loan sharks, and in one especially boring case, helped an old lady discover who had keyed her car. It was her son. So to investigate an abduction, to feel useful, made it more enjoyable than it should've been.

I leafed through the file Thalia was compiling. It wasn't much more than a few notes, but at least she was keen:

Between 10:00—11:00am Wednesday 13/7/16, the Tothovas (Graham, Maria, and Joy), parked on Stanmer Park Rd, and walked up to the Fiveways. About this time they noticed a blue Ford Transit-style van loitering on Hythe Road. It was double-parked, with engine running.

"Later the three of them were shopping in Fiveways Fruits, then Mrs Tothova crossed the road alone to shop in Barfields Butchers. When Mr Tothova found himself alone in the greengrocers, he assumed that his daughter had gone to the butchers with her mother. Around five minutes later, Maria returned, and discovered that Joy was missing.

They searched the nearby shops, and phoned 999 at 11:21.

Biographical research revealed that Graham Tothova was born in Derby, one of three boys and a girl. His parents, Paul and Lynn, were both still alive. His father owned, and still ran, a limousine dealership, and Graham was the only one of the boys not to join the family business. His sister was married, lived in Burton upon Trent, and didn't appear to work.

It sounded like a coma-inducingly boring upbringing, and no doubt there was some family politics involved in working at Paul's Limo's (the extra apostrophe giving it real class) that he had been keen to escape. His parents didn't even have enough imagination to give him a middle name. The interesting surname came from his Slovakian great-grandfather.

Maria Elizabeth Tothova, on the other hand, had been born Maria Elizabeth Redburn in Dubai. Her father, Stephen Redburn, was a British businessman who sold oil refining machinery to dubious regimes, and her mother, Emilia De St Croix, was a Maltese diplomat.

Her particular presence made a bit more sense to me now: her father had given her the height that comes with money, and her mother had given her the sweet smell of class. No wonder men like Ben McCready went gaga over her. And here she was, in Brighton, married to Graham the son of a car salesman. That must hurt ambitious men like McCready more than anything.

Both her parents were deceased, both from lung cancer, and she only had one brother. Thalia noted he lived in South Africa, but what he did there Google didn't say.

It was just the three of them in Brighton: Maria, Graham, and Joy. I had no idea why their daughter had been abducted. I couldn't see any connection with their charity. With their church. With them having moved from Fiveways to Hove. With their families. With their friends. With councillor Ben McCready. Nothing. I couldn't see how they had pissed anyone off. Quite the opposite. It was like the girl had fallen down a manhole.

Whatever the motive, I wasn't going to find it by sitting here staring at the bookshelf. I looked down to the cobbles. To the masses. It was a sunny Sunday afternoon, I should be out eating lunch somewhere. Fish & chips on the beach? Maybe not the beach, too many idiots. So maybe somewhere nice, here in the Lanes.

I felt like spoiling myself on a day like this, so to hell with it, I was going to blow a week's food money: late lunch at English's. If it's good enough for Peter James, then it's got to be good enough for me.

7

DNA

HALFWAY THROUGH my fruits de mer it started raining. And after an Aperol Spritz, and some pudding, and coffee, it was still raining. I paid up and stood in the door, looking out across East Street. It was a monsoon out there, tourists scurrying under the nearest shelter, until so many had gathered under the restaurant's awning that they blocked my view.

I held a newspaper over my head as I jogged back through the Lanes, round puddles and through waterfalls, until I made it inside. Upstairs I threw off my jacket, dumping it over the back of a chair. Then just as I had taken my shoes off someone banged on the street door. I wandered out onto the landing, but before I could shout down it opened and three men and a woman stomped up to the landing.

'Joe Grabarz?' a man in a dry white shirt asked.

I stood there in my wet socks. 'Can I help you?'

'We're here to search your office.'

He tried to get past me but I took a step back and blocked the doorway.

'You're not searching anywhere.'

He raised his well-groomed eyebrows. 'You haven't got anything to hide, have you?'

'Your wife's not here, ok? She left an hour ago.'

'Very funny.'

'Thank you.'

I drank him in for a second: the stiff, starched collar; the ironed-flat clothes and the ironed-flat sense of humour. The other two men were just the same and the woman only differed anatomically.

'Step aside!' she shouted from behind them.

She, along with the rest of them, looked far too well turned out to be behaving like this. It was pretend toughness. The type that has never seen the real thing. They weren't going to push me out of the way or hold me down, they'd run and find an adult.

'Do you know what I have in my pocket?' I asked her.

'Excuse me?'

'Brass knuckles.' I was lying, they were in my jacket on the back of the chair. 'Do you know what they'll do to your face?'

She took a step back. 'He said you wouldn't hurt a woman.'

'Who said?'

Before she could answer, one of the silent types pushed the first guy out the way and ran to get past me. I grabbed him and threw him back into the bannisters with a bit too much force.

They ran to help him; he was wedged half through, his head hanging out over the stairs. His body had snapped the balustrade and bent two bannisters out of shape. It took all of them to get him free.

'You're a bully,' the woman hissed as they carried him back down the stairs. Seconds later the door slammed.

I was back in the outer office checking my jacket. My brass knuckles weren't there after all, I must have left them in my desk, maybe.

The street door opened again downstairs.

'Another satisfied customer!?' someone called up. It was a man's voice, foreign, I didn't recognise it.

'Hello?' I called.

Footsteps wandered up the creaky stairs, across the landing, and in the open door.

'Mr Grabarz?'

Planted there was a short, almost bald, jowly man in a mac. He sounded German.

'Yes.'

'Hermann Vogeli.' Swiss, I remembered. He extended a hand, 'Nice to meet you.'

I shook it. 'You too.'

We stood in silence for a moment, my heart rate slowly returning to normal. He didn't say anything. Didn't even move. I was calm again now. I needed to learn to stay that way. I made an oath right there and then: *I will stay calm.*

'Come into my office.'

I put my shoes on the radiator. It wasn't on, but that's what I did when they were wet.

'What was that about?' he asked.

'Joy Tothova, who else?'

'Who?'

I sighed. 'Never mind.'

We wandered into my little office and he sat in the little chair opposite my little desk. I had left the windows open so I quickly checked on them, but it was ok, the overhang of the roof protected me from flooding, and despite the rain it was still as hot as hell.

'We were expecting you the other night.'

'Yes, I'm very sorry. I missed my ferry.'

Ferry? How far had he come? 'You didn't tell my assistant very much.'

'It's a private matter, I always prefer to speak to people personally. Don't you?'

I just shrugged, I wasn't really listening. 'Would you like a drink or anything? Tea, coffee?'

'No, thank you.' He slipped a cigarette and a lighter out of his jacket, 'Do you mind if I smoke?'

'I'm afraid I do.'

He froze mid movement, 'Really? I would not have thought so.'

'I don't personally. But I can't say the same for my next visitor.'

'Of course.' He put it back in his pocket, placed both hands on his knees, and looked out at the rain. It was falling parallel to the windows, a silent curtain.

'What a horrible day,' he mused, 'hot and wet. My uncle used to have a house near Dufourspitze that I would visit in the summer. It never rained when I was there. It was so high that we were above the weather. We would stand on the roof and look down at all the clouds that were laid out around us like a carpet.'

He was in his fifties at least, but he could have been older, everything about him was second hand and poorly treated. His face looked like cold meat left out in the rain, and hung off his skull in the way that it would if he had put it through the wash too many times. He dressed like the most boring form of businessmen, the type that sleep in airport hotels, where everything is as grey as the air on the runway. Except he had come by ferry. He had probably spent last night in a Dieppe Formula 1 with distant view of the punishing surf. He worked in a business park in a cold trans-European city where no language was common and experiencing it

97

was a sedative. He was a photocopied photocopy of a beige man. One that had yellowed in the sun like Sellotape.

'My uncle,' he continued, 'was a pioneer in what they now call ultramarathons. Because he lived at such high altitude his body processed oxygen far more efficiently than "der niedrige Leute", "the low people", as he used to call them.'

I smiled politely and made small talk. 'Your English is very good, I always wished I'd learnt a language.'

'My job takes me all over Europe.'

'What is your job?'

He gave a coy smile and raised his fingers very slightly off his knees. 'We'll get to that.'

I was too tired now to make a thing of it, the heavy meal and the drinks were hugging me to sleep.

He scanned across my bookshelf: various editions of *Kelly's Directory of Brighton & Hove*, *The Encyclopaedia of Brighton*, The Pevsner Architectural Guide to the city, other things like that.

'I see history is a hobby of yours.'

'It's my job,' I told him.

He smiled. 'History defines us all, doesn't it?'

'If you let it.'

He frowned, then changed the subject again: 'Have you ever been to Switzerland?'

'No.'

'You must go. Dufourspitze is beautiful in the

spring.'

'I'll add it to my bucket list.'

He went to open his mouth again but I cut him off:

'What was it you wanted to see me about?'

He tried not to smile and his fingers drummed on his kneecaps. 'Would you indulge me a little storytelling?'

I sighed. 'Why not.' I wanted a drink, but that might be impolite.

'My story begins in Spain, in Rojales, near Torrevieja. Have you ever been there?'

'I'll add that to the list too.'

'Well, Rojales is a poor town. And for the Spanish to think it poor, you know it has to be poor. It wasn't all their fault, the economy was hit hard. But for whatever reason you want to give, there are no jobs. And now most of the young people have left, half of them came here to find a job. Living in that town there is a woman, María Dolores Suárez, only she's not living anymore. A famous tragedy in Rojales, she was only forty-one. And when someone dies and they have something to pass on, they have to find a next of kin. Only when it comes to María's death, they cannot find any next of kin. Everyone knows she has no children. No brother, no sisters. But she's got something to pass on. That's when they hire me.' A thumb left his knee just long enough to point toward his chest.

My feet were sweaty, I fanned out the ends of my

socks with my toes.

'I went to Rojales. I asked every old bat living there, and I found out that María had what you call a half-sister. Older, the same mother, but family. So then I had to find her, Nadia del Toro, and I found her not too far away. In El Chaparral. If you need to know what El Chaparral is like: the people there dream of living in Rojales one day. So I found her, but when I found her, I found her in the graveyard. She had been dead for more than thirty years. But María has something to pass on, and I had been hired to find the person who gets it.'

I could feel this story stretching into infinity. It had got darker in the room now, grey clouds growing over the sky like mould.

I took out the brandy bottle from the third drawer down and poured myself a short drink out of boredom more than anything else.

'Do you mind?' I interrupted him.

'Of course not.'

'Are you sure you don't want anything?'

'Nein, danke schoen.' He continued: 'Right next to the graveyard where Nadia was buried is the town's only nursing home. Run by the church. Sitting in a chair staring at a dead tree I found the oldest woman you've ever seen. She was as wrinkled as a prune, couldn't see a thing, her eyes were like pearls. These old people know every story in the town, and they know every story in the graveyard because they know they will be moving there soon. It was her who told me Nadia's story. Nadia had been a young person once, and she came to England looking for a job like all the others. She came here, to Brighton. She stayed in Brighton for three years before she came back home. But when she came back home she kept herself away from people. No one was allowed to see her. People got worried, but they didn't get worried enough, and one day she took too many sleeping pills. She was a nurse, she knew the dosage.'

I took a sip of my drink, I didn't really want it.

'In the investigation a friend turns up. Carmen. Now, Carmen is a gypsy, and not well liked in El Chaparral; you know what gypsies are like. No one seems to think she was particularly good friends with Nadia, but then no one in the town cared enough to stop her killing herself, so I will ignore that. Carmen gets on the stand and she says Nadia had a child.'

I could see where this was going now. Another bloodhound job for Grabarz, the best nose in Brighton. In a minute he'd pull out a hat or a glove so I could get the scent.

'She was raped. In Brighton. Nadia, she says, was raped by a Pole. She left the baby in the hospital. This is why she killed herself, Carmen says.' He coughed suddenly, spluttering. 'Could I have some water?'

I got up to pour him a glass from the sink in the cupboard. I passed him the water and he took a small sip and then hovered the glass over my desk.

'Coaster?'

'Don't worry about it.'

He put the glass down.

'So, I checked the records here. They are all online. Nadia was here for three years. Accounting for the nine months, still I had twenty-seven months to look through. I looked for orphans named Del Toro but there weren't any. So I searched for orphaned children with Polish surnames instead, and guess what, there was only one:' *Holy shit!* 'Joseph Grabarz.'

I felt like time should freeze at that moment. That the rain and the footsteps and the spiders in the corner should all look up and shout WHAT THE FUCK!? That I should be granted a few millennia to process and contemplate and finally come around to some decision about considering possibly thinking about an idea of what I might want to do next. But it didn't, time kept charging forward like a freight train to the stomach.

He leant back in his chair. I was already leant back in mine. The wind drifted in through the open windows. Hurried footsteps were sloshing up and down the alley. The rain pattered on the glass and splashed on the cobbles down below. The rain was endless. Much like the silence that was sitting in between us like a morning fog. I felt cold for the first time in weeks.

Stay calm. I tossed back the rest of my drink. I wanted it now. The brandy lit a welcome fire in my chest.

'Let me see if I understand this correctly,' I started steadily, 'you think, because of some uncorroborated story that some blind old Spanish lady told you, that I might be some other, now deceased, Spanish lady's half-nephew? Is that correct?' I thought I had made it sound sufficiently ridiculous.

'Yes. It is for me to determine the inheritor of her estate. And I say that you are the inheritor of her estate.'

'Let me guess, I just have to pay you a small fee to release that inheritance?'

'Nothing like that.'

I poured myself another drink. My phone vibrated on the desk. A text. I ignored it.

'So, if you're correct, how much would I inherit?'

A little smile danced across his increasingly smug face. 'You misunderstand me, Mr Grabarz. Maybe it's my English—'

'I doubt it.'

'—but, you see, the men who hired me lent a considerable amount of money to Miss Suárez, and they would like that investment back.'

I tried to keep my face stony. 'Excuse me?'

'I am afraid to say that you have inherited only debts.'

I nodded. 'How much?'

'After the sale of her house, and her remaining as-sets, the final amount is estimated to be a little over seventy thousand euros.'

'I see.' I nodded again. 'Get out of my office.'

Vogeli must have been smiling about something else as he pulled the cigarette and lighter out of his pocket, probably out of habit more than anything else, put it in his mouth and lit it.

'We'll accept it in installments,' he chuckled.

I slapped him across the mouth, knocking the ciga-rette across the room. He was so shocked he fell off his chair.

I towered over him. 'I told you to get out of my of-fice.'

He scrambled backwards out the door, into the re-ception area, and then back up onto his feet. He took his time brushing himself down.

'I don't want to see or hear from you ever again,' I told him.

He wasn't impressed. 'I'll be sending you a letter, Mr Grabarz, with the exact figures,' he straightened his washed out tie, 'and I'll include all research materials for you to examine.'

He was fully straightened now, what little of him there was. He patted down his errant wisps of hair.

'Good evening,' he spat, then marched out of the room.

I heard the street door shut as I went to the sink in the cupboard to throw some water on my face. I took a look at myself in the beaten-up mirror:

Did I look half-Spanish? What did that even look like? It was bullshit. It was all bullshit. A scam.

I had broken my oath to stay calm. In fact I had probably broken a record for the fastest broken oath in history. But that was just a practice run. From now on. Again: *I will stay calm*.

Then I remembered someone had text me, they needed my attention far more urgently than this. Who was it?

"*Be at mine in 21 minutes*," it said.

She had given me four extra minutes for the rain, I had wasted more than that already.

I barely locked up, ran into the rain, to my bike. Twice in two days? That was unlike her, normally it was once a fortnight, if that.

I rode as fast as I could; zipping down the middle of jams, doing fifty in the thirty zones, sixty in the twenty zones, splashing, skipping, roaring my way there, but still I didn't make it to hers until three minutes after the deadline.

I rang the bell. The butler opened the door just a crack. I went to step in out of the rain but it wouldn't budge. The chain was on.

'Miss Todman asked me to give you a message,' he said with twitching lips that wanted to smile, 'you're late.'

And then he slammed the door in my face.
I broke my oath again.

8

The Policeman's Curse

I PROMISED MYSELF I would never end up back here. The place made me feel sick. The anxiety. The oppression. The cheap, rough texture of anything you touched. Grey under yellow light, the walls and the furniture and the people were so desaturated it was like being colour blind. It was only a few weeks ago that I was in custody. They had kept me the full twenty-four before charging me. Not that it made any difference.

I wondered how many hours they were going to keep me for this time. I had already told the trout-faced desk sergeant that I wanted to speak to the officer in charge of the Jilani case. She had given me a long, suspicious gaze through the glass shutters, seriously considering that I might be here to confess. Then she picked up the phone, dialled, and whispered down it so I couldn't hear what she was saying. She watched me the whole time, making sure I didn't leg it. Then ten minutes passed. Then another ten. Then I got up to ask what the hell was going on, and was told the detective was on his way.

Then, another ten minutes later, the door into the bowels of the station opened casually and a Rodin leant on the frame, gazing down at me. Someone had painted the statue to look like a real man. They had even added stubble. The finished effect was of a grizzled, stony face; forty-something years old. Hard jaw. Sapphire blue eyes. Thick eyebrows. And slightly greying reddish-brown locks, the type that were combed back once and stayed there because he told them to.

I knew this face. It was a brilliant likeness of the bastard who had dragged me to court on circumstantial evidence. Sure, I had committed the crime, but that wasn't the point. This was the man who hadn't batted an eyelid, hadn't protested a jot, when I was marched out of court an "innocent" man. A statue then, and a statue now. My nemesis. Richard. Fucking. Daye.

I didn't say anything.

'This way,' was all he said and he marched through the steel door into the corridors.

Phones rang. People milled about. We were moving too quickly for me to take it all in, but I had memories to rely on. I felt like every officer we passed was staring at me, about to shout my name, but of course that wasn't true. It was just paranoia tickling me.

We descended at least two stories, and after this labyrinth of low ceilings and easy-fall-down stairs the people disappeared and we arrived in an empty corridor, trudging silently to the end, to the last door. His office.

The place stank of smoke. Maybe it was just because they were a different brand, but I was sure that I didn't smell like that. It was heavy, like wearing someone else's wet coat.

'Take a seat,' he offered as he took the one behind his desk.

There was only one other and it was opposite, half plastic, and leaking yellow foam out of a million slashes. It looked like an advert for a chair rescue charity.

It was dark outside, but it was darker in here. It was so dark down in this basement that I could barely see around the room. Everything was a haze of green and grey and brown and black. There were a few dented filing cabinets. A peeling wood effect unit with a dirty white kettle perched atop and a bevy of powdered drinks stuffed into a scummy mug. Underneath was a selection of chocolate bars, and other high calorie snacks for the all-nighters.

There weren't any photographs or certificates on the wall, just a pinned up Ordinance Survey map of the city, extending from Southwick on one side to Saltdean on the other. And from the sea to the South Downs.

Only when my glance made it all the way round did I spot that there was another man in the room, right next to my face. He was barely older than I was, and had a topknot and a warrior beard about ten years before either was fashionable.

'That's just DC Watson,' Daye said, 'ignore him.'

'Hey, dude,' the man said with a killer smile.

Their niceness unnerved me.

Daye marked the celebration of my visit by lighting a cigarette. It looked as thick as a cigar and the brand might have been called Wet Dog. I fished out one of my thin rollups.

'How do you get away with smoking in here?' I asked. I had to drag my voice up from a deep well.

'The smoke alarm has been broken for ten years. I keep forgetting to tell them.'

I looked up but the place was so dark I couldn't even see where it was.

I lit my cigarette and smoked it gently. We were all sitting there, all existing separately for now. Us two smoking, and the constable chipping away at a mountain of paperwork, the Anglepoise lamp on his desk the only source of light.

This must have continued for more than a couple of minutes, both of us enjoying our cigarettes, blowing out the smoke until the walls and the ceiling and the floor became even more imperceptible. The three of us wrapped in grey blankets.

Daye was as comfortable there as an old oak. You know its roots run as deep below ground as the branches span above, and if you tried to rip it up it would bring the whole earth with it.

Slowly, the tree began to move, a face emerged out of the fog, and a voice as rough as bark.

'You wanted to talk about Mahnoor Jilani,' it said.

'That's why I'm here.'

'Hmm,' he rumbled. I could feel the vibrations. 'Why?'

'Personal interest.'

'Mmm…'

Then he took the longest drag of a cigarette that I have ever seen. It lasted for what seemed like minutes, and then he pushed it out through his nostrils, down onto the desk and across it, where it curled up and licked the sides of the room like dry ice on a Hammer Horror set.

'Why are you really here?'

'I'm a family friend,' I assured him.

'Hmm…' Those strong eyebrows were raised at me. 'I think I'll give you one more chance, and then I'll ask you to leave. Why are you interested in the Jilani case?'

What did it matter anyway? I was probably only lying out of habit.

'Someone has asked me to look into it.'

'Someone?'

'Honestly, I don't know if I'm allowed to tell you.'

He nodded, in a way that suggested it didn't matter anyway. 'There's a phrase: never send a boy to do a man's job.'

'I'm twenty-two,' I reassured him.

He agreed: I was twenty-two. 'Why exactly did they ask *you* to look into it, Mr…?'

'Sweet.'

He nodded. 'Mr Sweet?'

'I guess they must have asked everyone else.'

This got a slight smile out of him. 'Fine. Why have you agreed to do it?'

'This is pretty one-sided at the moment,' I remarked.

'It is, isn't it,' he replied.

It was no use: I had to jump through his hoops if I wanted to get any further, so I kept jumping: 'If I find the girl they'll pay me.'

'So what are you, Mr Sweet, a private detective?'

That got a slight smile out of me, but nothing more.

'And what are you doing here?'

'I thought I could help you.'

'I see, so you don't want *my* help?' he said with a grin.

I sighed. What was the point of lying to him? I couldn't trick him into thinking I was a professional. Or even remotely good at this. He had sat there opposite a million other punks, who all thought they were twice as smart as I thought I was. But it didn't do them any good, and it wasn't going to do me any good either. He was like all professionals at the top of their game; like a tailor who can tell your measurements without a tape, or a doctor who can diagnose cancer from a cough. The point is: Daye knew you were going to lie before you even opened your mouth.

'I want your help,' I admitted.

He did nothing but tap some ash into an ash tray. He was a class act.

'I have twenty-four hours a day,' I continued, 'seven days a week, that I will be spending trying to find this girl. And we both want that.'

He looked at the wall for a while, as though there was a window there. I wondered what he could see out of it. DC Watson was still scribbling.

'Very well,' Daye started, 'I just have one more question.'

He didn't even look at me.

'On the fourteenth of September, did you, or did you not, break into a property on Reynolds Road, Mr Grabarz?'

Bugger. Buggering fucksticks. He had given me the opportunity to lie and I had taken it. Now he was giving me an opportunity to tell the truth. More than I would have done. Although it pissed me off when he called me a boy, he was right. I *was* a boy. But like all boys I thought I was a man. A big man. And I deserved the same respect that all the other big men got: another reason looking back on this makes me feel sick. If young me walked into my office today I wouldn't give him the time of day.

However, man or boy, the useful thing about having nothing is that you can bet it all easily. I barely nodded. That was all he needed, and that was all he was going to get.

He stubbed out his cigarette, nodded, and then stared out that imaginary window again, lighting another as he went. I didn't know how he finished them so fast: my thin wispy rollup wasn't even half done. I guess he'd had more practice than me.

'Will you help me?' I asked.

'No, it's ridiculous.'

I bit my tongue, just muttering: 'Excuse me?'

'You could get hurt.'

I laughed, which took him by surprise. 'You'd be the first to care.'

'Maybe so…'

'Look, I'm doing this anyway, so really you're putting me in greater danger by not helping. And don't give me any of that "it's nothing to do with me" crap because that doesn't sit with someone like you. You have the policeman's curse.'

He tapped more ash from the end of his cigarette. 'Which is?'

'You care.'

Watson had stopped scribbling, he was listening with his back to us.

'Now, I've come and asked for your help politely. You want to find her. I want to find her. Where's the conflict?'

He stared at me for a long time. I could feel the clockwork of his brain ticking over like a difference engine. Then he closed his eyes to calculate the result, or whatever the hell he was doing.

He opened them again. He had reached an answer. Finally, steadily, calmly, it came: 'To answer the big questions: is she alive? where is she? and who took her? first you need to answer the little questions. Where was she taken from? Was she targeted, or taken at random? If she was taken at random, how and where did she gain the abductor's interest? If she was targeted, why was she targeted? If you can answer those questions before you leave this room, I'll help you.'

It sounded like fun. 'Do I get to look at the case file?' I asked.

He frowned, he hadn't thought about it.

'It's hardly fair otherwise, I can't answer those questions without the same information you had.'

He stared at me for a few moments, then through me for just a second. 'Andy, fetch Mr Grabarz the case file, and then you had better make us all a cup of tea.'

It was fascinating to read. I had never read a police

file before. It had pictures, statements, interviews, forensic results, every piece of evidence catalogued, every person profiled. I pored through it.

When my tea finally arrived it was garnished with the flat shimmer of limescale. Flakes luxuriated in a huge mug, that looked like it held almost a pint. It made me think that Daye probably ran on tea and cigarettes and Watson had bought this mug to push back making tea from every twenty minutes to every half an hour. Daye was also one of those odd people who has whole milk, which is at least better than being one of those people who has skimmed milk. Other than that it was the colour of clay. The correct colour. A person is always as weak as their tea.

The first question was easy to answer, a warm-up of sorts. The tea was still too hot to drink.

'According to this statement from a pupil at Mahnoor's school,' I thought out loud, 'she "walked home alone like always". If she walks home alone it would be fair to assume she was taken off the street.'

'It's never fair to assume,' was Daye's response.

Fine, not so easy then, if he was going to play it like that. But half a pint of tea later I was studying pictures of their hallway, and pieces of evidence taken. Especially item number seven.

'Her school bag was in the house. With her keys inside. So she did get home. And she didn't go out again.'

'Good,' was all he said.

'Is that a fair assumption?' I asked pointedly.

'It's not an assumption: it's a deduction.'

Whilst I finished the rest of my tea I read a very long interview with Mrs Jilani, where she confirmed that none of Mahnoor's clothes were missing: that meant she was still in her uniform. Then a very short interview with Mr Jilani. He seemed to know almost no helpful details about his daughter. There were a lot of I-don't-knows and she-might-haves. It made a part of my brain itch, like a thought was clawing to get out. I could hear it through the walls, but as much as I tried I just couldn't find my way to it.

In my searching I had inadvertently opened the door to another thought: 'She was targeted.'

'Why?'

'There were no signs of a break in, and nothing was missing, so they weren't waiting in the house for some-one else, and she didn't disturb a burglary. They just knocked on the door and grabbed her.'

'She would scream.'

'They chloroformed her. Stuck her in the back of a van.'

'That image is hard to avoid, isn't it.'

'She always walked home alone, but they took her from the house. Why?'

He didn't say anything, except to offer me another cup of tea. I said yes and Watson boiled the kettle again. It was the slowest kettle in the world, and made far more noise than necessary, it was drowning out my thoughts. All I could picture were calcium crystals swirling around the glowing element.

Why would they take her from the house? If it was me, the only reason I would follow her home would be if I needed to know where she lived. I looked at the other pieces of assembled evidence. It was mostly the girl's things. Nothing too exciting.

After I had finished my second pint of tea I was bursting for the loo. And that's when I realised Daye's cruel joke: I wasn't allowed to leave the room.

I shifted in my seat, attempting to crush away the sensation in my bladder. I could sense a small grin dancing across his face. *Come on, Joe, let's wipe that smile off his face. Think. Think, goddammit!*

'They didn't know what she looked like!' I said it before I had even realised it myself.

'What makes you think that?' Daye asked, not fully able to hide the surprise and interest from his voice.

Come on, brain, catch up! 'They were waiting outside the house, waiting for her to get home,' I was blurting it out now, 'It's kidnap!' I shouted.

'Slow down,' Daye said.

But I couldn't slow down, I was bursting with thoughts and piss. 'They couldn't wait until the next day, they had to take her there and then. And there's no other reason to abduct someone you've never seen before. It's not about her! They're ransoming the dad.

That's why he's so shit in his interviews. So... so... what's the word?'

'Evasive?' Watson offered.

'Yes!' I was on a high now, those desperate thoughts free to tear up the corridors of my mind.

'Go for a piss,' he told me.

I couldn't stop smiling.

Halfway through urinating the smile left me, it didn't add up. I told him as much when I returned.

'No,' he agreed.

'Where's the girl? If he couldn't pay, then fine, but why not tell the police as soon as the ransom demand came in. And if he could pay, and did pay, then where is she?'

'Mmm,' Daye murmured in agreement.

I gestured to the file, 'Can I take photocopies?'

He barely shook his head, 'No.'

'Can I take some notes then?'

'No, you cannot.'

I didn't push it, finishing my cigarette and stubbing it out in his ash tray.

'He's a taxi driver,' I said under my breath. 'Living in Whitehawk. Who in god's name would blackmail *him*?'

He didn't reply, he was staring out that window again.

So I asked him: 'What's your feeling?'

'My feeling hasn't found the girl,' he replied modestly.

'So I'll feel free to ignore it.'

He smirked, put out his cigarette and took the only breath of fresh air I'd seen him take. Not that the air in this room could ever be called fresh. I mean, it was stretching the definition to call it air.

'I think he paid,' he said at last. 'I think he paid, but they didn't give her back. And now he's too ashamed because if he had told the police then she might still be alive. And if his wife finds out she'll never forgive him. And that's why *she* hired you, and not him.'

Smart bastard. But that wasn't a surprise by now. At least we were making progress.

'But you've been through his bank accounts,' I said, referring to the file, 'and no large amounts have been paid out.'

'Yes. And now you're in the same place we are.'

I waited for more, but it didn't come. 'Thanks for the help.'

'Don't flatter yourself. I just don't see any point in that poor woman paying you to do work we've already done.'

'What should I do now?'

'My official advice?'

I shrugged. 'Why not?'

He looked me dead in the eyes. 'Tell Mrs Jilani you are very sorry, but the girl is dead. There's nothing you can do. Then go home, and never think about it again.'

It was cool and quiet as I stepped out into the evening. A gentle breeze caught the sound of distant seagulls ruffling their necks and drifting asleep on their perches, ready for another day of battle with people who hate them. The moon was beautiful that night, it's pitted silver surface resting silently in space. It looked close enough to hop a bus to. Maybe from up there I could get some perspective on this whole damn thing.

Another bank account. A secret bank account. What was Mr Jilani up to? Daye had given me a challenge whether he wanted to or not. And when I'm awake, and healthy, and reasonably sober, all of which I would be tomorrow morning, then I like a challenge.

9

The Little Questions

"LETTER FROM KIDNAPPER" screamed the headline of Monday's morning edition. The story was even on my television, but it was the paper that had received the letter, and they printed it in full:

To the parents of Joy Tothova,

We have your daughter. She has not been hurt. But we will enjoy hurting her if we have to. I am very disappointed at the police. They have no idea who we are. They do not understand. Especially that fat old man who first was investigating. The blonde woman is more clever. But we are more clever than her.

We at first did not wish to involve the media. But you have offered £100,000 to the person who finds Joy. We have her, and we now claim our money.

You are beautiful parents. She is a beautiful girl. She has been asking for her pink bear. We do not wish to hurt her. But if you do not pay us the money then we will have to hurt her. This newspaper will receive instructions. But if you involve the police, and if the newspaper tells anyone else, we will send you your English rose in the post, petal by petal.

Yours,
   Mancini

I didn't know what to think. But thankfully the paper had managed to shake out of bed a professor of Criminal Psychology at the University of Sussex, who had given them her "initial reactions".

She said that "the use of 'we' suggests multiple abductors", but that "the use of 'I' in the fourth sentence of the first paragraph suggests that it is in fact one abductor, who is trying to appear as more than one. Most likely to appear more powerful."

The fact that the author seemed to be aware of the change in senior investigator from Daye to Price suggested that they were "following the investigation closely". However, the fact that they did not use their names suggested that they either "do not have the mental capacity to recall them", or that they "do not place much importance on names". This suggests "a prepubescent mentality". The suggestion that they are more intelligent than DCI Price suggests "arrogance, delusions of grandeur, or simply a reduced ability to make accurate judgements". I thought that was a pretty strong compliment to Price.

Despite all this, their use of the phrase "involve the media" was "curiously adult", and their specificity in quoting the exact amount of money "suggests an understanding of the details of the situation that is not present in their descriptions of the investigators". Their use of the parents' own offer of money suggests either a "childlike simplicity" or a "distinctly adult sense of irony." So he's either really thick or really smart, basically.

The professor explained that the description of the Tothovas suggests this person "had not seen the parents before the media coverage", because it appears "as a revelation". The mention of the pink bear toy "appears as a form of evidence to prove their claim that they have the girl". The police would have to issue a statement on that.

The fact that the author of the letter claimed separately that they "did not wish to hurt her" and "would enjoy hurting her" suggests a conflict of personality. But the professor made it clear that she could make no medical diagnosis. In other words, he or she is definitely mad but they might not have a name for it. The professor instead suggested that the author had a "troubled personality". Who doesn't?

She brushed past that by saying that the use of the newspaper as the conduit of communication between the author and the parents seems to suggest "a lack of knowledge of the parents address, or of a more secure form of communication". This, in her opinion, was a strong mark against the validity of the letter. Communication directed at individuals but sent via the media was common in hoaxes, as "the number one desire is publicity". The naivety in demanding that the newspaper not "tell anyone else" did not seem genuine, she said. But she stressed, or more accurately the paper stressed, "there was no way to rule out the possibility that this was a genuine communication from the kidnapper."

I couldn't believe the paper thought it was real. Even with my low opinion of all hacks, I couldn't believe they would publish it if they thought it was. I mean, even they wouldn't want to risk seeing the girl hurt, it would be bad for business.

There were two things the professor didn't remark on, or at least not that the paper published. First, the use of the phrase "English rose", and the extension of that metaphor into "petal by petal". And second, the use of the name "Mancini". It had to be a reference to the 1933 murder of Violette Kaye by a man then known as Toni Mancini, actually Cecil Lois England. He murdered her and kept her body in a trunk at the foot of his bed, which he used as a coffee table despite complaints from friends about the smell and the leaking. That was at 52 Kemp Street, by the way, just down from the station. I wonder if the person living there knows that.

History lesson aside, these facts had a distinctly personal touch. The rest of the letter was a performance, a fictional character, but those words, they were the real person. We've all read something like it before: those stories where the interesting narrator breaks character because the self-righteous author can't help butting in.

Last night was a bit of a blur. After Mr Vogeli's visit and after Monica Todman's butler had slammed her door in my face, I'm pretty sure I rode my bike back to the office and went and got smashed. I mean, it's a good bet. And it's about all I had to go on.

Sitting at the kitchenette table, reading the newspaper, eating avocado toast, drinking an espresso, all whilst ignoring the hangover that was trying to crush my skull, I made an executive decision: it was time to stop following the Tothovas around. It had taught me a lot about them, but it hadn't got me any closer to finding the girl. And it's not like I was getting expenses.

I knew the questions I needed to answer, the same ones as always. To answer the big questions: is she alive? where is she? and who took her? First you need to answer the little questions: where was she abducted? Was she targeted, or taken at random? If she was taken at random, how and where did she gain the abductor's interest? If she was targeted, why?

Everyone knew the answer to the first question: Fiveways. But where and when exactly was really speculation. Graham Tothova was at the greengrocers, Maria Tothova was at the butchers. Joy was being abducted. There was a five minute window. Five minutes out of sight and she was out of sight forever.

With great effort I stood up and wandered to the bedroom window. Finally, the slice of bread was gone. The baby seagull was next to the puddle where it had landed. Glistening, still a little wet from yesterday's shower, but asleep. I studied his wings, the way they rested near his tail feathers: I had heard before that if their wings don't cross at the back then they can't fly yet. His didn't. He had glided down from roof to roof in order to get the bread, but he couldn't get out. If his parents didn't come and feed him he would die. I threw him another slice of bread and went back to the kitchenette.

Hangover be damned, today was a new day, time for a new oath. From now on I was going to be a sensible, serious, only mildly sarcastic detective. I would walk to the office, get my bike, head to Fiveways, and start figuring this shit out.

This plan was slightly scuppered when I stepped

outside to see my Honda on its side, no kickstand, on the traffic island in the middle of the circus.

Ahem, I thought. Well, I guess I didn't quite make it to the lock up last night. The tarmac and the bike showed signs that it had been dragged from the middle of the road. Time for a swift exit. The circus was as busy as always, and no one seemed to be paying any attention to me or it, so I hauled it up, got it running, and zipped along and up Ditchling Road. Today was another of those hot, hot days; when there's even more heat coming up at you from the ground than there is from the sky, and everything wants to melt like living in a Dalí.

Less than two minutes later I was at the Fiveways and my bike was parked on the pavement, just round a corner enough not to be noticed by any warden checking up on the freshly painted restrictions.

The Fiveways area is so named after the crossroads that connect Preston Drove, Stanford Avenue, and Hollingbury Road to Ditchling Road. It has the reputation, strongly enforced by its residents, of being like a village for people with liberal views. A village of terraced houses with very little greenery.

Artists living at Fiveways were supposedly the first to open their homes to visitors and therefore start the whole Open House phenomenon that sweeps the city during the Festival. And that's probably the best summary of character when it comes to Fiveways. It's a local place for local people, who don't shop at supermarkets, and can't see that that's because they can afford not to. The place has a butchers, a greengrocers; a bakers, and an artisan bakers. Five estate agents, two coffee shops, a deli, a pub, a wine bar, and a specialist wine shop. Two hairdressers, a men's hairdressers, and two barbers. An arts & crafts shop, an antiques and second-hand books shop, and a strange combination gifts, cards, and plant shop. A women's clothes and knick-knacks shop, a children's clothes shop, and a second-hand clothes shop; but you know, the posh kind where the items cost more than you would want to spend if they were new. The list goes on: a podiatrist, an independent toy shop. The practical capitalist necessities: a bank, a Post Office, a hidden dentist, a dry cleaners that never seems to be open, and a Co-op for the bits the greengrocers don't stock. If that's anything.

And, whisper it, a Chinese, an Indian, a kebab shop, a fish & chip shop, a newsagents, and shock horror, even a bookies. But these last few places are ignored by the residents like muggles passing Diagon Alley.

The people at Fiveways are all artists. Of course, not actually, they're teachers and accountants and management consultants like every other middle class neighbourhood. But unlike Patcham or York Avenue they all paint, or make their own jewellery, or make their own pickles, or make their own smug sense of satisfaction. They all wear casual, ethnic clothes, and like the rest of Brighton are as white as snow. It's a co-opted form of radicalism, of anti-establishmentarianism. Anarchy in a White Stuff blouse. They think they're hip and young and unconventional because they eat Thai food and wear a poncho. But they're middle class. Just middle class Brighton-style.

The first stop I made was into the greengrocers, where I chatted to a lovely woman called Lil. She said the Tothovas were regular customers, but she hadn't seen the girl that day. Uniformed officers had spoken to them at the end of last week, none of them could remember noticing Joy, they were busier than usual for a Wednesday morning and had very little time to chat to customers, even the regulars. In the butchers a man who seemed in charge, Will, remembered serving Maria six chicken thighs and a rack of lamb. But he didn't see the girl, and like the greengrocers they didn't have CCTV.

I decided to be thorough and went from shop to shop, chatting to the owners and the staff. They were all lovely, and what struck me was how the staff in these places could be so normal when the customers were so weird.

No one had seen Joy, and only a couple of other shops had noticed either of the parents. Fiveways is not that busy, but it's not un-busy either. Joy had a choice of a million roads to wander down, following a cat or something. A five minute radius in every direction was an enormous area. And all a sick bastard had to do was see her wandering alone. That's if she wasn't targeted, of course.

Sitting on a picnic bench outside the pub I texted Thalia to ask if she had found out which school Joy went to. She hadn't.

There was another way I could find out but I didn't like it. I did it anyway.

The phone rang on the other end for some time.

'Alderney Investigations,' a chirpy secretary chirped.

I told him I needed to speak to Clarence.

He told me to wait one minute and put me on hold. I imagined a wide marble lobby with brass hand rails and a receptionist in stiff white uniform. I liked to imagine Clarence worked in an old movie. One of those set in that kind of posh hotel that doesn't seem to exist anymore and probably never did. With Clarence behind an executive desk with plush furniture and an oil portrait of some grave looking moustachioed man above the carriage clock on the side.

One minute later Clarence's voice broke through the music: 'Joe, how are you?' he panted.

'You sound out of breath.'

'I'm not in the office, my secretary put you through to my mobile.'

'Hot lead?'

'What if it was?'

I just shrugged. I hoped it was audible.

'At the risk of sounding direct,' he continued, 'what is it you want?'

'I'm hoping you know which school the girl goes to.'

'There's nothing to be found there, I'm afraid.'

'Can't I find that out for myself?'

'I thought I'd save you the trouble, I want to at least worry I might lose our bet. It's no fun otherwise.'

'Really, you've got this all sussed out, have you?'

'Let's just say, the answers will become clear to you tomorrow morning. Right around dawn. Know what I mean?'

'No idea,' I lied.

'Think about it.'

'Thank you, I won't. Several decades ago I asked you a question; if you don't remember, it was if you knew which school she goes to?'

He did, and he told me without hesitation.

'What do you want in return?' I asked.

'Nothing at all,' he replied, 'have a good day.' And he hung up.

The strange thing was I would've preferred to give him something. I don't like being in anyone's debt.

From the outside the school looked eerily empty. I couldn't work out from the date whether or not school should be on. It was the middle of July, and all I knew was that it was around the time they broke up.

The school wasn't that far from Fiveways, another remnant of the Tothovas' pre-Hove life. It was hidden down a long single width fifty metre drive which revealed behind a row of houses a playing field and then the one-story building. If it weren't for the sign at the top of the drive you would never know it was there.

This was a problem. If you ever want to pass unnoticed in a school or hospital or anywhere really, then the bigger the better and the busier the better. As it was, I couldn't even tell if the place was open.

I had parked my bike at the top of the drive, remembering to take from my saddlebag my go-anywhere, do-anything master key to all buildings: a red lanyard that says visitor, and a blue one that says staff. I put both round my neck, leaving the staff one visible. Then, despite the heat, I zipped my jacket half up to cover the actual badge bit.

I wandered to the other end of the playground, away from the sign that pointed to the reception, and then I was into the corridors. I wasn't really sure at this point what I was looking for, but I headed for the central information nexus: the staffroom.

In the corridors I passed a couple of staff who nodded to me and gave barely audible 'Hi's. The lanyard was working well; to teachers I was some office worker or PE coach, and to office workers I was some teacher or PE coach. What I was to PE coaches I couldn't say.

There were no children anywhere to be seen. I assumed today was that odd day after the kids finish when there are meetings and goodbyes and work to be done, when everybody is trying to judge how early is too early to leave. It amused me to think that all of us might be private detectives or journalists, wandering the halls, eavesdropping on each other; the school itself might be entirely deserted.

The staffroom was empty too. One whole wall was covered in pigeon holes and I used the time to search for any names I recognised, any yet undrawn connections between the school and the rest of the Tothovas' lives. There weren't any. After that I decided to buy a twenty pence coffee from a machine that buzzed, and coughed and spluttered it out into a flimsy plastic cup that made it feel like I was holding the hot coffee itself, before taking a seat. Someone had to come in at some point. Something had to happen.

The next twenty minutes tested that theory pretty severely. It was nothing but me and the shit coffee and the ticking clock that mocked my patience. As a child I had always imagined what the staffroom looked like, the one place you could never go. I had never imagined it so boring. Noticeboards. Plants. NUT posters. A discarded filter coffee pot. Big group staff photos from the last few years. I didn't recognise anyone.

Instead I imagined what my life would be like if I

had been one of these teachers; would I be the passion-
ate kind, or one of those who takes it because it's there
and they give you a good starting salary and loads of
holidays? I thought I knew the answer to that.

I picked up a newspaper from the coffee table in
front of me. It was a broadsheet, and it was just nice to
read a front page that didn't feature Joy Tothova for
once. Sadly it seemed from the front page like the world
was falling apart outside the Brighton bubble. Terror-
ism. Shootings. Brexit. Donald Trump. If we really
made an effort, this year could be our chance to make
the world significantly worse.

The door opened with a raucous laugh and I clung
onto the paper in an attempt to look occupied.

'That was an interesting goodbye speech,' a young,
slightly too posh, man's voice remarked.

'Was it?' a shrill female voice asked, 'I'm surprised
so many people clapped.'

'Yes, I wonder why that was,' he replied suggestively, as a coffee began to spurt into a cup.

'John will be happy.'

'No, he's not getting the job,' came the hushed reply,
'haven't you heard?'

'Heard what?'

'Matt Newton's getting it.'

'Really?'

'Yes, and we all know why, don't we.'

'Do we?' she asked. I thought the same.

'Let's just say that he does give Allyson a lift home every day.'

'Does he?'

I had very little idea what any of this meant but this man seemed to know the school gossip, so I listened until the woman decided that she did, after all, have work to do. To my immense luck he took a seat opposite me and I looked up from pretending to read the newspaper.

I recognised him from somewhere. And what's more, he recognised me.

'Hello again,' he said calmly, smiling with one half of his face.

Late twenties. Floppy black hair. Thick eyebrows. White shirt. Designer jeans. Shiny black shoes. *Work brain, work!*

'Tam.'

'Tab,' he corrected me. *Close enough.*

It was that posh twat from the curry night. 'How are you?' I asked.

'Great thanks, John. If that is your real name.'

'It isn't.'

His eyes had already glazed over with disinterest. 'What are you doing here?'

'Sniffing around.'

'I see. Do you work for the paper or freelance?' he asked, thinking he was clever.

'Neither, I'm not a journalist.'

'Oh really. Just another concerned citizen.'

'No, I'm a detective. But I admit I do do it freelance.'

His eyes darted up, at me, there was something different in them now: interest.

'You work here?' I asked.

'Yes.'

'Doing what?'

'Teaching.' He said it like it was obvious, like this was some kind of school.

'You don't have a pigeon hole.'

'Not yet. I'm training.'

'I see.'

Whilst I glanced away he reached up and undid one top button, revealing a little more pink skin. 'The school won't be very happy to find a detective in the staffroom. Even one as beautiful as you.'

'Who's going to tell them?'

He smiled. It certainly wasn't going to be him.

'You know Joy is a pupil here?'

'I do know that.'

'That makes you someone interesting to talk to.'

His blue eyes studied me. 'Now I know what someone has to do to be interesting to you.'

Gone was the gormless charity worker. The 'Oh really?', he was a different person. He was Mercury. And it wasn't interest in those eyes, it was attraction.

'We should go for a drink sometime.'

'How about tonight?' he asked.

'How about right now?'

A nervous smile danced across his lips. 'Right now?'

I nodded.

He thought for another moment, then it was 'Ok,' and he picked his jacket off the chair.

'They're such a perfect family,' he said into his gin & tonic. He had asked for it with a slice of orange instead of lemon or lime. It was about the most interesting thing he had said so far.

We were in the nearest pub, just two roads from the school. No doubt this place would be swarmed with the rest of them come three o'clock, all toasting to the long summer, and the hope they were never coming back. At the moment it was scattered with a few of those afternoon drunks who fall asleep and sometimes never wake up.

'They're such a perfect family,' he said again, 'they remind me of mine.'

I took a sip of the bright green Gimlet I had ordered. I had to insist on it made the proper way: half and half.

He kept going: 'Father, mother, and beautiful child. And me for good measure. My nan's the only one who ever loved me.' He offered me a boiled sweet, I turned it down.

Yeah, I felt like saying, *I'm sure your childhood was really tough, posh boy.*

'My sister was just like Joy. Just as innocent.'

His arm came to rest on my knee. I didn't know if it was a crash landing or a deliberate stopover. I let it sit there, this was the new me, the calm me; but I knew I had tried a similar technique myself and if it attempted to taxi anywhere else then I would give him the same slap they gave me. The difference was that I was drunk when I tried it. If I hadn't bought him his only drink I'd think he was drunk now.

'Can you think of anyone that would want to hurt her?' I asked.

'My sister?'

'Joy.'

He scoffed. 'Isn't that why everyone is so upset? No one can think of a reason.' He was staring into the drink, into the bubbles, and the ice. 'But something being perfect can be reason enough to want to destroy it, can't it? Ever seen a beautiful painting and wanted to rip it to shreds? Ever seen a matchstick model standing so brilliantly tall that you want to trash it? Ever seen a kitten so cute you want to squeeze it until it bursts?' His fingers gripped my knee.

'I can't say that I have.'

'That's not true.' His hand flew up from my knee to express his point dramatically. 'Everyone gets jealous. Everyone loves to break things. It's nature. Look at a toddler, if you build something they'll knock it down. Laughing.'

'They knock it down because they get attention.'

'Yeah well, we know where everyone's attention is now, don't we?' His hands were back on his drink.

'Sounds like your childhood might have fucked you up even worse than mine.'

'Your childhood? I bet it was terribly tragic, wasn't it? What was it like?'

I couldn't help smiling. 'Short.'

Tab looked at his watch, 'The others are going to be here in a minute. One of us had better leave.'

'I'll do the honours.'

'Before you do…' He grabbed my arm. Something I did not like. '…I don't know if this is important, but the police are looking for a van, right?'

'Right.'

'Chris, in the site team, he has a van. It doesn't belong to the school, and he doesn't normally drive it to work, but I've seen him park it at the school a couple of times in the holidays. I just thought… he would have seen her.'

I asked him what he looked like. He told me.

'Thank you,' I said, 'I'll check it out,' as I peeled him off me.

I waited at the top of the school road. I had checked,

and there wasn't another sensible way out. I heard the high-pitched buzzing of a moped down below and then one zipped past me. As much as they can zip.

I got a quick glimpse of the rider: tall, lanky, white guy, wispy beard and checked shirt. That was him all right. Tab had described him to a T.

I followed as gently as possible on my Honda. It was quite an effort to stay a distance from him, my bike being so ridiculously overpowered compared to his. He headed up Preston Drove to the Fiveways, and over the other side, then left along Stanmer Villas just before The Dip. And finally, a minute later he headed onto Golf Drive.

I pulled over to the kerb. Golf Drive is a dead end, and too deserted for him not to spot me following. If he didn't live there then he only had one good reason: Roedale Valley Allotments. I got off my bike, and wandered up the road.

Golf Drive has four weird terraced house-sized buildings just on one side, split into flats, and then nothing. I couldn't see his moped in front of any of them, so I headed for the nothing. I say nothing, there's a small car park at the end next to a recycling point.

The car park looks out over, and leads to, acres of allotments. They stretch up out of sight, all the way to Hollingbury Golf Course. They looked empty, but I assumed that there must be some odd people hidden amongst the rows of crops, beds, ramshackle sheds, and grimy greenhouses.

In the car park, again, there was no moped. But there was something else: a van. A white van. A Ford Transit. But a white one. It also looked far too old for the description. It looked like the type that used to ram raid shops. I half expected men with stockings on their heads to come pouring out. It was the wrong damn age and the wrong damn colour, but incongruous enough that I wanted to stay out of sight.

It was parked up against the furthest of the car park's only two lamp posts. The back doors were open, but before I could move to an angle where I could see inside, the lanky, wispy-bearded man in a checked shirt and now a baseball cap, stepped out of the back and shut them.

I knelt in the bushes by the side of the road, and waited. He was taking a very cautious look around. He didn't see me. He didn't see anyone.

He put the keys in his pocket and marched quietly down the path, through the open gates, and into the allotments. I waited five minutes, he didn't return. I wanted to wait ten, but I was too impatient. It was white. I stepped out of the bushes and into the car park, trying to move to a position where I could see into the allotments. It was no good, they were too overgrown, too full of bamboo sticks and polytunnels to see anything.

I orbited the van, it was in bad condition. Rusty.

Dented. More orange than white up close. And longer than the normal model. There was nothing interesting in the front that I could see through the windows. I noted down the number plate, then I tried the back door. It was locked. A new lock. And I couldn't pick the laser cut type.

I circled round to the other side and almost tripped over something: rubber trunking. The type designed to stop you tripping. The type they use to cover cables when they run across the floor in an office. Or a school. I kicked it over. It was covering a wire that ran from under the van, along the metre of tarmac, and into the base of the lamp post.

The clever bastard, he was powering something inside the van by sharing the power fed to the lamp post. In fact, he had probably diverted the power entirely, that way the van would be hidden in the darkness at night, avoided, and no one would spot what he was doing. What *was* he doing? The thought gave me shivers. And then I realised quite how quiet it was around here. Just the birds and the wind. No civilization.

The car park was full of other silent vans, and even more silent caravans with ratty net curtains hiding the inside, as though anyone would dare look. Were they abandoned, just kept here in this free car park, or were they all used for nefarious purposes? The two dwellings, I refuse to call them houses, a few metres from the car park were much the same. Wooden construction, single floor, like a holiday cabin. But with the same ratty curtains drawn; rusting, rotting children's garden toys, and dead plants everywhere. As though a sickness in the cabin leeched the life from the soil.

I took out my penknife and peeled a chunk of paint off the van. It was pretty much rust underneath, but what wasn't rust was blue.

I headed through the gates into the allotments. The little shop and tea shed were closed. Empty. I couldn't see anyone around. The path ran along the bottom of the valley, and the holdings rose up on each side. They looked pretty large, a couple of hundred square metres each.

I headed up the path, peering at each plot as best as I could. I passed tidy ones with neat rows of vegetables and strawberries, climbers like runner beans and raspberries. I passed a lot of untidy ones, with half broken greenhouses full of rubbish and rubble. Weedy, over grown, grassy plots; and neat, prim lawns.

Halfway up the path I hadn't spotted him, and I was beginning to worry that he was in one of the dark sheds that I couldn't see into. Or that he had ridden his moped up out the other end and onto the golf course.

It was hot again. Too damn hot. I stood for five minutes under the only tree I could find just to get some shade. Then I passed a communal tap with a leaky pipe that was spraying water onto the grass. I caught some of the spray on my hand and rubbed it on the back of my neck. It was good. So good I had to do it again.

Three quarters of the way up, I spotted his moped parked outside a smart looking, recently woodstained shed. He didn't come out until I had been standing there for three minutes, looking as imposing as I ever have. He was carrying a cutting of some kind and almost dropped it when he saw me.

'Chris Corpe?'

He swallowed a comical gulp. He was very skinny, pale, and his beard was the thin, almost spray-on type that only very young men or very old women can grow. The former in this case. He was weedy. I had absolutely nothing to worry about.

'Who are you?' he asked feebly.

'Show me what's in the van, Chris.'

He swallowed again, and sort of pretended to relax. 'I don't know what you're talking about.'

'The one you have wired up to the lamp post.'

He twitched slightly, ready to bolt. 'Are you the police?'

'I am so much worse. And if you don't show me what's in that van then you'll find out how.'

Two-hundred metres later, his hand was shaking as he unlocked the back. It swang open with a rusty screech.

There was no one inside. No little girl. What there was, was dirt. Soil, I mean. And plants. Two rows, under strip lights. Sodding marijuana.

I just walked off, I didn't even say anything.

'Hey, dude!' he shouted, 'we're ok, right?'

I didn't reply, I just kept walking.

Another sodding day wasted. This was beginning to feel like the Mahnoor Jilani case: no clues, no trace, no motive. Nothing. Surely this thing couldn't run for months. Not again. What did I do that time? I had tried to forget.

10

Nice Ideas

PEOPLE ALWAYS WANT to know. I can see it in their eyes. It irritated me, but at least he had the balls to actually ask. I had a rehearsed answer. He wouldn't like it of course, people always thought it was flippant. But for me, it was the truth.

When I had left Daye's office I had been full of optimism, full of purpose. All I had to do was prove that Tariq Jilani had a second bank account and things would begin to unravel, or fall into place, or whatever metaphor you want to use. But just in crossing the road it drained out of me like someone had turned on a tap. I couldn't face it. Not that shitty caravan. Not Debra's cold dinner under rain-covered foil left on the plastic step.

I stopped into The Jurys Out and took a spot at the bar, ordering whatever was on the tap in front of me. I figured the expenses the mothers were covering must include beer money. It was a human right. I was far less sophisticated in those days; I wasn't the cocktail drinker I am now. I was a beer drinker, and not the posh craft stuff, that wasn't even a thing yet. Not even real ale, just beer. The cheap stuff too. I drank it like water.

I lit a cigarette, I had had enough fresh air already, and started to mope. A few people frowned at me lighting up, half of them were likely policemen, but there was nothing they could do. The ban was on its way, but it wasn't here yet.

I felt sorry for myself, wondering how I was ever going to prove a second bank account. Picturing a whole load of hard work in front of me. It wasn't my style, I was much better at lazing around getting drunk. Today, a second bank account wouldn't even be a problem. It would be a chore. I was pathetic.

We were all pathetic. No one in this place was rushing home to a family or lover. We were all drinking, hypnotised by the muted television in the corner, and trying not to think. I saw a man crack an egg into his pint and drink it. I had never seen that before.

Pints later is when this topknotted, bearded young man drifted in and up to the bar, waving to a couple of red nosed, mac wearing real ale swillers on his way.

He ordered a cider and swivelled my way.

'Do you know what I did this morning?' he asked with a smile.

What was his name? It was the young guy from Daye's office, a DC. It would come to me.

'I jumped the pier, kitesurfing.'

'You'd better not speak to me,' I grunted, 'I'm a criminal; you heard.' I was in a bad mood.

'Get over yourself, dude. Look around,' he did it for me, 'half the people in here are criminals. All have been in court today, and here they are sharing a pub with policemen, lawyers, and even the occasional judge. They all just want a drink.'

I gave him my best attempt at a death stare. He met it with a smile that would melt anyone's heart. Luckily, I don't have one.

'Have you really been hired to find that little girl?' he asked.

'Yes, I have.'

'Why?'

'You know, if people keep asking me that I'm going to start feeling insulted.'

'I'm sorry.'

I sniggered slightly. 'You probably are, as well.'

He still had the smile on his face, yet it wasn't painted on. He was one of those people with a small personal summer inside them, the warmth of which was felt whenever they spoke.

'Why do you want to start a conversation with me?' I asked.

'You look like you could do with a friend.'

I didn't know what to say to that.

More pints later and the pub had emptied of the after work lawyers and coppers, and the disembowelled witnesses and defendants; all that was left were the career drunks. Them, and me, and the man on my elbow.

'Daye didn't tell me you were an orphan.'

'That's a lovely non sequitur.'

'He's not the type to discuss other people's business. Unless it's pertinent to a case.'

'How did you find out then?'

'Your police file.'

What followed would be silence to anyone listening, but to me it was the static charge that precedes a lightning strike. I could feel it building. *Here it comes…*

'What happened to your parents?'

'Nothing,' I replied by rote, 'I never had any.'

For the first time, he didn't smile. Nor did he push it any further, giving a few respectful moments silence before he changed the subject. My follicles went back to resting.

'What did you think of the boss?' he asked.

'Interesting guy, if he's not careful someone might end up liking him.'

'I like him.'

'Then I guess he's too late.'

'He's a brilliant detective.'

'And quite the conversationalist, I bet you have great long chats into the middle of the night.'

The top half of his face frowned, but the bottom half hadn't got the memo and smiled again. 'He's a thinker. Sometimes I feel that he could solve any case without leaving his office. He just sits and thinks, sometimes for hours, and then… boom, the answer comes out of him.'

'Not like you then.'

'I just do the paperwork.'

I smiled in disbelief. You couldn't insult this guy. 'The Signing Detective. Keeping the streets safe one form at a time.'

'Something like that.' He smiled again, he seemed to think I was laughing *with* him. 'He likes you.'

'How could you tell?'

'He didn't throw you out on your ear.'

'That would be your advice, would it?'

'I'm too soft to throw you out. But I certainly wouldn't help you.'

Maybe there was some grit in this man after all. His smile had changed a bit now, it was less innocent, more knowing.

'I thought you were my friend,' I told him.

The smile did a little shimmy, like sunlight on waves. 'He works hard because he cares,' he explained, 'you're doing it for money.'

'Does he not get paid?'

'Maybe I'm too idealistic.'

'Maybe he's a better judge of character,' I retorted.

'I'm sure he is.'

I was starting to like him now. But I still hated him.

'I have no problem with you,' he told me, 'you understand.'

'No? You're the first.'

'You were doing what you had to do to survive. I think he knows that. But for me, there has to be more to life than survival.'

'Some of us don't have a choice.'

'Everyone has a choice,' he almost snapped. 'The way I see it, you only have one real responsibility, and that's to make the world a better place for you being in it. That could be anything, it doesn't have to mean making poverty history, it could be art, it could just mean bringing some joy to people's lives.'

'Well, I'm not a comedian. I'm not a poet. I don't have enough money to join a pottery class. And they don't let people like me become politicians. No one wants me to change the world. Surviving is the only option I've got. Surviving or dying. This world has never given me a thing, so I don't owe it.'

'It's given you life.'

'You're right, maybe it does owe me.'

He didn't smile again. For the first time he wore a genuine frown, but it was clearly an uncomfortable fit. He had to break it in like new shoes.

'We're just overgrown monkeys,' I continued, 'and I take great comfort in the knowledge that in a hundred years no one will ever know that I existed. Nothing I could do will ever matter.'

He sighed. 'If this is all there is. If this is all we'll ever experience,' he gestured around the pub, 'if this is our universe right here; then surely everything we do matters. Right down to this conversation; to this moment, right here.'

'We'll have to agree to disagree.'

He went silent for a moment, my negativity broke over him.

'I understand you need money,' he started quietly, 'who doesn't? Especially when you're our age. I was lucky to get my job, most of my school friends work in supermarkets, or bars, or call centres. I mean, so did I. Then I lucked out, like some of my teacher friends, into something 20k plus. 20k is something I could only dream of, you know. Like a house!' He smiled again. Then out of nowhere, 'Have you ever tried to find your parents?'

I looked along my beer at him, he was genuine, it seemed important to him somehow.

'There's no one to find,' I replied.

'I'm sorry.'

'Don't be.'

'How did they die?'

That's not what I said.

He left it alone again, but I could tell he was itching to pick it back up. He went at it sideways instead:

'My dad made me who I am.'

'He's a copper?'

'No, nothing like that.'

'You said it.' He was starting to piss me off again.

'He's a good man, but he never did anything with it.'

'He raised you, didn't he?'

'I wanted to do something worthwhile.'

'But you changed your mind and became a police-man instead.'

'What did you want to be when you were young?'

'Left alone.'

'You got your wish then.'

'Not yet.'

He gave another minute silence in memory of a conversation topic recently deceased.

'Do you know why the boss helped you?'

'He's wants to get fired.'

'He has to know, he's one of those people.'

'My condolences.'

'If there's a mystery, all he wants is the answer.'

'That's all?'

'He's not bothered if you make it to prison, he doesn't hold any animosity towards people, he just has to know why.'

'And you said he cares.'

'He does care, I think. In his own way. You wouldn't

know it to look at him, but he always does the right thing. And how could he keep doing the right thing if he doesn't care?'

A sober thought danced across his face for a second.

'Take this one case. Not too long ago, actually. We caught a burglary in a fleapit. Seventies brick building, near the centre. Landlord found the body, called up. The boss even volunteered to take the case.'

He took a sip of his cider. I waited for the rest.

'When we get there the place is a total dive. This is ten o'clock on a Tuesday and the place is dark as hell. Stripped out, completely empty, just a mattress on the floor. The landlord doesn't know how long it's been like that, he only checked because the door had been kicked in. He says the tenant is a young girl, twenty something, Eastern European, Slavic name. Everything points to one thing. So we thank him and take the key and send him on his way. The lights weren't working, of course, so the boss pops out to get this little torch that he keeps in the car. I was alone.'

He was looking past me now, out the window, as though across the street a television was playing the film he was describing.

'There's something about the human eye or the brain that can tell a human form from all the shadows in the room. On the mattress. It was my first. It's amazing how the anticipation builds in you. The adrenaline.'

He sated his thirsty mouth.

'When the boss came back we could see even the bulbs had been taken. I looked about two feet above the body as he shone the light on it. It wasn't a twenty-something woman, it was a thirty-something man. And he was quite peaceful, not a mark on him. It wasn't scary at all. Overdose, the coroner said, heart attack basically. We searched the place, not that there was anything but his clothes and his gear. He didn't have any money, didn't even have any change. Although the landlord probably took whatever there was when he found the body. Overdue rent. Basically, it turned out he was a small time crook, fancied himself a pimp, but she wouldn't have it so he threw her out and used her place to shoot up. He had been selling her stuff right out the front of the building.'

He finished and sipped his cider again. He seemed to think he had said something.

'I'm sure there was a point in there somewhere,' I told him.

'Sorry,' he sighed, 'anyway, everything in the place is beat-up and broken, nothing new; I'm sure you know the kind of place. But then, lying there in the middle of the room is a brand new kitchen knife. A long thin one. Absolutely brand new, forensics say the blade has never been used. Not a print on it either.' He lent back and raised his eyebrows as though I was supposed to understand.

'I see. Thanks, that was definitely worth my time.'

'He still talks about it today. It's been ninety days. I've counted them. That damn knife. He just has to know what it was doing there.'

'Fascinating.'

'Well, maybe you had to be there.'

I sighed. 'What was it you were showing off about when you came in? Kitesurfing?'

'Yeah, I jumped the pier today.'

'Is that difficult?'

'Impossible. Unless you have the right conditions. I think I'm the first to do it. It was just some silly idea I had. You see, the winds that are required, I had to wait for a storm before I could do it.'

Now I started to like him again. He was at the very least *something*, and so many people are just nothing.

'It just goes to show...' he declared cryptically. What it showed he let me figure out for myself.

When I got back to the caravan I was soaked through, and the dinner left on the step was as cold as a corpse. Overcooked salmon, new potatoes, and broccoli. Not my ideal dinner: I prefer something with flavour. But I stuck it in the submarine's nuclear reactor, and devoured it desperately.

I had never had a bank account, but even I knew that to access one you needed a card. Or a book like they had in the olden days. He had to have some way of getting to the money. Back then almost no one used internet banking, so there had to be something physical to find. Even if it was a cheque book, even if it was a cheque stub, it was proof.

I laid in the short little bed under the thin little blanket, listening to the rain battering the tinfoil walls; and I concocted my plans of how I was going to find my proof.

Now, back then I didn't have as firm a grip on the line between what's illegal and what's wrong. Maybe I still don't. Maybe back then I didn't even know that line existed. Not like I do now, even if I trip over it occasionally.

I reconnected with Jake, a fellow thug from Big Dave's crew. He was a few years younger than me but because of his size people always thought he was older. He used to get served in pubs at fifteen by leaning his tattooed arm on the bar, the arm that had been tattooed at fourteen. It was a Christian cross with a banner draped across it that read "Chubbs", his nickname. Except the cheap job looked more like "Ohubbs" where the ends of the C were joined up by folds in the banner. When we wanted to piss him off we called him Ohubbs. But that unleashed the Hulk and we soon stopped.

This is all to say that I paid him to mug Mr Jilani. And I know, I'm thinking right now what you are. But I wasn't thinking it then. Luckily, it went off without a hitch and the wallet arrived on the plastic step the next day. It was cheap, unbranded, brown leather. Probably bought from a market stall somewhere.

I took out each item and laid them on the little fold-out table in the middle of the caravan, designed to play mind-numbing games of Canasta on when the campsite becomes a bog.

First was his Pakistani driving license, which gave me his vital details. I used a burnt match to scribble them onto the surface of the table.

The next obvious things were his bank cards. One debit, two credit. The debit one matched the account the police already had, and I knew both the credit cards had been checked: they were only ever paid off from the same account.

In the last slot was a Nectar card that had the same washed out and overused look as the escorts on West Street, and in a little hidden slot was a loyalty card from his barbers. He had earned a free hair cut or eyebrow threading. I kept for myself.

In with his cash, seventy quid, was a wodge of re-ceipts. I peeled them apart from each other one by one. A fast food voucher on the back of a bus ticket, a city-saver. He'd been into town on the twenty-eighth of October, whenever that was. It didn't matter. A note with his sort code on. I checked, it wasn't shown on his debit card. A million petrol receipts, all for a full tank and all with Nectar points. He was a taxi driver, after all. There was a lottery ticket, a pair of unopened plasters, a receipt for paying in some cash, same account again. That's what he needed the sort code for. Then some shopping receipts: the odd sandwich, the odd can of energy drink; and some parcel receipts, heavy ones. He eBay-ed from the mosque computer, selling rubbish for pittance.

None of it meant much to me. There was certainly no proof of a second bank account. But the lottery ticket interested me. One of the few things I knew about Muslims was that they couldn't gamble. By which I mean, Allah forbids it. I don't mean Muslims can't gamble in the way that white men can't jump.

A man with enough money to be blackmailed shouldn't be playing the lottery. A man cautious enough to hide a second bank account from his wife should also not be playing the lottery. Maybe you don't agree with me? Maybe you think everyone likes a flutter now and then. Let me put it this way then, smart arse: a devout Muslim, a "very traditional" one, would have to be pretty desperate to disobey God's command. At his lowest ebb.

The police had searched his house. They had done a thorough job. The man didn't have an office, so there was nowhere else he could hide anything.

It was four more hours before I realised I was being a fucking idiot. Of course the man had an office. If you

don't know how taxi driving works, here's a brief explanation: you drive people places. Only joking. What I
really mean is, you either own your car and pay the taxi
company a cut; or you drive someone else's car, and pay
both of them a cut. In this case, Jilani owned his car. It
was his office.

This time I reconnected with Ryan. A lanky little
shit who made a noise like a magpie every time he
thought he'd said something clever. He was a real dickhead. He used to call his penis his 'python'. I mean, that
says it all, doesn't it? But, much to my annoyance Ryan
was an excellent car thief. He wanted to charge me two-
hundred for the job. I managed to talk him down to
one-fifty. But it still meant I had to beg the mothers for
extra money, and there was no way I was going to tell
them it was to steal a car.

In fact, just saying, 'you don't want to know what it's
for,' was enough to convince them. Debra sent the message down the grapevine and the money came back. I
wondered who was paying.

Normally Big Dave had a garage where he kept hot
cars until they were resprayed and had their number
plates swapped, but a taxi was a little too hot for him. It
did stick out rather. And this was a private job, Ryan
was not to tell Big Dave, or anyone in his crew. I was
trying to go straight and the last thing I needed them
thinking was that I was trying to go solo. That would
be a great way to lose my good looks.

Ryan had parked the car in an out of the way part of the Sheepcote Valley Caravan Club site just next to the Whitehawk FC ground. I parked my moped half a mile back, at the Wilson Avenue entrance to the park. Mopeds are noisy, and people notice them in quiet little caravan sites. Especially at eleven at night.

I zipped up my thin little jacket and started my trek. I could hear the sounds of the road behind me, the soft rumble of rubber on tarmac, Wilson Avenue is busy. But from ahead I could hear nothing but the gentle hooting of what couldn't possibly be an owl.

I passed no one. Just some empty tennis courts on the left, with limp nets swaying in the breeze. Then a single-storey brick park keeper's house, or something. The lights were off. I wasn't sure what it really was, or is; those odd buildings never seem to be used by anyone but squatters and junkies. My people. Occasionally I would pass an abandoned caravan. Yellowed net curtains and blocked windows. What was inside, I didn't want to know. Above me, solitary wisps of cloud sailed silently across the ocean of sky, heading south. I wished I could sit on one and gaze down at the gentle nightlights of the city, drifting over the sea, to the continent, over the alps and beyond. But instead I was here, amongst the dark trees, surrounded by rough stony paths that lead in every direction off into the fields, to the hills, and over into the ghostly pockmarked landscape of the East Brighton golf course.

I passed the cricket field on the right, and the AstroTurf pitch on the left, and now I could see the ethereal outline of white boxes ahead. I couldn't see any lights, caravanners are always asleep by this time. Lights Out at 10pm.

I skirted round the outside, and through trees, to arrive unseen in the little tarmacked car park/dumping ground that contained nothing but a couple of skips. Nothing but two skips, and one taxi, of course.

The car was quite new, only a couple of years old. A Skoda. The standard turquoise and white. Turquoise being the officially agreed colour of the city. No dents, no chips in the windscreen. It was clean, except for some mud around the wheels. All four tyres were the same make. All things considered, Jilani looked after it.

Ryan had left the key in one of the wheel arches. I slipped on a pair of latex gloves that I had bought from a chemist and carefully used the actual key, rather than the central locking, in case it blipped and flashed its indicators.

The lights came on inside and I frantically spent the next thirty seconds trying to find the switch to turn them off, but by then they did it themselves. The first thing I did was root around on the floor. In the front there was nothing, and in the back there was even less. Underneath the passenger seat there was a Haynes manual. And under the driver's seat there was a pound coin. Clever bastard. It was an old taxi drivers' trick to leave a pound coin on the floor. Most people are nice and round up the fare to the nearest note, but you always get those tight types who demand their change. This way, when you gave it to them you always gave them a pound short. Most people don't notice. But if they do, you just pretend they must of dropped it, and what do you know, there it is, it must have rolled under the seat.

I couldn't see the contents of the glove compartment without using my Zippo and lightly singeing the plastic. It stank. I made a note to buy a torch. Inside was the official car manual in a nylon case, a pen, a roll of electrical tape, a Brighton A to Z, and a phone charger that fitted into the cigarette lighter. The little pockets behind the seats were empty except for a Visit Brighton leaflet, and there was nothing on the parcel shelf.

On the dashboard was the meter, his licence, tax disc, and something that would come to ruin taxi driving: a Sat Nav. Today in London they still make drivers pass The Knowledge, everywhere else they just give them a Sat Nav. Eleven years ago I had never seen one before.

The boot was empty. Completely empty. And spotless. I guess it had to be empty for people with suitcases. I looked underneath; his spare tyre was still there, and a full-size one, not a space-saver. It was looking a little bald though.

With a worried hand on my cigarette lighter I checked the wheel arches, under the bonnet, and even under the car, but there was nothing to find. I was going to have to get tough.

I whipped out my flick knife and hacked at the carpet. I ripped it off the floor like it was clothes off Jennifer Lawrence. Or someone who was big in 2005. Jessica Biel, maybe. But unlike Jessica there was nothing underneath. I used the same approach on the seats, but despite my passion there was still nothing.

I slumped into Jilani's now ruined seat and lit a cigarette, staring out at the skeleton trees jittering in the darkness behind the orange glow of my own pitiful reflection. So far all I had achieved was to steal a man's wallet and find nothing, then steal his car and disfigure it. I was not going to let that be it.

There had to be more. If I was Jilani, where would I hide something? I looked around from where I was sitting, I even put my hands on the wheel, the gearstick, and the indicators. This is the position he occupied for eight hours a day, six days a week. There was no space behind the steering column and the dashboard, but what about the central panel? I used my knife to get behind the radio, but it was a right pain and there was nothing but connectors where an after-market radio could be swapped in.

Below the radio were the heater controls, they couldn't be removed, and underneath that was a little well containing some breath mints and a carwash receipt. The plastic clicked as I turned over the tin of mints. It hadn't quite been seated correctly. I prised my knife under the side and it clicked again, allowing me to lift it out. It was probably designed that way so you could clean it.

I could see something underneath. Nestled in the wires running from the cigarette lighter and the heater, was a brown padded envelope, folded over on itself and sealed with wrinkled brown tape. I delicately lifted it out, my heart pounding. It didn't weigh much, but more than nothing. About the weight of a golf ball.

I unpeeled the barely tacky brown tape and tipped the contents into my hand. A phone. A robust, not very modern, mobile phone. I grabbed the power cable from the glove box. It fitted, but I daren't start the ignition to charge it up. I prayed it had battery.

I even had to have a look out the windows, as though the laws of fate had to have it snatched from me the moment I powered it on. But there was no one around. Just sleeping bodies in the caravans through the trees, and I knew there was nothing more than a fox awake for a mile in every direction.

I powered it on. The little green square inch of screen glowed eagerly. Contacts? None. Call history? Four outgoing calls lasting zero seconds. Messages? 27. The most recent was on 30th July. That put it about a week before his daughter was abducted.

"Wordsworth Street/St Patricks Rd," was all it said. *Hmm.* Poet's Corner, Hove.

The message before was from the twenty-fourth, the same format: "Balsdean Rd/Bexhill Rd". Woodingdean.

The one before was from the twentieth, "Grassmere Ave/Telscombe Cliffs Way".

I didn't know Woodingdean or Telscombe Cliffs well enough to know the roads, but the first two were adjoining streets. Was it safe to assume the other ones were? I heard Daye's voice ringing in my head.

Fine. I got out my pad and a stubby pencil and scribbled down each message. Contents, number, date and time. Then I replaced the charger, stuffed the phone back in the envelope, and wedged it back into its hiding place.

The fresh night air smelt almost sweet as I stepped out, and although it was bitingly cold it was invigorating to me. It was a good night. I had actually done something. I had found a clue, or a lead, or whatever detectives call them these days. In fact it was up to me, I was a detective now, I could call it what I wanted. It was something. I had found *something*.

I was so proud of my moral superiority, my upstandingness, as I pulled the cheap bottle of vodka from my jacket pocket. I untwisted the lid and threw it into the wild grass. Then I fed in the rolled rag to douse it, pulled it out, fed in the other end, pulled out my Zippo and lit it.

II

Victory & Defeat

'I DON'T BELIEVE IT,' he said with the e-cigarette glowing between his lips. It was followed by a short burst of vapour from his nostrils like a chugging steam train.

I didn't ask why not. We never asked each other those kind of questions. If he wanted to tell me, he would tell me.

'If she was raped,' he continued, 'how would she know the man's surname?'

'If she knew he was Polish then she might have known him. People can be raped by people they know.'

'But if she was raped, why give the child his name.'

'She might have hoped they would find him, then I would be his problem.'

'Hmm… I don't believe it,' he said with another puff of steam, this time from his mouth.

Daye was the only person I knew who ever sat in his front garden. I imagine people in the country do it sometimes, and people in Westerns sat on their wooden porches looking over their acre of dirt. But not in a city, not where people would see you. Not where you could see them. That's the joy of sitting in a garden, isn't it? Being able to imagine you're the only person on the planet.

But he sat outside his Woodingdean bungalow on his wicker chair, smoking his e-cigarette, and watching the people and the cars as they went past. It was the end of the day now and the sky was tinged pink.

'Morning, Inspector,' a man waving a newspaper said as he passed along the pavement in front of us.

'Morning, Frank,' Daye called back.

He was like a sheriff. If there was any trouble at Old Mrs McGinty's house then someone would holler for him and he would saddle up. Everybody leant on him. Roy Parker, Price, Hacker, Ben McCready and all the other fools in the council, at the paper, and at the PCC's fundraising junkets, were all underneath the stone ceiling, chipping away at pillars like Daye. But he would never give up, I could rely on that.

I had come to discuss the Tothova case, of course. He had some pretty strong opinions on it.

'Nothing is what it seems,' he told me, 'Price is a

TOM TROTT

good detective, but she's taking the whole thing too literally. She's letting the parents drive the investigation, and that's the last thing you want.'

'That's the sort of talk that got you bumped off the case.'

'Someone wants this circus; the newspapers, the TV coverage. Which is why I said those things, I wanted to make it a non-event. No abduction, no monsters in the shadows, just a lost little girl. Then they'd have to overplay it; a ransom note or a video. And that's when they'd make their mistake.'

'But there is a ransom note.'

'Bill Harker wrote that.'

'Hacker?'

'Yes. I'd recognise his drivel anywhere.'

'Would he really do that?'

He just looked at me.

'I suppose you're right. The man's a rat but I didn't think he would put the girl in any danger.'

'It's a good thing he's done it. I would have done the same.'

I gave him a look.

'Don't misunderstand me,' he explained, 'Bill's doing it for his own reasons: he still dreams of working on one of the nationals. He'll have his heart attack before that ever happens. But the fake letter is a brilliant idea, if the real abductor wants the ransom then he'll have to make contact himself soon or he'll be mistaken for one of the fakes. And there will be more. He may even feel the need to prove he's the real thing, and anything he provides as proof will give us ten times the leads we have now. If, on the other hand, all the real abductor wants is this circus then he'll be happy to let Bill create it for him.'

'What if he doesn't want the circus, or the money; what if he just wants the girl?'

'Then I think we'll probably never find her.'

He took another puff. He used one of those e-cigarettes that tries to look like a real one. They're getting rarer these days as people prefer them to look like a gadget. But I guess it helped suspend disbelief.

'Is there something I should know about their charity?' I asked.

'What do you mean?'

'How do I know? That's what I'm asking.'

He frowned, it was against his ethics to tell me anything beyond speculation, even if he wanted to. 'Let's just say, I don't know where they'll find the hundred-thousand.'

'Surely they could remortgage?'

He raised an eyebrow, 'Again?'

'Are you telling me there's no money in giving meals to homeless people these days? Surely the charity must have patrons.'

'I don't know, but they've already had a cash injection from the council. And I don't need to tell you which councillor was behind that. He put more than our money into it, he put his reputation into it too.'

I didn't know quite what to make of that.

'In all my years I never worked a case quite like this,' he sighed, 'it's not a detective you need, it's a good scene partner.'

'What about the Jilani case?'

'That was completely different.'

'A girl. An abduction. No clues.'

'That's just the packaging. Different girls. Different parents. Different motives. And hopefully a different ending.'

I nodded. He took another long drag. The orange LED faded into life and out again. A simulated cigarette. A pretend vice. He put it down.

'I have to smoke one of these a day. Sometimes two. How did you quit?'

'I just quit.'

'You would.'

He waved to another passing citizen. 'I'm done, Joe.'

I looked at him. He just stared ahead. His face had changed over the years. Marble had become oak. Gnarled, carved, but still solid. The sun had begun to set on it now.

'Finished,' he restated.

'No you're not.'

'I don't mean it in a bad way. I've been coming to it for a while now. I'm happy. It's not my turn anymore.'

He looked at me. Cars passed. People walked dogs. Nobody gave a shit.

'How can you do it?' I asked.

He wasn't insulted, I was still a boy.

'There's still work to be done,' I pleaded, 'how can you quit when He's still out there?'

'That's your fight.'

'You're part of this city, aren't you?'

He sighed. 'There's always work to be done.'

'Yes.'

'I've got grandchildren,' he said without apology. 'I want to enjoy my life again, whatever I have left. I won't do you the disservice of saying I've given everything I can, I haven't. You give up, that's what people do. At some point everyone gives up, I've made my peace with that. I'm no less human than the people I've dedicated my life to. You could destroy your body, your mind, but there will always be more that you could've done. You only get to maintain things in this world.'

'I don't believe that. If you can't win then what's the point in fighting?'

'You can win, Joe, you can win. But victory and defeat have one thing in common: they are both temporary.'

* * *

174

It was waiting for me when I got back to the office. I hadn't been in all day, but it looked like Thalia had. Either that or the envelope had slithered its way from the letterbox onto my desk. It was perfectly square and an inch thick. "For the attention of Mr J. Grabarz, from Hermann H. Vogeli" was inscribed across the middle in elegant slanting script. The ink was purple in the moonlight.

It was dark now, seeing as it was eleven o'clock, but I was in one of those moods I have where I don't want to turn the lights on. Out on the landing they were on, and the light through the rippled glass projected "J. Grabarz, No.1 Private Detective" in big letters across the floor of the reception room. What a joke.

No.1 Private Detective. I had chosen it because it sounded good. It was what people wanted to believe when they hired me. They wanted to believe that maybe this pokey fly trap was just a front, a way of keeping clients anonymous. Maybe they thought I was just a front too, designed to scare away the timewasters, the real detective was someone else. I could do with his help right now. I had been arrogant enough to think that Brighton's No.1 Private Detective could succeed where every police officer and concerned citizen in the city would fail. In fifty-seven minutes it would be Tuesday. Joy had disappeared on Wednesday.

I took the office bottle out of the third drawer down

and drank a toast to the poor little girl. The same seeping dread that was probably slipping into every police officer's mind that night slipped into my drink: the tide had turned against her, now we were looking for a body. Not even Daye could convince me that this defeat was temporary.

I swivelled round to face the windows. The corridors of the Lanes were empty. The sky was empty. There was no one in the world but me. A cruel wind was coming in over the sea.

Other men were giving their wives a back massage, talking through the turmoil of the day. Young men were chasing skirts and trying to find the bravery to kiss one. Children were being tucked into bed, being told that there were no monsters to fear. That old lie. They didn't know He was out there somewhere. Stalking. Prowling for fresh meat. We're all pawns in His game.

I had my own misery to attend to. I picked up the square envelope. It felt as heavy as a brick. Turning it over; he had even sealed it with wax. He didn't lack a theatrical side, that was for sure.

Daye didn't believe it, that was a good excuse for me not to believe it. After all, he was a much smarter man than me. But somewhere, deep inside, in the darkest corner, some part of me knew it must be true. I've always known there was something wrong with me. They say the secret ingredient when making a baby is love. I'm what you get when you leave it out.

My phone vibrated solemnly in my pocket. I dredged it up. It was from Monica Todman.

"I will forgive you" it said.

That at least made me feel slightly better. I knew she couldn't resist me. I even smiled.

It vibrated again. Another message. Another message from Monica Todman.

"If…"

Oh I see. I waited for the next one. It didn't come. What did she want? Did she want me to make a suggestion? *Fuck that.* I wasn't playing her games. I knew that would drive her even more mad.

I had to wait twenty minutes for her to give in: "…you crawl on your hands and knees from your office to my bedroom."

Then the phone rang. I nearly fell out of my chair.

I took my time sauntering over to Thalia's desk, just in case it was her.

'Hello?' I answered. I never say any more after office hours.

'Good evening, Mr Grabarz.'

The accent sent a shiver down my spine. It was as precise and playful as a cuckoo clock. I don't know why I didn't just hang up there and then.

'Mr Vogeli.'

'I'm surprised to have caught you, it's very late to be in the office.'

'And yet you called hoping to find me. You must be

overjoyed.' This was the new me. The calm me.

'Ja, I'm very pleased. Have you got my package?'

I left a pause. 'Oh that, I believe we have it some-where. I haven't had the chance to look at it yet.'

'I'm sure you'll find the time.'

'There's this missing girl at the moment, you must have seen it in the papers. Big case, lots of people in-volved. I can't say when I'll get around to it.'

'It is quite urgent.'

'What isn't?'

There was a little trickle of a laugh. 'Yes, yes. That's right.'

The conversation went silent. So silent I believed I could hear the static bouncing up and down the line, stretching from my office to the lane, to the street, and all the way to wherever the hell he was. I hate tele-phones. There's nothing more intimate than having someone's mouth pressed up to your ear, blindfolded, no eyes to read.

'When I delivered it,' he finally returned, 'I gave it to your secretary. I must say, she is quite a woman.'

I gripped the phone tighter.

'She reminds me of a whore I fucked in Hamburg once, Johanna, she was quite a woman too. Chunky. What is her name?'

By this point I was gripping the phone so tightly I thought it might shatter. I wanted to bite into it. I kept silent.

'Thalia, I remember now. Thalia Sweet. What a beautiful name.'

Static came back. Or was it the meshing of cogs?

'Do get back to me as soon as you can, Mr Grabarz. Auf wiedersehen.'

I was knocking so hard I had split my knuckles. And she was fucking angry when she answered in nothing but a slip.

'Jesus Christ, Joe!'

'Do you always answer the door dressed like that?' I asked.

If she could look any angrier, she did then. But she had no idea how I felt, I had almost punched a hole in the desk when I put the phone down.

'It's gone midnight, what the hell do you want?'

'When that letter was delivered, from Mr Vogeli, did you speak to him?'

'You came over here and woke up all my neighbours, who by the way already hate me, to ask me that?'

'Yes. And I'd like an answer.'

She took a few moments to exhale all her anger. I was serious, and she knew it.

'Yes, why?'

'If you see him again, call me straight away. Don't speak to him, don't let him get near you, just go somewhere public and call me. Are you alone?'

'Excuse me?'

'Is there a man in your bed?'

'Yes there is. What is it to you?'

'Who is he?'

'No one you know.'

'How much do you know about him?'

'Not much. We haven't been doing much talking.'

'Fine. Where did you meet him?'

'Tinder.'

'Where's that?'

'It's an app.' She stopped short of adding 'you moron!'

She was breathing enough air to flush the corridor. I quite liked her angry. Her breasts were heaving under thin lace. I tried not to notice them.

'I want you to sleep at mine,' I told her.

'I know that.'

'For your safety.'

'I can take care of myself.'

I paused to emphasise my point: 'If you see him, call me, ok? I'm sorry to have interrupted.'

I disappeared from the doorway.

'Joe, wait.'

'What?' I was already halfway down the corridor.

'I might as well tell you this now. Maria Tothova's brother showed up on my Tinder tonight. I can't remember his name.'

'Spencer Redburn.'

'No, that's not it.'

'That's the name you put in the file.'

'Yes, but that's not the name he has on his profile.'

I stepped steadily back toward her door. 'I thought he was in South Africa?'

'According to the most recent thing I could find.'

'How can you be sure it's him?'

'I saw his photo enough times when I was sorting out the file. It's him.'

My mind fizzed with possibilities. Was this something? Maria Tothova's brother. Not in South Africa. Here, nearby. A different name. Hiding.

'It said he was seven miles away.'

This was not nothing.

12

Q&A

PETER KALOGIANNIS WAS the most unusual kind of taxi operator. She was Greek, transgender, but hadn't changed her name. In fact she did nothing more than wear makeup. She was a one-woman gender convention-busting tour de force. But in one way she was disappointingly conventional: she wouldn't talk without a picture of John Houblon.

'He owns his Hack and as a result he gets to work the evening shift,' she explained. 'Journeyman does the day and another does overnight. That's unless they can get a better shift on someone else's ride.'

I was sitting in what I was sure was garden furniture, in a cramped office, two storeys up, built into the corner of some Victorian building not far from the Seven Dials. She was wearing tight unisex jeans and a thick turtleneck jumper. Her silver glitter eyeshadow was shimmering in the white glow of a square, beige computer monitor that looked like it was running Windows 95. I recognised it from the last time I used a computer. The rest of the office was full of street maps and filing cabinets, dirty mugs and cigarette butts. I was working on one of my own.

'Is that the best shift?' I asked.

'Depends,' she shrugged, pausing to take a drag of her own. 'Some drivers do well overnight. Some like the airport run. Some have regulars for the school run, so they do well during the day. Sunday morning the rates change so you can do well if you catch the church crowd. But conventional wisdom says Saturday night is the best, and Tariq likes the evenings. He's a conventional kind of guy.'

'What are his hours?' I asked.

'He does six till two mostly. Journeymen do two till ten, ten till six,' she shrugged.

'But he hasn't always liked the evenings: he used to work the day shift, am I right?'

'Yeah, for a few months.'

'Let me guess, he stopped around August?'

'Something like that,' she said with an impressed smile.

'When did that start?'

'I don't remember exactly, but it was around Christmas. I figured he wanted to spend the winter evenings with his family. He's got a daughter, don't he?'

'I need the exact date.'

'I don't remember.'

'You've got records, haven't you?'

'Yes.'

'Check them.'

There was silence. She didn't move.

'I've just paid you, haven't I? Work for it.'

She didn't appreciate being treated like a prostitute, and got up with exaggerated sophistication to begin checking through the drawer of a filing cabinet. I hadn't learnt yet that when you pay someone, they always like to pretend you haven't.

'Twelfth of December, two-thousand-and-four. Good enough?'

'You mean you can't give me the hour?' I said with a smile. It was returned, and with a look that went much lower than my eyes.

'Whilst you're there, who drove the evening shift when he was on days.'

'I can tell you that one without looking,' she said. 'Nobody.'

'No one?'

'Nobody. Even when I needed a bigger fleet around Christmas he wouldn't let any of them use it.'

'Is that unusual?'

'For him, absolutely.'

'Why?'

'Because he would get paid. I even offered to pay him extra. But don't tell the others that, darling,' she added, striding back to her desk. 'Of course, I'm in the same position now,' she sighed, 'It's November. He better have a new car by Christmas week, let alone New Year's Eve.'

'Well, hopefully we can clear this up quickly and pay out his claim.'

She gave another smile, and her pencilled eyebrows disappeared into her hairline. 'Save it, honey. Insurance investigators don't pay for information.'

I bit my cheek and nodded. I was twenty-two, and looked it. Who could I possible impersonate? A student? I didn't look clever enough.

'And he wouldn't let anyone else drive it until he went back on the evening shift?' I asked. 'The whole time?'

'That's right.'

I had been through all the messages, plotted them on a map you couldn't fold out fully without hitting the caravan walls, and they were all intersections. Street corners to you and me. He started getting them less than a week after he changed to the day shift. Less than a week after he stopped anyone else from using his car. There was only one explanation. I don't even have to tell you.

I got up out of the chair. 'Thank you, Peter.'

'You're welcome, honey.'

I stopped with my hand on the knob. 'Why did you never change your name? If it's not too rude to ask.'

'I don't mind, people ask me all the time. They don't get to choose their name, but I can, and they don't understand why I don't.'

'And what's the answer?'

'My parents gave it to me.'

It wasn't until I was five minutes from Debra's caravan that I realised I was being followed. It was a beat-up Volvo estate, no wonder I hadn't noticed.

I took a sharp turn here, a sharp turn there, indicated one way, went the other. I even went into a left turn only lane and turned right if you can imagine such a thing. But the bastard still followed me. I parked up by London Road station, back when you could park around there, and wandered into The Signalman. The Volvo was pulling up as the doors swang shut. I stood just round the corner by the quiz machine and waited for the next person to enter.

The next person was a forty-something man with already white hair and a baseball cap to try and hide it. He wore a fleece, and trousers with loads of pockets. He was the least threatening person in the world.

'Who the fuck are you!?' I shouted as I pushed him

against the bar.

People froze. The landlord was close, ready to inter-vene, but the man gave him a wave with his fingers.

'It's ok,' he said. Then he smiled yellow teeth at me. 'I'm your best friend.'

'Really,' I mocked.

'Oh yes.' He looked at the landlord, 'get this man whatever he wants,' then he looked back at me, trying to reach for his pocket, 'do you mind?'

I let go and he held a twenty pound note ready.

'A pint,' I barked. 'And a double whisky.'

'That's the spirit, make that two.'

The Signalman is quite a nice place. Not too posh, but nowhere near a dive. It's rival is the The Open House, on the other side of the bridge that crosses the train line. But that's posher, just like the neighbour-hood. I've always been more comfortable on the rougher side of the tracks.

'Cheers,' he said, when the landlord carried our drinks to a table.

'So, who are you?' I growled.

'I told you: I'm your best friend.'

I stood up.

'Who else would know you stole Tariq Jilani's taxi and torched it in the grounds of the caravan club?'

I sat back down.

Yellow teeth smiled again.

'And who are you going to tell?'

'No one.'

'I'm so lucky to have a great friend like you.'

He nodded. 'And since we're such good friends, why don't you tell me what you were up to just now at the taxi office.'

I took some time drinking my pint. It gave me a chance to interrogate myself first. There was nothing this man could possibly tell the police that Daye didn't know already. I go talk to him about the Jilani case and three days later the man's car is stolen. You didn't have to be a detective to work that one out. He might not be happy about it. He might even try and get me on it. But then I didn't steal the thing, Ryan did. When I had finished drinking I realised I'd wasted my time thinking about that, and not about this arsehole.

I reached over and held the man down.

'Here, what are you—' he struggled as I pulled out his wallet. He gave up once I started going through it.

'I always think it's good for friends to be on first name terms, Bill.' I found his business cards: 'You're a hack.' I threw the wallet back onto the table. 'How the hell did you find me?'

He grinned, then shrugged. He couldn't possibly tell me that.

'You found out about the car obviously. So you went to talk to the taxi company and you saw me coming out, and what, you didn't like the look of me?'

'I was right, though, wasn't I?'

He was right. He had walked into The Signalman with nothing.

'But what makes a big shot Chief Crime Reporter like you interested in a burnt-out taxi?' I asked. 'Unless you knew who's taxi it was, and knew someone was looking into things.'

He didn't respond, just sipped his beer. I was near the end of mine already.

'Or knew that there was something to be looked into,' I offered.

'There's not a crime committed in the city that doesn't cross my desk. Sure, a burnt out taxi isn't particularly interesting, maybe a drug angle though, maybe reckless kids, that sells. Then I see the name. I remember it, the guy certainly has bad luck!'

He laughed a foul little laugh. One that didn't inspire a shred of warmth.

'So,' he continued, 'I decide to call my friend at the police station, find out if anyone has been looking into his daughter's case. And what do you know, a DC pulled the file on it just this week. Someone's been slipping him notes under the table, and I don't mean ones that say "I love you".'

His teeth were more than yellow. They were brown at the roots.

'I went to the taxi office to find out who was asking questions. But I didn't need to. You saved me twenty quid. Now,' he spat into his glass, 'If one of my own was kicking around an old case I'd like to think I'd know about it. Who are you working for, kid?'

'Myself,' I answered.

'Freelance, huh? I started out freelance. Then again, I never torched any cars in the pursuit of a good story.'

'What do you want?'

'I wrote the original article on the girl. I'm the only person in the whole world who reported on it. Share what you've got with me and I can take it to the nationals for you, I've got friends. Fifty-fifty, joint byline.'

Like that he came into focus: he was the same as everyone else. He'd eat his own shit if you paid him.

'I don't remember seeing your article,' I told him.

'It was pushed to the centre. Was always going to be that way.'

'Why's that?'

'Because no one gives a damn about a little Muslim girl less than a month after 7/7.'

At least now I knew why I hadn't heard about it. It was up to this guy and his editor, his editor and the shareholders, the shareholders and the readers; and none of them wanted to see this girl's face on the front page. It would confuse people. It didn't fit the narrative.

'And what's different now?' I asked.

'Nothing, but I'm hoping you've got something juicy involving the father. You know he's got a record back in Pakistan. Criminal, that is.'

'What for?'

'Beating a man half to death.'

'You've got proof?'

'Well I can't exactly slip a DC twenty quid for that file, can I? It comes from a reliable source. Give us a few days, I can have three, maybe four, prozzies swear to him picking them up in that taxi.'

'But that isn't true.'

He almost spat out his pint. The treacle-dark laugh bubbled and subsided, I was serious, he couldn't believe it.

'People don't read newspapers to get news,' he explained.

'Is that so?'

'Unlike you I'm old enough to remember when they did.'

'I wasn't aware they read them at all.'

'Well, some do. They read us to make sense of everything that's happening. That's our job; to take the facts, the right facts, and show people how the world works. That's more honest than just straight reporting. And if the facts don't quite fit how we know the world really is? Then maybe they need a little massaging. If you can read the facts and get the wrong impression, or read my story and get the right idea, which contains more truth?'

I could see now that his teeth were least rotten part of him. 'That's our job, is it?' I asked, 'As journalists.'

'We're not journalists, my friend. We're storytellers.'

I stood up. Then I downed my double whisky.

'Thanks, Bill. But no thanks.'

He didn't even look that disappointed.

I left and managed to get back to the caravan before the whisky hit me. I'll never forget that conversation; I didn't meet him again for a few years, although I started to notice his name in the paper more. The funny thing is, when I did meet him again, he didn't remember it at all.

13

Entropy

THE BULL IN DITCHLING is a great village pub, full of low beams, dark corners, and local ales. I'm not an ale drinker myself, the stuff tastes like dirty bathwater to me, but I enjoy the relaxed atmosphere that comes with it. Real ale is not sophisticated, the food served with it isn't sophisticated, the setting isn't sophisticated, and all that takes the pressure off you. The Bull offers this with all the walked-in mud and grass, creaking wood, and other things that make a village so charming; but with Wi-Fi, and a car park, and only seven miles from Brighton.

I was sitting at the bar clean-shaven, fingering a glass of white wine, wearing a thick pale blue shirt, turned-up cream chinos, and slip on shoes with silly tassels. Everything about me said I was a delicate little flower, allergic to mud, unequipped for the country life, who would have a meltdown if he stepped in a puddle. I was so deep in character even Daniel Day-Lewis would be impressed.

Through the back of my head I was watching the man who was sitting alone at a reserved table, playing with his phone. It was ten o'clock Tuesday night.

'Fuck,' he ejaculated. Then he shot up, his chair screaming along the uneven floor. He had to stand next to me to tell the barmaid: 'You can give my table away.'

'She stand you up?' I asked.

Unfazed, he replied: 'If you can believe it,' in passing, as he turned to leave.

'Want a drink?'

'No thanks,' he said, stopping to type into his phone.

'Got something better to do?'

'Not exactly.'

'Then let me buy you one for the road.'

'What for?'

'Christ, do you normally take this much convincing for a free drink?'

He glanced at me for the first time, but didn't say anything.

'Go on, leave,' I told him, 'I was only trying to be friendly.'

He tucked his phone away, facing me now. 'And

why do you want to be friendly with me?'

'I just moved here, I thought I should get to know some locals. But you can fuck off if you want.' I smiled.

'I'll have a beer. Something in a bottle.'

The barmaid picked one out of the fridge.

'No, no, from the back,' he said, 'I saw you put those ones in ten minutes ago.'

She knocked over a few getting to it, but he had an ice-cold one in his hand in under a minute.

'Did she give a reason?' I asked.

'Family emergency.'

'What does that mean?'

'Who cares.'

'Are you going to meet her again?'

'I hope so, she looked hot. But there's plenty of others on there, it's like Netflix for pussy.'

'Tinder?'

He nodded. 'I thought she was a sure thing, she messaged me.'

'Problem is, you don't know if people are who they say they are.'

'Who is?' he asked rhetorically. Then he took a long swig of his beer. 'Where are you living then?' he asked as he finally took a stool next to me. I'd expected him to leave one in between us but he didn't, and as he asked the question he leaned even closer to me and didn't blink.

He was a handsome man, or had been once. Maybe

he still could be behind his mad beard. He was forty-something and his skin had been tanned a deep brown. His hair was short, golden, and curly at the ends. Grey eyes were sunken into their sockets beyond his age, and veins showed around his temples, his skin pulled too tightly across his skull. His body was tall and lean, his muscles not big, but toned; his body didn't carry an ounce of fat or water. This was a man who had spent years walking long distances over long days under a hot sun.

'I've just bought a little farmhouse over near Streat. Farm came with it too. How about you?'

'I'm renting a little farmhouse myself,' he answered, 'for the present.'

'I could have sworn you were a local,' I lied. 'You have the country look.'

'Whatever the hell that is, I'm pretty sure I don't have it.'

'I suppose you don't exactly blend in here.'

'What, amongst these buffoons and transplanted city types like yourself? What a pity.'

'You're not enamoured to the country life then?'

'This isn't the country. In the real country they don't have a Waitrose down the road. In the real country you can look to the horizon all around and not see a soul. That's nature.'

'It sounds barren. Not many amenities.'

'It's great if that's the way you like it.'

'Is that the way you like it?'

He didn't answer straight away. 'I can take it or leave it,' he said.

He had almost finished his beer already so I bought him another. We talked about the pub, and Ditchling, and women, and other things divorced from who we were or what we were doing here. Whenever I asked him a straight question, his answers reminded me of what the SAS call "the grey man". It's part of their training to resist interrogation. *Be the grey man*. Be kind, but not helpful. Don't anger them. Don't interest them at all. Occasionally he swung out into territory where he expressed an opinion, but he always circled back to indifference. He was a tough one. Some people you can cleave in two, but I would have to pull him part with tweezers. The only way I could draw him out was on seemingly unimportant, abstract issues of philosophy; life, death, little issues like that, and even then his answers were a vague form of pessimism that I could easily get from myself.

Three bottles later I was speaking about my fictional school days, hoping he would reciprocate.

'Where was that?' he asked.

'Westminster.'

'Is that a private school?'

'Very,' I laughed. 'How about you?'

'Boarding school. Just like the gardener and the cook, my parents paid for the very best children.'

'Where did you go? We might have met before.'

'I doubt it.'

I held out a hand. 'I'm Matthew, by the way.'

He shook it. 'Me too, but people call me Matty.'

'Interesting.'

'Is it?'

'Is that a South African twang I've been hearing?'

His eyes darted up from his beer. 'You need to clean your ears out.'

'I thought I heard something.'

'No.'

'There's something there.'

'Just me.'

I nodded, leaving it be. 'Matty… Matty Ross?'

'Yes.' He put his bottle down.

'I saw your listing on Gumtree today, you're selling a load of farm equipment aren't you?'

'You've got a good memory.'

'I remembered because I used to be called Matty at school.'

'What's your surname, Matthew?'

'Granger, why?'

'No reason.' He picked up his bottle again and finished it. His fourth. 'So you're looking to buy farm equipment?'

'Absolutely. I have bought a farm after all.'

'Why is that?'

'I think I'll enjoy it.'

'Farming?'

'Absolutely.'

He snorted, he clearly didn't think I was cut out for it. Then he gave me a sideways look.

'I'm hoping to start a vineyard,' I explained. 'My father owns one in Klein Karoo, I'm planning to use some cuttings.'

'Those varieties won't grow here. The soil is completely different.'

'Maybe I should employ you.'

'I'm not interested.'

I finished my second glass. It tasted like vinegar, I've never understood the point of white wine. 'Did the equipment come with the farmhouse?'

'Yes it did.'

'How come you're allowed to sell it? If you don't mind me asking; I thought you were renting the place.'

'The owners aren't interested in selling it off as a farm, they can make much more selling it to a developer. I offered to clear it out for them on the condition I keep any profit.'

'They should have sold it to me.'

'They should have.'

'Well, I'll pay what the stuff's worth. I'd have to see it first though, you know, to check it's not just rust.'

'Good idea. What are you doing right now?'

* * *

He was too drunk to drive, and for some reason he trusted me, so five minutes later I found myself piloting his pickup truck along the dark country lanes.

The sun had set behind the downs long ago, and even the residual glow had faded from the sky. Just the rolling treadmill of tarmac; twenty feet that weaved this way and that, up and down like a carnival rollercoaster. And the dry stone walls, and black grass, and the rising tsunami of hills to my right that told me we were heading east. He had given me the address before he went to sleep. He *was* asleep, I could swear, but maybe he wasn't. I don't know what to think, considering what happened that night.

Why did I say I had come by taxi? I didn't think my Honda was in character, but I could have made it in character, I wrote the damn part. I could have loaded it onto the back of his pickup, and then I would have an escape route. But who could have predicted a pickup truck in this country?

I shouldn't have been in his car. I shouldn't have been driving into the darkness. But I had to see his farm. I just didn't know why.

A rabbit bolted across the road, I slammed on the brakes. He jolted awake. We were at a crossroads.

'Which way?' I asked.

'Left,' he stated. Then leant back on the window.

We trundled along a bumpy, muddy, stony track up

a shallow incline. Ahead I could make out pitched points silhouetted against the sky. Buildings of some kind. Then the feeble headlights finally reached them and revealed that it was in fact a farm. And a proper farm, not one you would draw, but the type you actually see; with open-sided buildings and steel gates and water butts, troughs, and coiled hose connecting taps tied to wooden posts. In the swinging headlights each item was illuminated separately as a characterful element waiting to be placed in a setting. A hedge. A hutch. A rusted sign that used to say "Eggs sold". A discarded plough.

I nudged him awake. 'Is this it?'

'You can pull up anywhere.'

I parked up against a stone building, turned off the engine, and opened the door, leaving the lights on for now. The sound of cicadas was deafening. Another great thing about this heatwave: now we had tropical bugs.

'There's a torch in the glovebox.'

He told me this, but didn't get it out from right in front of him. Instead I had to lean over and get it. I turned it on before I turned off the lights. Then I stepped out onto mud, wishing with all my heart I wasn't wearing this costume.

'You want a drink?' he slurred.

'No thanks, you help yourself. I better look at that stuff.'

'Sure thing. I'll let you in the store.'

He headed away from the main buildings and I had to follow. We started to wander the length of a field, torch light quivering out in front of us, tiny insects swirling in the beam. At its end I could see a small stone and corrugated steel shack.

So far as I could tell the farm consisted of a cluster of three buildings. A small stone cottage, an old wooden barn, and a steel open-sided barn. I don't know if barn is the right word, but it was something you kept animals in. To the north was all green fields, leading almost a kilometre down toward the road we had left: just an empty, meaningless ribbon of slightly different darkness. To the east was a thicket of trees, how large I couldn't tell. To the south were the downs, we were already on the base of them. And to the west, the way we were walking, other than the shack, was nothing but more fields. This one was nothing but dirt. And in the middle of it was a tired scarecrow, patiently defending the dirt.

The store didn't have any lights, or paned windows, and "letting me in" consisted of drawing a bolt and peeling back a rusted corrugated sheet. Inside was a tangle of deep orange shapes, like the torture chamber in any film that has "chainsaw" in the title. I didn't know what any of it was, except a tetanus shot waiting to happen.

'Wow, I don't know where to start,' I said. Truthfully.

'You'd better have a look through it.'

I nodded pretty unconvincingly and started to move toward the stuff. With the torch in my hand it was mostly spikey shadow puppets that danced across the roof.

'Have you ever had a red espresso?' he asked.

'I don't think so.'

'I'll make us a couple,' he said, and trudged off.

I watched him disappear toward the house until he was engulfed in darkness, and I turned back to the torture porn dungeon. Honestly, I didn't know what any of this stuff was so it's impossible to describe it, the only comforting thought was that my character wouldn't know either. He'd get a man in to look it over. I'd tell him that. But first I better wait at least ten minutes to make it look like I tried.

The wind whistled through the gaps in the steel and the stone, and the tiny window smaller than a piece of paper. I thought about how many generations had farmed on this land, and how it only took one generation of fools to turn it into an early-retirement pad for some dick-swinging London arsehole and his second wife. They'd add a glass extension of course, because people love the idea of a cottage until they realise they've got nowhere to hang their aren't-I-so-fucking-beautiful photos. It would become an occasional snug.

Centuries of history reduced to character features. I thought the scarecrow should inherit the land, he'd worked it the longest.

Having spent my time constructively, I stepped out onto the field again, heading back toward the house, using the scarecrow as a guide in the blackout. Then the scarecrow did the strangest thing and I almost shat myself. He raised his hands up high, like the congregation at church, grasping toward the sky. I shone the torch at him. It was Redburn, of course. He hadn't made it to the house, he was transfixed by the stars. Staring upwards, he didn't register me. He didn't even look at me when he spoke.

'That's all we are, you know. Stardust.'

I didn't argue.

'We're just atoms held together. Temporarily. An alliance of matter that will decay and disperse. We're two successful germs on a ball of dirt.'

I looked up at the sky. It was magnificent. Where the earth was shades of darkness, the sky was bejewelled with pure light on brushstrokes of blue and purple.

'I was out on patrol,' he continued, 'long distance, wearing a pack as heavy as a corpse, sleeping under the stars, after the most significant event of my life. You look at them and you stare and you stare and suddenly you feel like you're on the bottom of the world, underneath, and you're not looking up you're looking down at the lights, and you could fall off the earth and plummet head first into all of that.'

I didn't say anything, not wanting to break the spell. Our heads were cranked upwards until there was nothing in our vision but the expanse. Unrooted, unanchored; we could be anywhere in the universe.

'But I was greeted instead by the revelation that taking someone's life is just fulfilling the law of entropy because there was never life there to begin with. Our consciousness, our hopes, our dreams, all our intelligence, and even the great big four letter word, love, is an emergent property. There's no such thing as life; from a microbe to us to a cactus to coral, we've had to invent definitions to fit what we want to believe. There's no life on earth, there's no life anywhere in the galaxy. We're all just an emergent property. A mirage in the eye of the universe.'

A steady light, maybe a satellite, too far away to be a plane, was sailing gently across the vastness as he continued: 'Scientists used to believe that there were a hundred to two hundred billion galaxies in our universe, each containing a hundred billion stars. And just when you can wrap your head around how insignificant that makes us they discover they were wrong. There are ten times as many galaxies as they thought: two trillion. You are ten times as insignificant as you thought you were and you were already infinitely insignificant. And you're never going to be anything more; no one cares about the most important germ in their toilet. And the only sane response is to take comfort in the fact that nothing you've done will ever matter.'

'Everything we do matters,' I whispered.

He scoffed. 'On what scale?'

'The one we live on.'

He smiled in the way you would smile to a witty child who's wrong but doesn't understand why.

'I'll sort out the tea,' he said, and marched back into the darkness.

I followed a few feet behind and watched as he stepped into the cottage. I only had a couple of minutes to search the barns.

The first was the open-sided one, and there was nothing in there but a few pens where you would keep pigs or sheep when you need to keep them somewhere for some reason. There was nothing on the floor but wisps of hay. Nothing twinkled in the torchlight, I felt nothing beneath my feet. It hadn't been a working farm for some time. Hanging off the steel gates to each pen were one or two meat hooks. They could just have been somewhere for the farmer to hang his tweed coat, but they didn't half give me the creeps. They were ice cold to touch, and sharp. Occasionally they clanged in the wind.

I turned to the wooden barn. It was overgrown with weeds and vines that reached from the earth, wrapped around the sides, and gripped the roof like the tentacles of some subterranean kraken. I ripped them from the rotten doors, and they came away with ease. The vines were dead, the kraken having swallowed too big a prize. Still it took all my strength to open one door one foot. I had to claw my way inside.

Without the torch I couldn't see a thing. Wind blew. Wood creaked. I clicked it on. My pale yellow light was met instantly with a red one. Shining at my face. I pointed the torch at the ground and the red light dimmed to a soft glow that helped light the barn. Against the walls I could see stacks of rotten logs, the type that crack open to reveal a million woodlice and one valiant centipede wriggling through the mass. But mostly I saw the ground had not been managed and the same tentacles that grasped the outside were everywhere inside. A dense, dead forest of skeletal hands.

The red glow was a reflector. A reflector from the back of a vehicle. A blue van. Not a Transit, mind. A Renault Trafic, eleven years old. It took up most of the barn and its presence was what had forced the tentacles into thickets.

It had windows in the back doors, I shone the torch in through the glass. It was empty. Entirely empty. Nothing but walls, floor, and wheel arches.

I clambered around to the front, pushing my way through thick woollen cobwebs, and shone the torch in through the windscreen. There was nothing here either. There was nothing to say the van had ever been driven.

Something slammed outside, a door or a gate, and I
felt a sudden urge not to be caught finding this. Before
squeezing through the door I took one last look at the
thing. On the back windows, in the yellow glow, small,
insignificant finger smudges glistened on the inside.

* * *

The door to the farmhouse opened off the latch with a
gentle push. I faced a set of narrow stairs. On a small
telephone table was a rotary phone with the zero worn
off, a pot of pens, and the cardboard from a notebook.
On the shelf underneath were the Yellow Pages and a
phonebook. Underneath me was thin, worn green carpet. To the left was a low doorway, not quite level, that
led into a small living room.

The room was quaint inside, but far from clean. It
had all the exposed stone walls and wooden beams you
could want, and with thin leaded windows that whistled in the breeze. It was packed with blankets and
throws in a way that told you it was never warm. There
was an open fire, but it wasn't set up to be used. Instead
an electric radiator ticked away in the corner. Around
it sat a television, radio, stacks of dirty bowls each with
one fork, a pile of laundry, dirty mugs, newspapers, Fri-
day-Ad, empty cans of Carling Black Label, shoes, and
a clock chiming one in the morning. All the appearance

of life, with nothing personal. No photos.

The kitchen was even smaller, and even less interesting. Every white good was grey, the oven rusted and so old it didn't even have a window. The chessboard linoleum floor was curling up at the walls. Mouse droppings dotted around the bag-less bin. It was a grimy place for cooking lonely meals. Both rooms were empty of human beings.

In my time as a detective I've learnt to walk quietly without doing the full Scooby-Doo, so I moved upstairs in a way that wouldn't look suspicious if he jumped out of a wardrobe.

There was a bedroom above the living room and a bathroom above the kitchen. The bedroom was piled with throws as well. There were enough layers of blankets on the bed to keep a strong man pinned. There were still no photos, but there were a lot of books. Sartre's *Being and Nothingness*. *The Stranger* and *The Myth of Sisyphus* by Camus. Kierkegaard, Nietzsche, Heidegger, they were all there. Even some Beckett. But they were all strewn across the floor, half-read, abandoned, trampled on. He hadn't found meaning in them. Except the Beckett, they were on the bedside table. He had some Pinter stacked up, ready to read. *No Man's Land* was next. He'd enjoy that one.

In the bathroom was a sink with a crack running across the base. It was full of curly golden wires and on the side sat a small pair of scissors: his mad beard had been a whole lot madder. There was a roll top bath with a tide mark less than six inches high. No products except a bar of coal tar soap. I could imagine him standing in the bath, strip-washing. He wasn't the type for bubbles. Or even lying down.

The man himself was nowhere. He wasn't in the wardrobe. So I headed back down to the living room and peered out the little windows into the darkness. I saw my own face, eye sockets in shadow. When I strained to look through them all I could see was a bush swaying in the breeze. *Where is he?* The breeze whistled through the lead, onto my eyeballs. *What is he up to?*

The quiet was cut by an angry buzz. It sounded like a bee in a shoebox and was coming from under my feet. I looked at them, but they didn't offer an explanation. Next I heard footsteps, rising up stairs, getting louder, moving across the room, and then he appeared from the cupboard under the stairs. He was holding an espresso in each hand.

He held one out to me without a word. I took it. It was in a clear glass cup, and sitting on a red glass saucer. Both looked clean. I was happy to drink it. That said, it looked like espresso, but it didn't taste like it. I didn't know what it was, but it didn't taste dangerous.

'What did you think of the store?' he asked.

'I don't really know what to think. It's probably best if I send a friend round; someone who knows what they're looking at.'

'Maybe it's not such a good idea to sell it.'

'I can send someone round tomorrow.'

'Give it a week.'

'Are you sure, it's no trouble.'

'I won't be here.'

I nodded. Then I finished my drink in three short sips.

'I'd better call a taxi,' I announced.

He nodded. 'You're better off using the landline, cell coverage round here is patchy.'

'Cheers.' I was happy to use the home phone, revealing I had anything less than the latest iPhone would break character, I was playing someone with more money than sense.

I went and made the call. The bastards said it would be forty-five minutes.

'Help yourself to anything from the kitchen. I'm going to turn in,' he announced when I told him. He was standing up and stretching. 'You can let yourself out.'

I nodded. 'Sweet dreams,' I added once he had reached the bottom of stairs. He didn't reply.

I followed his steps up, and into the bedroom. They moved around whilst he got undressed. Then into the bathroom. The bath tap ran for less than a minute. Then back into the bedroom. Then they were gone.

I glided silently toward the cupboard door. It had a new Yale lock. I had left all of my lock picking gear with my bike, back in the car park of The Bull. I had left my penknife, my brass knuckles, my Maglite, everything. But I still had his feeble torch.

I gently slipped out the front door, my thumb over the latch until the last moment. Then I paced the grass around the house, hoping the cellar had some kind of window. Round the back I could see three small arches curving no higher than a foot off the ground. They were barred just tightly enough to keep out even the most determined fox.

I shone the quivering urine-coloured beam down into the darkness. I could only see one detail at a time. Through this keyhole of information I saw stone, old wood, dirt, then an MDF worktable. It was nothing more than a table top with two sides; he had probably built it himself. On it I saw the chrome-effect trim of a push-button coffee machine, then two more glass cups, bigger than the espresso ones. Next to them there were two small gas hobs, and a gas bottle under the table.

I searched the two corners I could see. The one at the bottom of the MDF steps, was empty; and in the other was the clean, white glow of a china basin under a copper tap. On the ground was a camping stretcher, and on it a thick thermal sleeping bag. Next to it was a one bar heater. I couldn't see the half of the cellar closest to me as I couldn't get the beam or my head at the right angle, but I had seen enough.

I returned the torch to his pickup and waited by the gate for the taxi. There was no way I was going back inside unarmed. Every now and then I would look back at the bedroom window, but there was nothing to see.

The bloody taxi driver was late by over half an hour. It was almost three in the morning.

'I had trouble finding the place,' the old geezer groaned.

Me too.

As we started trundling down the lane I leant over the back, watching the house recede into the darkness. Just then the bedroom light flicked on. He hadn't been sleeping at all.

14

There Are No Happy Answers

TARIQ JILANI let himself into his family's pokey Whitehawk flat. He had just got back from a big argument with his boss; he wanted her to pay some of his insurance costs, she told him that was never going to happen. He stomped into the living room, taking off his jacket, and sifting through the junk mail. He separated the pizza flyers and takeaway menus from the credit card offers and other crap that someone had bothered to print his name on. As he went to throw the envelopes onto his armchair, he looked surprised to see me sitting in it. It flashed across his face, but then it was gone. Then he threw the post on the sofa instead, as though I was only just above it in his list of chores.

'Who are you?' he asked calmly, the way a chemist

asks for your address.

'I am the angel of justice,' I told him.

He didn't look impressed. 'Whose justice?'

'Your daughter's.'

He didn't move an inch, but everything behind the façade crumbled like a bombed-out factory. I watched his knees unlock, and finally, he sat down onto the sofa, staring at me from behind hollow eyes.

For once I had entered legally. I had arrived in that afternoon window, not too long after school finishes, when normally Krishma would be looking after Mahnoor. She had been less than pleased to see me; we had agreed Tariq would never know. I lied, telling her I would leave before he got home.

Their flat could be described as two-bedroom. I mean technically. But the rooms themselves were more like cupboards, and the essential pieces of furniture were enough to create submarine-like corridors through which you bent yourself out of shape to move around.

As I squeezed through to the kitchen, I could hear cartoons in the living room. CBBC. It dawned on me I had never really spoken to Krishma, and never even seen Tariq. They were just abstractions. An addendum: every missing girl has to have parents, of course. Now here she was, standing in the kitchen, making me coffee, with the sounds of children's TV in the background, because those had always been the sounds of four o'clock, and silence would be deafening. This would have triggered enormous sympathy in any other human, but that part of me doesn't work. I used to wonder if there was something left out when they made me. Not that it did me any harm.

She was even smaller than I remembered, and last time I saw her she was sitting down. She walked with a stoop, which brought her below five foot. Her hair was as long as she was and hung in a plait down her back. Any longer and she could play Rapunzel in panto, except no one was going to climb up and rescue her. She was ungroomed, which is something I have absolutely no problem with; she looked like she was supposed to look; but she didn't have any of the happiness or beauty that emancipation brings.

Her stoop almost hid the fact she had a black eye.

'Are you ok?' I asked.

She ignored the question. 'Theresa say you not found anything,' she told me, placing the coffee on the worktop I was leaning against.

'Mahnoor isn't her daughter. You deserve to know everything first, then you can decide what Theresa needs to know.'

She didn't nod, or do anything really.

I continued: 'The police think your husband is involved.'

'I know, detective tell me.'

'Daye?'

'Yesterday. He smell of cigarettes.'

I nodded. 'What do you think?'

She stared at me for some time. 'I know he have second phone. He say is work phone, but he get angry I touch it or move it. Sometime he get message and he go in night. A wife knows. Is she white?'

I wasn't listening, my attention drawn to a knife block sitting in pride of place by the side of the cooker. It held five different sizes. Four of them were in place. Where the fifth should have been there was just a narrow slot. There was no dishwasher, and I couldn't see it in the sink or on the side.

'That knife block, it looks expensive,' I mentioned offhand. I don't suppose by anyone else's standards it was expensive, but it would be for them.

'My birthday present. Tariq get cheap because knife is lost.'

'When was your birthday?'

'September.'

I had dots: the taxi, the phone, the disappearance, and now this. I was here to connect them.

I convinced her she needed to go food shopping this evening, and she needed to take her time doing it. But first I had to ask her:

'Why did he hit you?'

Her eyes were deep wells, so deep you couldn't see the bottom. 'I was crying too loud.'

What a big tough man, I thought. *What a big, tough*

man.

Sitting opposite me, his face was drawn and gaunt, disappearing into shadow around his eyes and in his cheeks. He was just skin on a hat stand. His eyebrows and his beard were turning grey, and the hair on his head had already gone. Radioactive decay. Which has a longer half-life, I wondered: grief, or guilt?

'You're one of them,' he stated.

'No. I'm unique.'

'They sent you here.'

'I was sent by God himself. And he was in a vengeful mood. I will visit his vengeance upon whomever deserves it. If that's you…' I let his imagination finish the sentence, 'If it's not you, then you want to start talking.'

'What do you want me to say?' he asked, his voice not at all aquiver.

'Last Christmas, you started picking up private fares. You got the address by text to a burner phone that you hid in an envelope, underneath the plastic tray in the centre console of your car.'

His eyes widened.

'This seems like it was a happy arrangement until three months ago, when your daughter was taken. Are you going to start talking, or do I have to guess the rest?'

He had been growing pale over my last few sentences. This time his voice was aquiver when he asked:

'Wh-w-wh…'

'Start from the beginning. Christmas.'

'I didn't want an-any of this to happen. I just wanted to look after my family.'

'Between beatings.'

'I love my daughter!' The anger gave him back his strength.

'Then tell me what happened.'

He seethed.

'Want to tell me to fuck off? Go ahead, everyone does. Or maybe you're wondering why you should say anything to me? Good question. Why should you say anything that might help find out what happened to your daughter?' I let that land, giving him time to work it out. 'Unless you already know.'

His nostrils flared, eyes locked on me like a cat. He was still angry, but he took his time responding:

'You people.'

'Yes, me people. Is there more to that?'

He licked his teeth. 'My mother was a thief, never had a job. My father, I never met. My childhood was short. I didn't want that for my daughter, I was going to look after her. As soon as I found out Krishma was pregnant I moved us to England. Here I could look after her, there are so many opportunities, for all of us. And yet the only job I can get is driving a fucking taxi.'

'Let me guess, back in the old country you were a doctor.'

He didn't brush past that, staring at me until the

moment dissipated. He wasn't finished being angry yet. 'I work hard every day—'

'Everybody works hard.'

'They don't get the shit I do. I thought it was bad enough, but after 7/7, people won't get in my taxi if they see a white man free. They spit at my wife. The other kids won't play with my daughter. And you pretend you are tolerant. I used all my money buying that car, buying the hackney license on eBay. Forty-thousand pounds! I lease it out day and night, it is never off the road; and yet the money gets shorter and the rent gets higher. We had to move into this place. All those promises, they were promised to me and I promised them to my daughter. None of it came true, so I'm not sorry I took another chance to look after my family.'

'You're wasting time, telling me your fucking sob story when your daughter is missing. Who gives a shit about you?'

'My daughter—'

'Tell me about Christmas!' I shouted. That must have been interesting for the neighbours. 'You can waste her time telling me about how hard your life is, about how hard you work, but you can't just admit to what you did. And I know the reason you won't tell anyone, won't tell your wife, it's because you're worried they'll think it's your fault. Because you already know it is.'

'That's not true.'

'Then tell me, because last I checked I'm the only person who cares.'

'And me!'

'What have you done to get her back?'

'You don't know.' His eyes shimmered. 'You don't know.'

'Then tell me.'

They pooled, begging me not to make him do it.

'Tell. Me.'

He breathed in through his nose long and smooth, but it came out of his mouth in fits. He tried to nod, but he wasn't in control, and his head just sort of shook. He swallowed a few times, licked his cracked lips, screwed his hairy hands into each other, then started:

'He was just a fare, you know, like all the others.'

'Where did you pick him up?'

'Downtown, taxi rank on East Street; he wanted to go to Ditchling Beacon. On the way, he kept asking me questions. He wanted to know about Pakistan, about Krishma and Mahnoor. How much do I make? Where do I live? I talked to him, it's good for my English. When we get to Ditchling Beacon it is nothing but a car park at the top of a hill. It was empty. And he doesn't get out of the car. He asks me if I want to make some money driving his friends around, just one evening a week or so. He says he will pay me five hundred pounds every time, but I have to be on-call twenty-four seven.'

'What did he look like?'

'He was just a kid.'

'Not good enough.'

'He had a spider tattoo on his hand.'

'Better.'

'I said I would have to think about it, and need time to stop leasing the taxi. He offered me payment for the first two jobs upfront if I said yes right there and then. A thousand pounds. He showed me it all in fifty pound notes. I had never seen one before. Afterwards, I drove him back to East Street.'

The floorboards creaked above us. Their neighbours were stomping around, shouting occasionally. Outside the net curtains it was dark. An occasional siren wailed. This was a miserable little submarine, grounded at the bottom of a miserable ocean.

'Who did you pick up?' I asked.

'There were loads of them. That young man. A few men, mostly white. One black man. One black woman. One white woman. Two old men. A Jew. There were a lot of others that I only drove once. They made me turn off the lights inside. No Muslims.'

He jumped up and pulled out a drawer by the television. He felt around in the back of it until he found a half-smoked packet of cigarettes. He sat back down, and shaking, put one in his mouth. But he didn't light it. I would be smoking except that every time I went to roll one I saw Bill Harker's teeth.

'Then there was Him,' he whispered. Then he lit it. 'He never spoke. I never saw him on the pavement. He always waited for me to pull up and then appeared from nowhere. He would pass me the address on a printed slip.'

'What did his hands look like?'

'He wore plastic gloves.' He was staring now into the glowing end; holding it upright and watching the paper ripple and disappear, replaced by a growing tower of ash.

'What happened?'

'It was the middle of the night, I got a text as usual. I went, and he got in the car. I recognised his smell.'

'What did he smell like?'

'Like flowers.' He was still staring at the cigarette. 'He passed the paper, as always, with gloves on. And I drove. On the way I pulled behind Western Road to avoid gas works and in the road this man steps out in front of us. He screams something, so I wind down the window, and quickly his hand reaches in and he un-locks the door and then he has a knife at my neck.' His hand pawed at his throat. 'He forces me to hand over my money, so I do. Then he opens the back door and holds the knife to the man in the gloves. He has his wallet ready. Then the thief runs off. I grab the radio to call in to the office, and when I turn around my passenger has already gone. I didn't see him go.'

At this point I'm going to take over telling the story

because frankly I tell it better; for starters, I'm not breaking down in tears and saying each word through desperate gasps for air.

He never received another text after that night. But he kept the phone handy just in case. Instead his wife came home to find their daughter missing, and inside his glove compartment he found a printed letter. It read: "He lives at—" and then an address, "Kill him, or you will never see your daughter again."

'You didn't do it?' I asked.

His eyes shot up to look at mine. It took him a while to answer. 'I tried calling from the phone, to speak with them, but the number doesn't work. So I bought a knife block at the market, in cash. I took one of the knives, then I went to the place. He didn't answer the door, so I kicked it in, nothing was going to stop me killing him! But he was already dead.'

'What did you do with the knife?'

'I don't know. I thought that they would give her back. He was dead. They had to. But I never heard anything. No letters, no texts. Nothing.'

'Why didn't you go to the police?'

'What could I tell them?'

'You could show them the letter.'

'I tried to kill a man. They would send us back to Pakistan, how could I find her then?'

'So instead you did nothing?'

'What could I do!?'

'Something! You could have done *something*.'

He didn't want to argue with me. He didn't give a shit what I thought. His daughter had been abducted, probably long dead, but what really upset him was someone suggesting it was his fault. *Some people.*

'Well, you can start now,' I told him. 'Where did you take them?'

'Everywhere.'

'Where exactly?'

'All different places.'

'You can remember some of them?'

'Yes.'

'Then write them down!'

I threw a notebook and a pencil at him. He picked them up, thought for a few moments whilst he opened the pages, and then started scribbling.

'What are you going to do?' he asked.

'Something,' I spat. 'I'm going to do *something*.'

15

The Other Brighton

IT WAS FOUR in the morning when I made it through
the door. There was no point in going to sleep. Instead
I stood naked in the living room, staring out the window, waiting for the sun. Occasionally I would wander
into the bedroom and look out across the flat rooves.
The baby seagull wasn't moving, I was worried about
him. I went to chuck another slice of bread but found it
was my last one. What the hell, he needed it more than
I did; not that he seemed to notice it. Just once the wind
picked up and he pulled a wing in tighter. He was alive,
just not hungry. Just tired. I knew I should sleep, but
sometimes that's more work than staying awake. And I
didn't want the old man to find me.

In the living room I pulled a drawer unit over to the

window so I could sit on it high enough to lean my head out. The wood was nice and cold on my arse cheeks, and I was smoking my first cigarette in eleven years. It tasted like shit. It tasted like the past.

The night was dark blue, starless. The streets were empty, the world silent. Pigeons huddled asleep in the covered corners of dirty grey façades. Foxes padded zigzag across the road. Quiet lights stretched down the streets, toward the sea, where more quiet lights twinkled on the horizon. It was all mine, and what was I going to do with it? Just watch it. Let it be. It wasn't really mine of course, it belonged to the magician that had disappeared the little girl. This false peace was just the held breath before the reveal.

Slowly the sky behind the cinema bled orange and cars started drifting down the road. Shops were getting deliveries now and those unlucky enough to work in London were heading for the station.

Once the real noises of the day started, I made myself an espresso and ate my last avocado, sans toast. Afterwards I threw on a pair of boxers and headed downstairs to pick up the post. I was the first today and did my duty by putting it in the box by the window. I had the usual junk mail and the morning paper. Today's headline was some controversially approved planning permission. The council was actually going to build homes people could afford, so no surprise it was a big scandal. Nestled amongst this stuff was a small but impressively weighty envelope. My name was hand-written, and it had been hand delivered. It wasn't the hand of Hermann Vogeli, I was pleased to notice. It was a woman's hand.

I sat at the kitchenette table and slit it open. It was a calligraphically written letter on wonderfully textured notepaper, and the hand that had written it smelt of sugar and spice. It read:

Dear Mr Grabarz,

It has reached our attention that you are amongst those concerned citizens who have been doing everything possible to help find our daughter. We feel eternally blessed to be living in such a kind and caring community.

We can never repay the love that people have shown us, but please allow us the opportunity to thank you in person. You are invited to our Find Joy event at two o'clock this afternoon at our address. Food and drink will be provided.

Kind regards,

Maria & Graham Tothova

After a lazy morning of showering and shaving, I got dressed. I put on the same combination of shirt and jacket I had worn to the church because it was smart enough for Hove without making me look like a prick. Then I started walking into town to get my bike.

I passed through Pavilion Gardens on my way. The scene was tragic. Council workers in plastic trousers scooping up piles of the now rotting flowers, muddy teddy bears, and spent stubs of burnt candles. It looked like the first day after Glastonbury. The party was over.

I swang by my office, but there was nothing waiting for me except a fresh layer of dust. We always left the street door unlocked during office hours so any walk-ins could wait on the bench on the landing. But it was gone one o'clock and it was locked, meaning Thalia hadn't been in today. I decided I should probably text her, but I also decided there wasn't enough time. I was already late.

I headed to my lockup, got on my Honda, and cruised gently toward York Avenue. I was actually nervous. I had no idea what this event was, or how many people would be there, or how they had heard about me, or what they thought I had done, and I hadn't even had time to think over one of these questions by the time I arrived.

I was able to park my bike on the same square of tarmac by the block of flats, and the same old lady was staring through the same net curtains wearing the same face, and trying to spot the magnet that was gathering smartly dressed people toward the house. I gave her a wave and she disappeared.

I saw a couple disappear down the side of the house, so I followed suit, emerging into the back garden. It was mostly grass but with bushes and flowers down all sides, shielding any view of the outside world and giving a secluded feel to this secret garden. In the middle was a large willow tree, with four children hanging off it, playing. There was no trampoline, no slide, no sandpit; nothing made for children except a wooden swing that also hung off the willow. Stylishly oxidised copper furniture poked out of bushes in a way that suggested it grew there. Sun streamed through the gaps in the willow projecting crepuscular rays onto the kids. God rays to you and me. This was a place where in twilight elves lurked and fairies larked.

But right now, rich people were lurking and larking instead. Fairy lights and fucking bunting was hung along the back of the house, across the patio. Two large boards on easels proclaimed the words "FIND JOY" above *the* picture. Below it was a website, a phone number, and a social media hashtag: #FindJoy. It sounded like a self-help book.

There looked to be around thirty people, all dancing through this little pocket of tranquillity, but I didn't bother looking for people I recognised because two trestle tables were set up against one side, and a barbecue was smoking bitterly next to them. On the tables were piles of sausages, burgers, chicken legs, and the unusual middleclass options: fish, halloumi, salads, that sort of thing. And by salads I don't mean bowls of chopped vegetables with dressing; I mean bowls of

couscous and beans and other things with some vegetables hidden in the middle alongside bits of fruit and
walnuts and other things that aren't at all salad. Everything was busy going off in the sun, and the occasional
fly was circling the piles of meat so I began picking up
as much as could fit on my paper plate without it buck-
ling.

I had to circle around an old man in a suit who was
helping himself to the not-salads, and whilst I was
looking for the non-existent ketchup he spoke:

'You,' he said in a surprised and offended tone.

I looked up. It wasn't a man at all, it was that old
woman from the church, wearing the same ill-fitting
suit jacket. The one who had sussed me out the first
time.

'Relax,' I told her, 'I was invited.'

'Did you bring your invitation?'

'No, but I stamped my hand for re-entry.'

The frown that was permanently stamped on her
face did its thing. 'I can't see why they invited you. It
must be a mistake.'

'You're probably right. Whereas, you: you must
have done loads to help find the girl.'

'I helped organise this,' she gestured around at the
people.

I poured myself a plastic cup of what people incorrectly call Bucks Fizz.

'And what is this?' I asked. 'A garden party, how is

that going to find her? Wait, let me guess, she's some-where in the house and we have to go around blindfolded.'

'These are the most important people in the city.'

'And what are they going to do? Issue a proclama-tion? Order the kidnapper to give her back?'

'These people are very successful people, they could help raise a lot of money.'

'Oh, I see: you're going to buy them a new daugh-ter.'

'This is a chance for successful, important, intelli-gent people to share ideas and coordinate a strategy to find her. To generate leads and follow them up. And I don't see how someone like you could help with that.'

'Someone like me?' I asked. Then I put down my plate whilst I got out a business card, showing it to her before I placed it in her breast pocket. 'Joe Grabarz, private detective, pleased to meet you. If anyone at the WI loses a ball of wool give me a call. Now if you don't mind, one of us has to do our job.'

I don't have a lot of pride, but I allowed myself just a taste of it then. She wasn't impressed. Though she was even less impressed with my plate:

'Aren't you going to have any salad with that?' she asked as I picked it back up.

'I can't, I'm on a strict things-I-want-to-eat-only diet. Nice chatting with you,' and I moved off into the mix.

Most of them were that breed of ever-so-pretty middle class types, plus a plumbing business owner or some such who had leapt above his oik status by earning so much money and wearing a suit. They humoured him because he had shown the necessary deference by adopting their tribal customs. I wafted through these groups, smiling benevolently with a mouth full of sausage until I smelt something rotten. I turned around when I heard the foul mucus gurgle of his voice. A few steps away from the rest of them, Hacker was standing with two photographers. A flash went off in my face.

'I don't believe it!' he almost screamed as he saw me.

'Funny,' I drawled, 'your readers say the same.'

He cackled, showing those yellow teeth. 'They invited *you*. Still, it seems a good idea to invite *someone* who lives in the real Brighton.'

'Is that a compliment?'

'Just a fact.'

'A fact? I'd be careful, you might get a reputation.'

With another smile he muttered something to the photographers and they moved off to snap some more.

'Writing your next piece of fiction?' I asked.

'A short story, if you're asking. Slip me a few quid and I'll put your name in it.'

'How can it be short with all these important people here?'

He groaned. They meant as little to him as they did to me. 'This'll be enough for the faithful, might run as a teaser under the masthead if I'm lucky.'

'Have they been discussing a media strategy with you?'

He scoffed. 'Find the girl. Or arrest someone. Then you'll get some media. There's your strategy.'

'No national interest?'

'I wish.'

'Last week people were breaking down doors, holding a vigil in the centre.'

'That was last week. People have very short attention spans these days.'

'Still, people covered the letter he wrote.'

'Yes, pity he hasn't written another one.'

'Well, I'm sure if your circulation really drops he will.'

He looked at me. I gave it right back to him. *I have no idea what you're implying*, he seemed to say. *Yes, you bloody do*, I replied. After a few moments he turned back to watch his photographers.

'What happened to you?' he asked. 'You used to give us all sorts of good copy. "The Police's Dirty Habit", you remember that?'

'You were never interested in me, you were only interested in embarrassing them.'

'Maybe a little bit,' he smiled once again. 'I write what people read.'

'And which comes first, I wonder.'

'I ask myself that every day.' He sighed ironically.

'Mitchell, come over here.' He gestured to one of the photographers, who jogged over. 'Take Mr Grabarz's picture, and make it a nice one.'

Bill snatched the plate from my hands and the flash went. Then he gave me it back.

'"Tenacious private detective Joe Grabarz was amongst those invited", how does that sound?'

'But will people read it?' I asked.

This time there was a note of melancholy in his laugh. 'Nobody reads this shit anymore.'

As I moved back toward the pretty people I could swear one of my chicken legs was missing.

The other side of the willow tree, half hidden from the rest of the guests, a shampoo commercial-style array of one stunning blonde, one stunning brunette, and one stunning redhead, all in those dresses so tight they have to walk upstairs like a crab, were enraptured by a young-ish bearded man in a suit so sharp you could cut yourself.

'Afternoon,' I nodded to the women.

They turned their nose up at me instantly. They could smell my poverty.

'Mr Grabarz,' the man intoned. It was Ben McCready.

'Your Majesty,' I replied. 'You were just going over the council minutes with these ladies were you?'

He didn't engage, he was playing The Serious Man for them. 'I advised against inviting you, Mr Grabarz.'

'Well, I always advise against voting for you, so that's ok.'

'You're not in my ward.'

'Neither are the Tothovas. Where are their councillors, are they here? Or did you advise against inviting them too?'

He sighed. 'I don't know what Maria and Graham thought you could bring to this.'

'A detective, what could he bring to the search for a missing girl?'

'Over there, by the rose bush, *they* are detectives, Mr Grabarz. *You* are a joke. You're just a thug who wanted a police badge but couldn't be bothered to earn it, so you stencilled your door and managed to exploit enough desperate individuals to pay the bills.'

'It's like you can see into my soul,' I told him.

I could have told him my half-baked thoughts about him. I could have told him that if I didn't know better I'd say he had spent his entire life without his parents or his peers listening to him. He was so smart, he was always right, and still they never listened to him. So he worked hard, did all the right things, and got himself elected to some minor position of power, and now people have to listen to him, don't they? Because he's important. He wants all the respect that comes with being respectable but he still wants all the pussy that comes with power. The world is still the playground for him and he wants to swing his dick around with the rest of the boys. But a new, special kind of dick that pretends not to be a dick at all, but instead progressiveness and modernity and equality because that's what women want to hear and like all men he'll say whatever women want to get into their pants. It was all part of the game, and he and his mates would brag about how they fooled women into thinking they were someone they wanted to get fucked by. I could have said all this. But this is the new me. The calm me. And I didn't want him to know how far he got under my skin.

'Enjoy the rest of his speech, ladies,' I said with a smile, 'just don't give him your number.'

I moved toward the rose bush, I didn't want them to think I was scared, even if I really didn't want to speak to them. Immediately I could see Price and Roy Parker, a couple of other people who stood like policemen, and Graham Tothova. They were deep in conversation.

'What are we talking about, gang?' I asked.

The conversation stopped instantly. They all stared at me. I tried to keep the grin on my face. Price looked as incredible as ever, her athletic body piercing through her blouse and tailored jacket. Parker looked even more like a corpse. He hadn't looked so bad at Saturday's press conference, but he had probably been wearing makeup. The other two officers were doing their Serious Man act like McCready. Only Mr Tothova looked like he wasn't about to stab me with a wine glass.

'Thank you very much for inviting me,' I told him.

He was confused, but calm. 'That must have been my wife,' he apologised, 'what is it you do?'

'Mr Grabarz is a detective,' Parker answered in the tone of a Victorian schoolmistress, 'according to his business card.'

'That's the trouble,' I told Mr Tothova, 'anyone can get them printed these days. Roy's says he's a police-man.'

'At least I didn't have to pay postage and packaging on mine,' he sneered.

'Perhaps this isn't the best time to throw insults around,' Price interjected, 'I'm sure Joe just wants to help.'

'Thank you,' I said, and gave her a little smile that she didn't return.

'So,' she said, 'what leads have you developed? Any information you can give us?'

That bitch. I had nothing to give them, and she knew it. And I couldn't put it to her the other way around because we were all here to help the police, that was the point. She stared at me through glacial blue eyes, her blonde curls hanging loose off duty, her ski-slope nose, those thin pink lips. She was fierce like a vixen. My god, we could have been something fantas-tic. In bed, I mean.

'Not at present,' I stated matter-of-factly.

'Oh,' she offered in mock-disappointment so subtle that those who didn't know better would think it was genuine. 'Any theories you can offer instead?'

Now she was just being mean. 'Not at present,' I repeated.

'Shame. Maybe the bogeyman took her. What's his name? Matt? Mark?'

'Detective,' Roy said in quiet reprimand.

'I'm sorry,' Price apologised to Mr Tothova, 'but you see, Joe has a theory, don't you? About crime in the city. Do you want to tell them?'

The other officers sniggered. Price pretended to wait for an answer, I did everything I could to keep the embarrassment out of my face, but now people were staring at me and I felt my cheeks getting hot. Stupid fucking cheeks.

'He's a conspiracy nut. He's even managed to convince some of the more tragic officers: Richard Daye is one your believers, isn't he? And Daye's old DS, Andy Watson, down in his little basement. Not that they would be stupid enough to tell anyone, would they?'

'Only someone they trusted,' I told her.

That hurt her, I was glad to see. But she shook it off: 'So you see, Graham, he's exactly the sort of level-headed individual you and Maria should be listening to. If only he had anything to say.'

I stayed calm and quiet enough to look like the decent one. Then I raised my glass in farewell to Mr Tothova and stepped silently away. I couldn't help but smile at how upset Price must be. I was supposed to argue back. I was supposed to be unreasonable. But now she looked unreasonable. Maybe not telling people what I think was going to be fun after all.

The garden was as hot and humid as a bayou, so I hid under the shadow of the house.

Everyone hates me. *With good reason*. I was glad at least they hadn't invited Tab, otherwise I might never get away. Small mercies. I went to drown myself in Mimosa but spilt it on myself as I did a sudden dance on the patio. It was dotted with glass tiles. They were only a few centimetres square but dangerous enough. *Who the fuck has glass patio tiles?* I thought. *Fucking death-trap*. But the lid on this thought was slammed shut by a voice that seemed to come from another world:

'Mr Grabarz.'

I could only see her silhouette. The sun was streaming through a tree behind, obscuring her in golden haze. I inched closer, moving the sun behind a tree, revealing her.

Golden blonde hair that ran straight down to her stomach. Ever so pink wind-chafed cheeks with the tiniest dance of freckles. White layers of thin silk. Around her neck and in her hair, dark silver jewellery studded with marcasite. An opera necklace disappeared behind her high neckline but between the layers of silk; you could see where a pendant figure hung below her petite breasts. An angel.

'Mrs Tothova.' I almost bowed. 'Thank you. For inviting me.'

'I was told that when the police can't find someone, you're the person to see. Why waste the time?'

'Why indeed.'

'You will of course be rewarded, as will everyone who contributes to finding Joy. We'll share the money fairly.'

'I'm sure your charity could spend that money in a much better place than my bank account.'

She blushed a little. 'Let's hope everyone is as generous as you, Mr Grabarz.'

'Call me, Joe.'

'Maria.'

'I do appreciate you inviting me, Maria, although I don't think many of your guests do.'

'Who cares what they think?' she asked calmly. 'She's my daughter. I'll spend all my money, all these people's money, let cameras into my house, I'll even whore myself out—' she stopped suddenly, 'I'm sorry.' A single tear had escaped.

'Don't apologise,' I told her, 'not enough parents care as much as you do. Believe me.'

I don't know what gave me the nerve, but I leant in and wiped the tear from her cheek. Her eyes floated up toward mine. They seemed to contain the entire universe, anything there was to know could be learnt by gazing there. I wanted to step inside them. Her teeth showed beneath her lip as she inhaled a hushed, excited breath.

Then her eyes shot off behind me. I looked round. There was a flurry of black and silver as ten or more uniformed officers flooded into the garden, surrounding Parker and Price. I moved to wade into the mess. But as I did they broke and disappeared like starlings, scattering back down the side of the house at speed, Price and Parker's heads bobbing in the middle, people whispering in their ears, Price pulling her phone out.

Bill was running after them, also on the phone. I grabbed him.

'What the hell is going on?'

'Some kid who works at the school has a blue van registered. They're on it now, he's tearing up the city centre.'

Tearing up the city centre?

'It's an actual, genuine police chase—this is the story we've been waiting for!' he squealed, and he was gone.

I tried to calculate the dread I was feeling. *A panicked boy, with marijuana in the back his van, and the police chasing him.* Adrenaline shot into my veins. *Not good. Not good. Jesus Christ! This is not going to end well.*

16

This Is Not Going to End Well

I BROKE INTO a sprint. Down the side of the house, out the front, across the road, onto my bike, helmet on. I fired it up. *Town centre. Town centre?* Time to play follow the sirens. *Got to find them first.* Engine revving. *Let's go!*

I shot down York Avenue, posh houses zipping past each side, left onto Lansdowne Road, narrow, but wide enough for two cars. *Don't want to die today*. Thinking ahead, this becomes Upper North Street, running parallel to Western Road, the high street, that cuts right through to the clock tower at the centre of town, should be able to pick up the scent from there. *Already on Upper North Street. Think faster. Sirens!* They were near, but where? I shot a glance down each connecting road as they whipped past my right, giving me a brief window into what was happening on Western Road. The sirens were loud now, but each glance was empty. There was no traffic. Nothing. *Where are they?* I twisted the throttle open, letting out a deafening roar and shooting round the car in front—*truck!*—and back onto the left, just missing being pancaked by a removal van. I had fifty metres of clear road now and I ate them up in a single bite. Montpelier Road cut across at traffic lights ahead, they were green—*lean forward, look to the right*—the wide avenue zipped past and for just a second I saw blue lights. *Found them!*

I was running parallel with them now, weaving, dodging, at the next road and the next and the next I saw the flash of blue and heard them wail. I needed to ride even faster to try and catch their quarry. *Traffic ahead!* I had to brake, switch onto the pavement, thank fuck it was empty, I did *not* want to kill anyone today. Back onto the road, I kept looking right, but I couldn't see the blues anymore, the sirens were quieter. *Fuck!* I came out at the end of Upper North Street onto Dyke Road. *Shit!* I had to turn right, head down onto North Street, the middle of town, I was going to be even further behind. *Pedestrians!* Near miss, bloody tourists! I zipped down past the clock tower, onto the high street, expecting to hit the usual stationary buses, but they were all squeezed against the side of the road, everything: taxis, vans, the lot. The usual summer crowds filled every inch of pavement but all had the backs of their heads to me, staring down the road the way I was heading, toward the blue lights that had just disappeared. I leant forward into my bike, opening the throttle as far as it would go and rocketing down the hill, the streams of vehicles and department stores just blurs, my visor giving me only what was in front of me. *Clear, clear, clear, zebra crossing! Fuck, fuck, fuck! Too fast! Don't step out! Clear! Traffic moving. Shit.* Slowly they were beginning to wake up, the chase had passed, and the buses and the vans were pulling out from the side and closing in on me and—but I was out. Onto the Steine.

The Steine is just two long stretches of grass with statues and flowers and stuff in them and the roads circle round them clockwise in a one way system. I skidded left, moving sideways, barely in control of my front wheel, zipping past the Pavilion on my left. *Bus lane in a second.* Another blur of tarmac and amber lights, then the bus lane gave me mostly empty road to bomb down and when I had made it within sight of St Peters I could see the ocean of blue lights ahead, flowing like a torrent of water after a single white van less than twenty metres ahead of them. They must have thought he resprayed it after the press conference, still it was clearly too old.

The sound of ten angry sirens was deafening. *Faster, faster, faster!* I was within twenty metres of them. *What the fuck are you going to do if you catch up to them? Shut up!* Onto London Road, another high street, single lane, down the narrow gap of traffic. *Red lights! Through. Everyone alive.* Two lanes now, the circus ahead, we were about to go past my window. *Who cares!?* The road splits here, one way again. *Holy fucking shit!* I don't know how it happened but metal crunched, glass smashed, cars were jerked in directions they shouldn't go. Some kind of accident, police cars smashing into each other, one on the pavement, no time to pay attention—*avoid dying!*—onto the wrong side, through the sea of lights. Now we really were going past my window. *Oncoming traffic!* Shit. *Pavement!* Narrow escape. Under the viaduct. I was alive and still moving but I was on the wrong side of the block. *Think, where does he come out? Left. If he has any sense he'll stay down London Road!* Left, wrong way round the corner, dodged more oncoming traffic—*Bus!*—almost dead, missed, still alive. *There's the van!* He's not smart, he's veered right, into Preston Park Avenue, running along the top of the park. He's trying to lose them.

I skidded right, let out a roar catching up, got in close behind, my front wheel almost kissing his back doors now. If the police had got this close surely they would have seen the paint job was done years ago, the white layer was shedding all over the road. Not that it mattered, he was driving like a madman and they had to stop him whatever colour his van was. *Too narrow!* I pulled back two metres, there were parked cars along both sides, the van filling the road in front of me: one piece of traffic and that unlucky driver is dead. One football from the park, one child not looking, and they are dead. And so am I. *This has to end.* I accelerated, I had to pull level with him, maybe if he could see me he would stop. He had to know this wasn't about the drugs. Doing sixty miles an hour, at least, I slipped into the sliver of space to the right of the van—*breathe in*—pulling level with the driver's door. *Maybe I should bang on the door! Maybe I would fly off my bike!* Finally he saw me, for a split second. He was scared. He was confused. Then I realised all he could see was a maniac on a motorbike riding dangerously down his side, he didn't know who I was. Was I police? Did he care? *Shit, shit, shit! Got to take off my helmet. Too dangerous! Fuck it, this is all too dangerous. One hand off the handlebars—too late!* He inched the wheel to the right, closing the gap between me and the parked cars, I had to brake, didn't I? *Brake or die!? Brake or die, Joe!?* I braked, slipping down the side to the back again. He was metres ahead of me once more, heading toward the crossroads at the end of the street. I looked in my mirrors: no sign of blue. Just me and him. And the crossroads. Traffic from the left. Traffic from the right. This was the gauntlet, right here. Blind entry, it was like driving through a meat slicer, if one of us was going to die it was going to be here. *Here we go!* He made it. So did I! *Fuck. Me.*

Surrenden was next, and much safer: uphill, dual

carriageway, massive houses, grass and trees in the middle, few pedestrians. There was a college further up, but I remembered with relief it was the holidays. *Sirens*. I checked my mirrors; all I could detect in my glance was a shimmer of blue. They were back. And they were gaining on us. The arrogant bastards were putting their pursuit driving course into practice. They lived for this.

After ten seconds the road took a sharp turn to the right, and got steeper. The weight of the van slowed it, and I took my chance. I pulled up my visor, wind in my eyes, and pulled level with him again. I banged on the window. He paid attention this time. *Pull the fuck over!* I said with my squinting eyes. Or at least I hoped I did. But it didn't matter: if he recognised me, he recognised me as the man who knew what was in the back of his van, and it wasn't until this split second that I realised I was probably the one person he wanted to see less than the police. *I am so much worse.* He moved his hands to the left of the steering wheel and gripped it tight.

'Wait!' I shouted.

No time. I tapped the brakes as he wrenched the wheel to the right, trying to ram me onto the grass, but I was too quick, I dropped behind him again, sandwiched between him and the police cars that had finally joined the party. He put his foot down again, revving the thing raw, and rivalling my Honda for noise.

The van screamed its way over the top of the hill,

and onto Braybon Avenue, a steep and winding roller coaster. The road rolled back down over the hill, we swang to the right, then to the left, the sirens were quieter now, the police had slammed on the brakes. They knew what was coming.

Then the road was steeper, and our speedometers jumped, then it curved back up. A dip. A step. Whatever you want to call it, my stomach did a somersault. Then I watched in horror as the road dropped away from the van. One wheel was in the air. Then two, then three, a pirouette. Then four. It was floating. Then my bike was floating. And I was floating away from it. The van was turning gracefully through the air, heading for a bungalow on the right. Number 48. Then my head hit the tarmac.

Everything was quiet. Everything was dark. It was a long dark that stretched away from me, full of wind and storms. Out in this deep darkness someone had rung a bell. A giant one the size of a house. It reached me as the deep reverberating hum of a bell rang centuries ago atop a monastery in the Himalayas, the sound still bouncing off the mountains of my mind. Then the darkness was on my face, and there was no depth, no world, no bell. I felt around. I could feel grass in both hands. But my feet pushed against stone. Or concrete. A step of some kind. Then I knew I was lying face down on a verge, my legs dangling off the kerb.

I was wearing my motorcycle helmet. I pulled it off. Everything was sirens, and screaming, and bright lights. I pushed off the ground, hurting my arms, slowly up onto all fours, hurting my knees. Then I breathed, hurting my chest. Had I been in an accident?

I looked up. What I saw didn't make sense. Half bungalow, half building site. Half building site, half van. Ambulances. Police. A howling woman being held back from the rubble by two officers. Around the rubble, paramedics worked, and around the van. The road was closed both ways.

I saw all this through the windows of a car. Had no one found me? Or seen me? Or they didn't care. What had I been doing? I tried to walk myself through today's events. *I got an invite? Yes, that's right. From who? The Tothovas.* I took it forward moment by moment. *My flat. My office. A barbecue. Lots of meat. Stupid salads. People. An old man in a suit. Hacker. Ben McCready. Roy Parker. Price. Bitch! Glass patio tiles. An angel. Fuck!* My heart was going to break my ribs. I had no idea what I was doing here when there was a girl to save.

I leant on the bonnet, then finally got up onto my feet. I still seemed to be invisible. A small boy was being loaded onto a stretcher. A small girl onto another. The driver of the van was slumped over the steering wheel, bloodied. He seemed to be invisible too.

I looked around for some way to sneak off. Something silver glistened in a front garden. My Honda was upside down in someone's garden! I limped over and righted it, poor thing. It was hurt, but it wasn't fatal.

I looked around again. There was no way I could push it through the road blocks unseen. There was only one way out: Steve McQueen style. I put my helmet back on. *Ok. Ok. Here we go!* I fired it up. Heads span as I launched out, onto the road, uphill toward the roadblock, up along the side of someone's wall, into the air, over a police car; over the craning, unbelieving head of a uniformed officer on a radio; and back onto the tarmac. *Out!* It was pretty damn impressive.

Siren's wailed, but they were too late, I would be lost in ten seconds. I headed right, onto Woodland Way, and from that into Withdean Park, bombing downhill through the trees and across the grass toward London Road. Toward Hove. A strange, whimsical thought had mutated, festering in my mind, in the darkness. It possessed me: *Nobody has glass patio tiles.*

17

When Ghosts Come Back to Haunt

'WHAT DO YOU THINK of the name "Petra",' she asked as I was leaving.

'I thought you liked your name.'

'I do. But I've got a fella, and he doesn't like it so much. Do you think I should go for it?'

'I think you should do whatever you want to do.'

'If only life was that easy,' she sighed.

'Isn't it?' I asked rhetorically, and left.

It was obvious what I had to do now, that's why I went to see Peter again on the off chance, but sadly the rest of her drivers were behaving normally.

Although they were thorough enough not to use one of hers again, there was still a pattern to follow. It only took me two days of paying, threatening, and flirting, to find him. A different firm, but the same story: used to lease out his car, the type who would let you wipe your arse with his pillow if you paid him enough, and suddenly he had stopped leasing it, suddenly he didn't need your money thank you very much. He was a Mr Gentjan Hajdari, a half-Albanian, half-Macedonian immigrant who had moved to Britain ten years ago with his family. After Srebrenica he was afraid Eastern Europe was no longer safe for Muslims. He always wore one of those strange German Army parkas, and had a habit of disinfecting the car seats every couple of hours. I even saw him cleaning his air vents with a paintbrush.

There was nothing to do but follow him through his shift, which was nine to five. Just like Jilani, the regular job was pocket money. Keeping up appearances. It must have been part of the deal, after all, there was a reason they used a taxi driver and not a chauffeur.

Nothing ever happened during his shift, and after it hadn't happened I would follow him back to his house in Coldean. Coldean is a suburb squeezed into a valley between Wild and Stanmer Parks, and Ditchling and Lewes Roads, hidden away and only accessible by car from one road. Because it's cut off it doesn't attract people or investment in the way other areas do. Some residents optimistically call it Coldean Village. Coldean Shanty Town might be more appropriate.

He would pull into the driveway of his strangely half-timbered bungalow and I would find a new place to wait on one of the roads above in case tonight was a night he got summoned. In the morning I would head back to the caravan and grab a few hours sleep, then catch up with him again around lunch. He always ate at the same place, an Arab deli with Al Jazeera on the TV. He was one of the few people left in the world who wanted to engage with people, not eat something out of a packet in his car. He always took a full hour for lunch, which I admired. A French hour and a half is even better.

On the fourth day I took my usual piss-warm shower in the caravan, hitting my head as always on the way out; dressed, jumped on my moped, and zipped off to wait down the street from the deli. He sauntered out, nicely full, as always. Where Jilani had been stress-thin and balding, Hajdari had the build you would expect of a man who spent his days sitting down and his lunches sitting even further down. He always walked out of the deli with a smile on his face, often chuckling to himself as he squeezed into his cab. Then he radioed in for a job and was off.

That afternoon passed as boringly as the others had, and like the past three days I went slowly out of my mind. I made a game of learning all the street names, that's how bored I was. By five o'clock it was already dark and I followed him up to the top of Ditchling

Road, where he had to queue forever as always, and I would zip past and right and take up an observation post around ten minutes before he got home.

Over the evening the lights would slowly disappear from the houses, and all feeling would slowly disappear from my fingers. Eventually I would be the only person out on the road. Today I had circled round to a couple of roads above. Looking down from this position I could only just see the rear of his taxi poking out, but it was enough. I waited.

It was a dark November night, thick shutters of cloud pulled across the sky, blocking out the moon and the starlight, trapping moisture until it clung onto your face. Yellow balls of light hung around street lamps but no light was thrown, and from the fog you expected Jack the Ripper or a Peeler, a headless horseman or a woman with her throat cut, to stumble out and grab you by the lapels. It was a suffocating kind of dark, a supernatural type, when ghosts come back to haunt and others go to join them. The kind of night when people die.

If tonight was the night Hajdari got summoned, and surely it would be, I was worried about losing him. So I wandered down to his and hid in one of the bushes until all the lights were out. Then I inched forward to the rear of the car, and punched out the red lens on his left light. It fucking hurt. A light came on in the house, but I was back in the bush. Once the light went off, I jogged back to my moped. All I had to do now was wait some more.

Around half eleven I saw the red glow of a rear light and heard the soft rumble of an idling engine. I gripped the handlebars. Or at least I tried to, my fingers were numb. Then a minute later he reversed out and drove off toward Coldean Lane. I was excited, but I kept my distance, able to follow the mismatched lights in the gloom. Together we headed down to Lewes Road, descending out of the fog. I eased back, headlight off, making sure not to hit his radar. He led us down toward town, through the Steine, all the way to the pier, and then left along the seafront until we reached Sussex Square. The silhouette of a large older man was standing in the doorway of one of the icing-white Victorian mansions. His white hair and moustache were glowing in the dim light of a sickly yellow bulb, beyond that his face was in darkness. He threw away a cigar when the taxi pulled up and walked jauntily toward it. At least someone was enjoying themselves tonight.

A moment later we were off again. Back along to the pier, round the Steine, but this time we kept to the left along London Road, taking a right where only buses and taxis, and a cheeky moped, are allowed. Then up Ditchling Road, almost all the way up, through the Fiveways, ascending back into the fog, past the school on the left, right to the outskirts of the city, then he took the last right before the road becomes a bypass, down a single lane that cuts across open grass toward woods. It's a dead end, so I sailed past the turning, pulling over in a private road that serves a row of houses opposite. There wasn't a single light on in any of them. The taxi's twin lights disappeared into the mist.

Two minutes later it re-emerged, with no passenger, just Hajdari turning right toward the bypass, on his way back to Coldean. Uncharacteristically cautious, I waited. Seven minutes later a second taxi appeared up the road carrying a fare and turned into the lane. I couldn't see anything more than a silhouette inside. It disappeared, reappeared empty, and left. Four minutes after that, another one did the same.

This wasn't just one driver. This probably wasn't even just three drivers. All I knew was that people were gathering here, somewhere in the mist, for some reason. A collective group using a rotating enigma code of drivers, to keep people like me off the scent. Who was I kidding? It was to keep people like the police off the scent. But like the enigma, once you had one word, you had the system. Jilani had been one car, one driver, but it was enough. I just had no idea who was on the other end of the line.

I had to get closer, but I couldn't just walk down the lane as any more taxis would see me instantly, even in this weather.

I started my moped and headed back down Ditchling Road, past the school on my right, passing another taxi on the way. Then I took a left and zipped the wrong way down Hollingbury Rise, which runs along the bottom of the woods, and left onto Golf Drive, pulling up in the car park at the base of the allotments.

I left my moped out of the light of the lamp posts and climbed the fence. The mist hung amongst the plots. I passed grimy greenhouses and wilted brown plants, faint outlines of sheds and other indeterminable shapes; the eerie crucified outline of a scarecrow. Heading up the middle of the valley, I rose gently into thicker fog as I headed north, I was waiting to see the car park at the top. Instead an old man's face hove out of the grey, gaunt and muttering, with misted glasses. I might have mistaken him for a ghost but he was carrying a black bucket of something. What he was doing in his allotment at midnight I didn't want to know, that was a job for a proper detective. In five seconds he was lost to the mist again. He was the only person I saw. He might not have been there at all.

I started to worry that I had lost the path and that I too would be haunting this place forever but the woods slowly encroached on my left and then the ground turned to concrete and I was standing in the car park. There was only one thing at the end of the lane, and only one thing this car park served: Hollingbury Park Golf Course. The club house is the only building: an L-shaped brick eyesore so boring you know it was built by the council.

As I stood there the grey fog began to glow and headlights appeared from the down the lane, I knelt down and they stopped just before the clubhouse. Another silhouette, this one a well-built man, climbed out of the back. He waited whilst the taxi turned in a circle, headlights sweeping round. I threw myself as flat as I could. When I looked up the lights were trundling back down the lane, and the man had gone.

I crawled forward until I could hide behind a row of four parked golf buggies, just by the tip of the L. I was looking at the reception, but I couldn't see any lights. I could only see one of the six sides though. I wanted to observe from the trees or behind a rise, but there was nothing close enough to see through the mist, so keeping low I began to circle round in the open. First the long side facing south, where I could hide behind the ha-ha of the stepped putting green. No lights on. Then I paced to the bottom of the L, but still there was nothing. I had to climb through some trees to check the next side, and still there was nothing, and then I was on the inside of the L and could see the last two sides. There didn't seem to be a light on anywhere. I was standing in a smaller car park for staff and disabled members. It was empty. The whole damn place was empty, just the unyielding flat black stare of the windows. I was chasing spectres.

Maybe there *was* another building, but I didn't think so.

I listened. There was nothing but muffled wind. Not a bird, not a car. Not even a breath. The reception doors were just round the corner. I know what you're thinking. I was thinking it too. I was a brave boy, and stupid, but not *that* stupid. I was going to do the smart thing. The safe thing.

I would head back down through the allotments, down to my moped, and the phone box at the bottom of Hollingbury Rise.

'Emergency, which service?' A woman's voice.

'Hello.'

'Do you need fire, police, or ambulance?'

'Police.'

Buzz, *click*. 'Police emergency.' A new voice.

'Yes, hello, I was just walking my dog and—'

'Calm down please, sir.'

'Sorry. It's just—I was walking my dog and… and I heard screaming. A woman screaming. Coming from the golf club.'

'Which golf club, sir?'

'A nine iron. Sorry, I mean, Hollingbury Park.'

'Hollingbury Park. Ok, sir, happy to help, the boys'll be right there. Fully armed and ready for business.'

'Oh thank you! Thank you so much!'

'Anything else we can do for you in the meantime?'

Sirens. Armed men. Storm in, drag 'em out. Key to

the city? Yes, thank you very much. Million pound reward? Don't mind if I do—

Gravel crunched to my left. *Footsteps?* I ran to my right. It was instinct. I ran past the entrance, round to the putting greens, and straight into a fist!

Everything went bright, then dark, then red, green, purple, and painful. My optic nerve was firing every colour into my brain, all at the same time. My clothes were being tugged. I tried to keep them on. Then gravity disappeared, and I was floating, my shoes just brushing along the ground. The colours faded. Fuzzy shapes replaced them. Then I could focus. Ceiling wheeled in front me: I was inside.

18

Beneath the Surface

I KILLED THE IGNITION. The engine burbled and died. Nothing greeted it in return. Not even a gust of air. There was no sound from the garden this time. No movement from the house. No traffic. No police cars. No one to be seen. No one to be seen by. Even the little old lady in the flats had gone, there was just the drape of her curtains.

I kicked down the stand and climbed off. Everything about me hurt. I felt like I had rusted. I pulled off my helmet and took the torch and toolkit from the saddlebags. I didn't know if I would need them, but I felt better when properly equipped.

I wandered down the alley the same way I had two hours earlier. Only this time I wasn't greeted by a throng of pretty, rich people. There was no one, and no sound to go with them. The serving plates had all been cleared away, but the tables were still up. I stepped over dirty paper plates and empty plastic wine glasses. Half-finished ones rested on the side, undisturbed by me or anyone else. The "FIND JOY" boards were still up on their easels, as was the bunting. The place had been abandoned quickly; dropped like cold chips.

I jogged up the patio stairs to the back door. It was one of those ugly modern fibreglass ones, which meant there was no hope of avoiding the lock. I knelt down, unrolled my toolkit, and went to work. It didn't take long, I'm too much of a pro.

This let me into an airlock-like wet room where you could hose down the dog before you let him in to mess up your white kitchen. There was a deep sink with a shower head on the taps, and several heavy coats hung up. There was a washing machine and tumble dryer stacked on top of each other, and the usual assortment of detergents and softeners. It was a modern extension, and they had kept the original back door, which they locked for added security, so I spent another minute picking this one.

Then I was into the kitchen, pocketing my tools but gripping the heavy torch in case there was someone to hit with it. The kitchen was mostly plain, sanded light wood, some of it painted a pastel, sort of peppermint, green. Anything else that was painted, a table leg for example, was white. There were glass Kilner jars that said sugar on them, or flour, or self-raising flour, or salt, pepper, paprika, and more, all with their contents decanted into them so that you wouldn't be offended by seeing a brand label and could pretend you were living in the nineteenth century. There was a Smeg fridge, none of your vulgar American-style shit here, Mason Cash bowls for baking, and Le Creuset for cooking. Only the best. I wanted to look in their fridge and see if it was packed full of vegetables the way they are on television; and chilli jam, and onion chutney, and other things that humans don't eat. On the table were the now empty serving plates, as well as the unopened extra boxes of wine and cartons of orange juice.

I moved through to the living room and gave it a cursory glance. Mugs were placed on almost every surface, they must have spent more on drinks coasters than I did on rent. The furniture was expensive and not at all child-friendly. The floor was the same sanded light wood boards as the kitchen and hallway, but with a large Persian rug covering everything except the last foot before the walls. There was an open fireplace, but being summer it was stacked with ornamental pinecones, some of them painted with a subtle silver glitter. There were a lot of candles that had never been burnt. There was no television in the room, it was no doubt banished to a hidden chamber like a demented step-child. And as a result there was a lot of free real estate on the walls, taken up by art. It was the sort of nice looking but not masterful stuff you might buy in an open house. There was also a prominent show off-shelf with trophies and a couple of medals, won by Joy, no doubt.

The only time I took I used to study the photographs. You can always learn a lot from what photos people choose to display. When you display what seems like every photo ever taken you are telling people that you don't think your real life lives up to the curated version, and nothing more specific than that. But the Tothovas had chosen only three, and it's when picking just a few that you have to ask yourself: what people, places, moments define us?

There was one of a young blonde teenager reclining on a beach, with a stunning dark-haired beauty in her forties reclining behind, and a pompous man in at least his fifties crouched next to them. They were somewhere in the Middle East judging by the characters in the background. The girl wore nothing but a modest swimming costume, her eyes squinting; the mother in a similarly modest but far more chic costume with Chanel sunglasses and a wide-brimmed summer hat. The father on the other hand was in a grey suit, yellow shirt, orange tie, and matching red face. The Redburn family, almost. I had to guess who was holding the camera.

Next to it was a photo of a young boy in a dark blue puffer jacket, almost up to the top of his wellies in snow, on a forecourt. Standing behind him were too larger boys in slightly more stylish cold weather gear and a girl. The boys were laughing to each other, the girl was staring off to the side; the young boy was the only one looking at the camera. The subjects: Mike, Steve, Tasha, and Graham Tothova. The setting: Derby, circa 1980s. Taking the photo: Paul or Lynn Tothova.

The last one was the new Tothova family: Graham in one of his boring shirts, Maria looking as beautiful and otherworldly as ever; and Joy, nothing but a bundle of clothes in Maria's arms, a knitted yellow hat hiding everything but a pair of screwed up eyes and a button nose. A low winter sunlight shone on the two of them, Graham was in shadow.

I padded back into the hallway, and into the room at the front. Here was the television, and the less fashionable furniture. All of the girl's toys, crayons, a painting set, and a dress up box. Graham's toys were here too: a state-of-the-art stereo system and racks of CDs. There were Blu-rays too, split into two distinct shelves; one was eighties action movies and the other was all world cinema. Nothing interesting in here.

I headed back into the hallway and crept up the stairs. I wanted to check the house was clear before I went where I needed to go. On the first floor there was Joy's bedroom, but I didn't dare do any more than lean my head in in case someone in the flats saw me or my shadow. There were posters and books and an oboe in a case. It was just your average young girl's bedroom to me, I don't know enough about what's popular to know how weird or not-weird she was.

The other rooms included a home gym and an office to run their charity from. I was sure this contained a treasure trove of interesting financial information, but I had no way of copying it and not enough time to study it if I had.

I climbed another set of stairs into the loft conversion. It was their bedroom, unsurprisingly fashionable, and an en suite. I wanted to look through all their drawers but I was confident the house was empty and that was all I was up here to find out.

I tiptoed back down both sets of stairs and with a quick glance front and back and a short listen, tried the handle on the cupboard under the stairs. It was locked, but this was the type of lock I could pick with nothing but a paperclip and my tongue. It was open in less than ten seconds. What greeted me was a wall of stuff: an old pram, an old hoover, a spare washing up bowl, wellies, strange old products for cleaning strange old metals, all the crap you always find in those cupboards. The pram was piled on the top and it was the first thing I reached in to remove. I pulled it out and the most extraordinary thing happened: everything else came with it. It was all one piece, superglued.

I had no time to admire the genius of it, instead with

my torch I searched for what had to be there. Sticking out of the floor there was a small eye hook. It wasn't quite what I was expecting, but it would do. I could see on the underside of the stairs, set down a few from directly above, its partner hook. A ball of string was part of the display that had been inside, so I cut off a piece with my flick knife, threaded it through the eye hook and heaved with all my might. The trapdoor lifted up easily and I slipped a hand under it, pulling it fully open and connecting the two hooks. I flicked on my torch and stared down at a set of rickety wooden steps, down to a metal door.

Step by step I went; each creaking, and threatening to buckle beneath me. Finally I reached the bottom and pushed open the heavy, rusted door, swinging the torch beam into the darkness.

I saw a flash of a cellar and maybe a person, I couldn't be sure. The only thing I was sure of was the cloth clamped to my mouth and that sweet smell.

19

The Society of the Twelve

ROUGH HANDS THREW me down into a chair.

'What is that?' a voice inquired.

'Found him outside, snooping around,' a voice behind my ear replied.

The room was dark, I could hardly see anything. I was at a table, I knew, and there were windows on the other side. The grey mist made them opaque moonlit panels, strange light fittings. There were four dark shapes in front of me, and between them colours swirled and twinkled in my retinas, a fog of blood vessels. My shoulders felt heavy.

The rough hands searched my pockets, I had nothing but my moped key, tobacco, Rizlas, filters, and my Zippo lighter. The key and lighter were passed into the darkness. Moments later they were shoved back into my pockets with the rest.

'Who are you, and what are you doing here?' one of the shapes enquired.

I didn't answer it. Things were beginning to focus. There were indeed four people opposite me and another behind, pushing my shoulders down into the chair. It was the shape in the middle that was doing all the talking. He had a pleasant voice. The room smelt of something. Lavender maybe.

'What were you doing outside? I won't ask again.'

I still didn't answer.

'Break his finger.'

The man behind clamped my right hand to the table, I clawed with my left to try and stop him, but he already had my middle finger in his grip. He folded it back until the joints were touching the hairs on the back of my hand. *Crack.*

Someone slapped me. I must have blacked out. I was tied to the chair now. My hands behind my back, the right one numb and throbbing. It felt like someone was inflating it with a bicycle pump. It might burst any moment.

I looked up. All five were now sitting at the table. The room was still a mystery, nothing but darkness and the white windows of fog, but light and shadow began to form on their faces as my eyes adjusted, pupils dilating.

'I told you I won't ask again,' said the man in the middle.

'I wasn't doing anything,' I told him.

'I wonder how many fingers we will have to break before I get a satisfactory answer. I'm quite prepared to find out.'

His voice had all the technical qualities of a young man, but the accent and the flow of speech was something from another era. Peter Cushing? Alec Guinness? O'Toole? Something along those lines. Class, that was it. The voice had class.

The larger man pulled his chair closer to mine and without getting up reached round my back toward my hands.

'I was only coming here to nick stuff!' I shouted.

The big man stopped, sat back again.

The exertion had pushed more blood into my hand, it throbbed harder and a wave of intense pain washed over me. I tried not to vomit. Instead I stared at the blur opposite. I couldn't see anything but his silhouette, inside it stars and galaxies seemed to wheel around. I was staring into a crack in the universe.

'A burglar,' it said. 'How disappointing. Take it outside and dispose of it.'

The big man stood up and before I could think he was dragging the chair out of the room, and me with it.

'No!' I screamed. *Think, goddammit! Save your life!* 'I know about the taxis!'

'Wait!' the voice commanded.

The big man placed the chair back on its feet. We were by the door. This was a function room, as characterless as they all are. Tonight its function was interrogation and torture.

'Bring him back.'

The big man did just that and plonked me down at the table.

'What do you know?' the voice asked. He pronounced the 'h' in that way that only truly trained speakers do.

Adrenaline was firing. My brain was firing. I could lose my life tonight. And suddenly I heard new sounds and there was more light in the room. Every detail might be important.

I could make out the people a little more clearly. On the left was a black woman in a sharp dark dress, wearing over it a brightly painted chunky wooden necklace. She wore gold Fulani earrings and her hair was clipped short. Her eyes were fierce and she looked as though she would have no qualms about driving one of her stiletto heels through my eye socket. We'll call her the African Queen. I know that name might be a little racist, but it's where my brain went, probably because of the film.

Next to her was the older man, probably in his sixties, that Jilani had picked up from Sussex Square. He was wearing a short sleeve shirt with a pen in the breast pocket, and a tie. He had white hair, a white moustache, kind blue eyes, and a large belly. He looked like Father Christmas without the beard, dressed to attend a regional sales conference.

On the other side of the table was another older man, even older, wearing a midnight blue crushed velvet suit jacket that caught the light, over a white shirt. His tongue would dart out of his mouth from time to time and I was worried it was going to shoot out all the way and hit me like a chameleon.

Next to him and closest to me was the larger man. He wasn't quite so impressive now that I could see him, but I knew what those hands could do. He looked like an ex-footballer, the type that has let themselves go a bit but still gets exercise running up and down the side of their children's games. Not someone I would ever give a second look.

And in the middle of them all sat the voice that smelt of lavender. He was backlit into silhouette and framed by a white panel of fog. My eyes were drunk on the moonlight but all it illuminated were the orbits of bone around his large dark sockets, his exceptionally high cheekbones, and where his cheeks hung off them down to his chin. This simple outline gave the impression of a cattle skull.

'I'm waiting,' he intoned.

I cleared my throat. 'Well, I know that you pay taxi drivers to ferry you to your secret meetings.'

There was a moment's silence whilst he thought about it, like a computer processing my words. 'And how do you know this?'

'I just figured it out. I'm smart like that.'

'Mmm… I do find deception incredibly tiresome. Especially from someone who lacks the proper experience. Something tells me someone needs to pay Mr Jilani a visit tomorrow. And Mrs Jilani.'

Shit. There was only one way to play this: 'It's a shame you can't kidnap their daughter again.'

'So it *was* the Jilanis. Thank you.'

Double shit. So he was cleverer than me, big deal. We all have our strengths, I had to play to my mine. And there's one thing no one can beat me at: being irritating. I had to get under his skin. If he *had* skin.

'I'm not the only one who knows.'

'Really?'

'And it's not all I know.'

'I see. What else do you know?'

'Why should I tell you?'

'Perhaps to prove that you're not lying. Which I know you are. Perhaps to stay alive, if you're still labouring under the impression that you can do so.'

I couldn't answer that.

'I thought so. How tragic.'

'You prey on desperate immigrants, always with families. Is that only as leverage? Or because you know they're more likely to take your money?'

It was his turn not to answer.

'You give them a burner phone, text them the pickup, and then tell them where you want to be taken. Or in your case, you pass them a little printed slip of paper. How am I doing so far?'

There was that little silence again. Processing. Then: 'The only thing that's interesting me is who you are. I believe that you're a burglar, by trade,' he gave a little scoff, 'if one can call it that. Perhaps in your circle. But what is your connection to the Jilanis? One imagines you didn't burgle them. Why would they hire a burglar to find me?'

'No one hired me to find *you*.'

'Of course: the girl. Sadly for the Jilanis, and for you, I can guarantee that you will never find her.'

'You should have given her back. Then we wouldn't be in this situation—'

'I never go back on my word,' he snapped, 'burglar.'

'And just because some guy pinched your wallet? What did you have in there, some receipts you wanted? Donor card?'

'You're being facetious, how amusing.'

'No, someone as shy as you wouldn't carry anything so identifiable.' I thought about the slips of paper, the latex gloves. 'Fingerprints?'

'I don't leave fingerprints.'

'Of course not.'

I thought about it for a few more moments. He kept

his face in shadow, he never spoke to them, he didn't even write the notes by hand, and he wore gloves at all times. Then it came to me, there was one thing he couldn't avoid:

'DNA.'

His cheeks moved ever so slightly. Maybe it was a smile.

'I bet that really frustrates you. Little bits of your skin and hair that can't be trusted to keep schtum. And if the police found that wallet they'd have your DNA on file forever.'

'But they didn't.'

'No, I don't suppose they did,' I sighed. 'When the guy overdosed, why didn't you give her back?'

'I always keep my word.'

He had told Jilani that if he killed the man he'd get his daughter back. He hadn't. That was that.

'Do you know who we are?' he asked.

'No,' I replied honestly.

'We are the Society of the Twelve. Do you know what that is?'

'No.'

'Perhaps you should read a book, once in a while.'

I have read books since that told me the little there is to know about the Society of the Twelve. It was an ancient governing board of Brighthelmstone, to be comprised of eight fishermen and four landsmen who were together "the ancientest, gravest, and wisest inhabitants" according to 1580's *The Book Of All The Auncient Customs heretoforeused amonge the fishermen of the Toune of Brighthelmston*. Their spelling, not mine.

This group of four men and one woman sitting in front of me were members of what I can only assume is a modern equivalent with a keen respect for history. Criminals. Businesspeople. Councillors? Police? I can only guess. But at the time the words meant nothing, so let's get back to it, no one wants another history lesson from me.

'What are we playing?' I asked.

I asked because there was a wooden box on the table with a set of gold hinges set flush into one of the sides. It could be a chess set, but then the board would be on the outside, and the outside was plain wood. That meant it wasn't drafts or Chinese chequers either. Could be backgammon, that would be on the inside; but you can't play backgammon with five people. I figured it had to be cards. Bridge and Canasta are both a maximum of four as far as I was aware, same goes for Hearts.

I looked between them. 'Poker?'

None of them answered.

'Knock-out whist?'

'It is a game of skill and bluff, and above all, subtlety,' the silhouette explained. 'It wouldn't interest you.'

'Worried I'd beat you at it? None of you look like the gambling type.' I looked at the big man, 'you, maybe.'

'And *you* are?' the voice asked.

'When you don't have any money you learn to make it whichever way you can.'

'Fascinating.' His voice was as dry as a martini.

'You think you're good at this game, don't you; I can tell. Want to put it to the test?'

'What on earth could you offer as your stake?'

'The only thing I have: my life.'

Silence greeted me once again. The outline of his cheeks moved in the moonlight. 'But surely that's mine to offer, not yours.'

'Well, we can disagree on that, but let's face it, it's the only thing on the table. Why don't we make it official?'

Silence.

'Does that not sound like fun?' I asked.

'It does rather.'

Father Christmas looked into the darkness and saw something I couldn't, then he reached forward and undid the gold catch on the other side of the box.

'Very well, burglar,' the voice said, 'let's play.'

20

Mother of Mercy

DARKNESS. Complete darkness. And the smell of damp. I was on a hard, cold floor. Something was covering my eyes. I reached to pull it off but my hands wouldn't budge. They were tied to something. I sat up against a stone wall, hit my head, and went spinning. I came back to earth. Then I groped what felt like a copper pipe. And now I wasn't sure if there was something covering my eyes. I couldn't feel anything.

What the hell is going on?

'Can't you figure that out?' a voice replied.

I scoured the darkness, but couldn't see anything. 'Who's there?'

I glanced to my left and almost jumped out of my skin. He was leaning right next to me, in spotlight:

Richard. Fucking. Daye. We were tied to the pipe to-gether.

'Where are we?' he asked.

'How do I know?'

'Where did you go?'

Shit. I remembered. Some of the houses on York Avenue were built with cellars. Those glass tiles on the patio, they were light wells, just like on Tidy Street. Just like half of North Laine.

'Why didn't you tell anyone?'

'There wasn't time. And I had to be sure.'

'Sure enough now?'

'Very funny.'

I considered the ramifications before I said it out loud: 'They kidnapped their own daughter.'

'Yes.'

'Why?'

'You're a detective, detect.'

'I don't know.'

'You can do better than that.'

'Can I?'

'Yes,' said Clarence, as he crouched down in front of me. 'What did I tell you?'

'That everything would become clear tomorrow morning. Right around dawn.'

'And what did that mean?'

'It was your poncey way of saying this was all to do with Firstlights. You're wrong.'

'What did I tell you about Firstlights?' Daye asked.

'They're in debt.'

'And?'

'Their house is tied up in it.'

'Everything they own.'

'And how does a charity get out of debt?'

'Donations.'

'From?' asked Clarence.

'People,' I told him.

'And how do people hear about a charity? What makes them donate?'

I looked at him incredulously. 'Publicity?'

He had a mad smile on his face.

'No,' I told him, 'people don't abduct their own daughters for publicity.'

'It's not publicity,' Daye stated definitively, 'it's money.'

'Publicity,' said Clarence.

'Money,' said Daye.

'You're both wrong.'

There was another voice. It was getting crowded in here.

'Still playing detective?'

'Fuck off, McCready.'

'This is where you belong: down here with the rats.'

'At the church you told me the Tothovas were "very important people". What the hell did that mean?'

'Exactly what it sounded like: that they're better

than you.'

'They're important. Important how?'

'To the city.'

'To you…?' It dawned on me: 'Goldsmid. Of course.'

'What about it?'

'The vote is split.'

'And where the vote is split…'

'…it's the perfect place for a third party to slip through the middle.'

'From your ward: Hove Park.'

'Exactly. And who would make a super-strong candidate?'

I looked at him even more incredulously than the others. 'The local charity-running angel whose daughter was abducted.'

I wheeled between the three them, unsure which to believe. Then I considered the lean, tanned man crouched in the corner, drinking a can of Carling Black Label, with eyes that burned in the darkness.

'What I can't figure out,' I told him, 'is where *you* factor into all this.'

He kept drinking, didn't even look at me. 'Into what?' he replied. 'The universe?'

'Just this part of it.'

'You'll have to figure that one out for yourself.'

'Maybe you were the one who was supposed to find her.'

He smiled to himself. 'Be the heroic big brother?'

'Keep the money in the family. Not that you'd accept it, of course.'

He scoffed. 'Sounds nice. Mummy and Daddy would be so proud.'

'No… I don't suppose anyone would believe that.'

I thought harder. The blue van, the farm in the middle of nowhere. His own cellar.

'You're the one who abducted her, aren't you. Or at least you will be.'

He betrayed a wry little smile, but there was sadness behind it.

'Why would you do it, throw your life away like that?'

'To get my soul back.'

'I wouldn't think you'd believe in a soul.'

There was that smile again, 'I don't.'

'JOE!' a voice screamed.

Thalia!? I searched the darkness but couldn't see her.

'Joe, he's got me. He told you. He *told* you! He would hurt me if you didn't give him the money—'

A hand slapped me across the face. My lips stung.

'Snap out of it, Mr Grabarz. You're losing your mind.'

I looked up into the pale, sweaty face of Hermann Vogeli.

'It's probably the chloroform,' he whistled in his soft

Swiss accent, 'it can make people quite delusional. What a pity.'

'What have you done with her?'

He just laughed. I was the most pitiable thing on the planet. He sauntered away into the darkness.

'No, wait!'

I fumbled across the landscape again.

'Hands and knees, Joseph,' she purred from another corner, 'Hands and knees. All the way from your office to my bedroom.'

'I'm a little busy right now, Monica.'

She reached across the room and slapped me. I went spinning. Round and round. And round. And round like a roulette wheel. Until I came to a halt. I was facing Bill Harker.

'What the hell do *you* want?' I asked.

'Nothing,' he shrugged.

'Well, give me another spin then.'

He did. Round and round. And round and round. I stopped on darkness again.

A cold wind blew.

Waves crashed.

No! No, no…

A banshee screamed. A shape was forming in the distance. A ghost on strings flying toward me like in a haunted house. The old man's face. Beady eyes, reptilian mouth.

'NO!' I screamed.

Then I grabbed the wheel myself and span. Round and round. And round. Still round. Round some more. Then a little bit more. Keep going. Slowing down. *Click, click… clunk.* Sweet silence. Darkness again.

But not quite. Dark sockets. Cheekbones. And the smell of lavender.

'When do you think they had the conversation?' that preening voice mused. '"Darling, I think we should kidnap our daughter. That would solve all our problems, wouldn't it?" "Oh yes, simply marvellous idea." Honestly. Whatever it's for; money, publicity, to be a councillor; it makes a mockery of the whole idea of abducting a girl. And the brother? Have you met a more pitiable snowflake in your entire life? It smacks of amateurism, no wonder a fool like you could stumble onto it. If you're going to do it, do it right, I say.'

I didn't reply. He enjoyed doing the talking.

'They'll have to kill you. You know that, don't you, burglar. It'll take them some time until they realise, they're probably talking about it right now. They can't buy you because they couldn't possibly trust you to keep your word. They can't fool you, you already know too much. They'll have to kill you. And they will, they've already gone this far.' He leant forward. 'It's him who'll do it. She'll make him.'

I couldn't hear him anymore. My face was hot and wet. I looked up into the eyes of a kindly Spanish lady. She was around twenty feet tall, a little plump, stroking my hair with her large, soft hands. I was lying in her lap and I knew that nothing could hurt me here. I was safe in her bosom.

I went to speak, but she put her finger to my mouth. It was time to sleep now. *Time to sleep.* So I curled up in her lap and sucked my thumb.

21

Lies & Death

THERE WERE NO CARDS inside the wooden box. Instead there were six leather cups and thirty dice. Father Christmas placed one cup in front of each of us and counted out five dice each.

'So what is this?' I asked him.

'Liar's Dice.'

'Sound's fun, but I can't pretend to know the rules.'

'At the start of each round we all use our cups to roll our dice, keeping them hidden from each other underneath. You can look at your own dice. The object of the game is to correctly estimate the number of dice out of all thirty that are showing any particular number.'

He reeled it off as though he might have written the instructions that came with it the set.

'One player starts the bidding,' he continued, 'stating how many of a number on the dice, or "face value", of his choice he believes are underneath all the cups. The next player must either increase the face value or increase the number of dice in the bid, in which case he may select a new face value if he wants. The object is not to exceed the total quantity of that face value underneath all the cups.

'If the next player believes that the previous bid is too high he should challenge it, by saying "liar". In this case the players reveal the dice under their cups one by one and the number of dice showing the relevant face value are counted. If the number is less than the amount bid, the player who made the incorrect bid loses a die. If there are the correct number or more, the person who made the incorrect challenge loses a die. The player who loses their die starts the next round, unless they have lost all their dice and are out, in which case the next player starts instead.

'Now, ones, or "Aces", are wild and are counted in every bid. Therefore, if a player wishes to bid Aces alone they must halve the previous bid, rounding up of course.'

'Of course.'

'Similarly, if the player wishes to change the face value of the previous bid back from Aces, they must double the quantity of the previous bid and add one. The game continues until only one player remains. Do you get it?'

'He gets it,' the silhouetted answered, 'let's play.'

'You promise a fair game?' I asked him.

'Of course. Within the rules.'

They each brushed their dice into their cup and placing a hand over the mouth, gave it a shake; the mystery man reaching out from the darkness with latex hands. Then they each slammed their cup upside down on the table, dice trapped underneath.

The vibrations sent a ripple of pain through my hand, both of which were still tied behind my back. I could feel the swell of a tsunami on the horizon.

'Do you mind?' I asked the ex-pro, nodding my head behind me.

'Not at all.'

He reached forward and picked up my cup and dice, shook them, and slammed them on the table. Then he tilted the cup ever so slightly for me to peek underneath. I had one 1, two 2s, a 4, and a 5.

'Thanks.'

'I'll start,' Father Christmas said kindly to me, 'that way you'll have the knack of it by the time it comes round to you. Two 4s,' he announced.

'Seven 4s,' the darkness bid instantly.

The overdressed reptile mused for just a second. 'Seven 5s.'

'Ten 3s,' was the ex-pro's instant bid.

My turn. What were my options? Eleven or more 3s

or 2s; ten or more 4s, 5s, or 6s; or five or more 1s. *One 1, two 2s, a 4, and a 5.* I tried to do the maths: with thirty dice the odds are five of each number, and if 1s are wild, the odds of any bid are ten. So his bid of ten would be stupid to challenge. That said, I didn't have any 3s, so I was looking for ten out of the twenty-five other dice. Except I had a 1, so he only needed nine out of the other twenty-five. Nine 3s and 1s combined. That sounded too easy. I had two 2s and a 1, that made three, so I bid:

'Eleven 2s.'

'Liar,' barked The African Queen, and lifted up her cup for all to see. She had no 2s and no 1s. Nothing for me.

Then Father Christmas lifted his cup. He had two 2s but no 1s. 'Two.'

'Three. Four. Five,' counted out the silhouette.

'Six, seven,' counted the reptile.

I only needed the ex-pro to have one, but he had none.

He lifted my cup to reveal the three I had: 'Ten,' then he threw one of my dice into the middle. 'Good start,' he muttered as he rolled my dice again.

Thanks.

Round two; it was my turn to call now, and I started to discern some of the tactics involved. If I bid fairly high, with six people in the game, it was unlikely to get back round to me. And if I bid a high face value, it became even less likely.

'Eight 6s,' I announced.

'Nine 2s,' bid the African Queen.

'Nine 4s,' offered Father Christmas.

'Nine 5s.'

'Nine 6s.'

It was getting back round to me. The bastards were playing as a team. But wait a minute, this put all the stress on the ex-pro and the African Queen. The ex-pro couldn't challenge the reptile, because one of them would lose a die. He had to bid. And if I bid, she had to challenge me for the same reason.

The ex-pro took a few moments to consider his options.

'Take your time,' I told him, 'I'm not in a hurry.'

'Five Aces.'

'Liar.' There was nothing else I could do. Eleven was too high, and so was six Aces. He lifted my cup, I said, 'None,' and we went round again:

'One,'

'No.'

'Two, three.'

'Four.'

The ex-pro didn't even lift his cup properly, he just threw a die in the middle and re-rolled, slamming his cup back on the table a little too violently.

I let the silence emphasise his mood; this was something I could work with, so I told him: 'Good start.'

He looked at me with dead eyes and rolled and

slammed my dice even more violently. He tilted it up for just a second, then it was his turn to bid:

'Seven 4s.'

'Do you mind?' I asked him.

'What?'

I nodded toward my cup.

'I already did that.'

'I forgot.'

'That's tough then, isn't it.'

'Either you untie at least one of my hands, or you lift it when I tell you.'

'You don't get to give fucking orders, mate.'

'You promised,' I told the silhouette.

'How about I break another finger?' He leant over toward me.

'That's quite enough,' the silhouette commanded. 'Lift his cup. I promised him a fair game.'

And you always keep your word.

The ex-pro lifted my cup with his Neanderthal hand until I nodded for him to stop. It didn't matter what was under there, with his bid of seven 4s he had already bid too high if they were playing the game to get back round to me.

I bid eight 4s.

'Eight 5s.'

'Eight 6s.'

'Nine 2s.'

The ex-pro looked at his dice. Then he pushed his

fat bottom lip up close to his nose.

'Come on,' I moaned, 'at the rate you think, I'll die of old age.'

A vein in the side of his head arrived to watch.

'Just my luck to be caught by the dumbest one of you. If I hadn't given myself away out there I wouldn't even be here.'

'Liar.'

The others all stared at him in shock, although they tried their best to hide it. The reptile glanced at the other four, as if to ask *are we really doing this?* But it was too late. The ex-pro had lifted his cup, and my cup, and counted them out. Out of twenty-eight dice, nine is actually below the odds, but they're only odds and the reptile lost a dice. And he lost it with a pissed off look to his left. Their plan was broken in three moves. Now things could get fun.

And they did get fun, if the word can be used to describe a desperate struggle for your life against a robot, a fictional character, a ghost, a lizard, and an arsehole. Which of course it can't. The reptile didn't want to be the first to go out, and he was angry the responsibility that was supposed to be the ex-pro's was now his. I'm sure that in a regular game he would challenge the cattle skull but there was no way he was going to do it this evening, so he was the first to go out, and was now smoking a cigarette in a flagrant breach of signs. By this point Father Christmas had lost two dice, as had the ex-pro, miraculously I hadn't lost any more than the one, the African Queen was on the same score, and the human shadow was still on five. Nineteen dice. My finger was throbbing again. My finger, my whole hand, even my stomach.

'You lot don't seem like gambling types,' I let them know, 'if you don't mind me saying. Although I guess you normally play for fun. But you don't seem like the types to play for fun either.'

'We're great fun when you're not around,' the ex-pro retorted.

'It's our little tradition,' explained the silhouette.

'Who started it?'

'It's my set,' said Father Christmas.

'Where did you pick it up?'

'Well, actually—'

'That's enough conversation,' the silhouette announced loudly but calmly.

I nodded gently. 'We wouldn't want to have too much fun.'

I had learnt pretty quickly that the sooner, and calmer, you stated your bid, the less likely people were to challenge you. This game was a good metaphor for life: you might be destined to lose, but act confidently enough and people will believe you can win.

So I did just that. Not that it worked on the African Queen, she was a computer; soon I had lost another die. She was playing the game far too mathematically for me to have an edge, so I decided it was time to shake her up. I stared at her for a few moments, whilst she shook her dice to start another round.

'What's a cold, robotic woman like you doing in a place like this?' I asked her.

She didn't respond. It was Father Christmas's turn to bid, which he did, and the play went round until it reached me. I took my time, umming-and-aahing, and making screwed-up faces.

'What do you think I should do?' I asked her.

She didn't even blink. 'Kill yourself.'

'I can see what you mean,' I told the ex-pro, 'you lot must be a right laugh when I'm not around.'

I bid, and the game continued in much the same way it had been going. Soon we were down to fifteen dice, halfway. Me, the African Queen, and Father Christmas all had three. The mystery man still had five, and the ex-pro was down to one; I had just successfully challenged his bid.

'There's no need to feel bad, mate,' I told him, 'it's just beginner's luck.'

'Shut your fucking mouth before I shut it for you.'

'You're a delicate little snowflake, aren't you.'

His hand gripped his leather cup until it was crushed out of shape.

'Here!' Father Christmas wasn't happy, 'those were handmade in Peru.'

'Oh, fuck off, Alan.'

The name landed like a bombshell in the quiet room. The fog still licking the windows.

'Bid,' the silhouette commanded.

'Three 5s,' he mumbled instantly. I wasn't even sure if he had looked at his dice.

'Five 3s,' I bid.

'Five 4s.'

'Five 5s.'

'Five 6s,' bid the silhouette.

That left the ex-pro with two choices as I could see things: six of anything, or three Aces; either of which were above the odds and I would have to challenge. It was just a matter of which he would pick.

'Liar.'

The room shook. The cigarette fell out of the reptile's mouth. Even the African Queen's eyes had widened.

He lifted his cup and counted. Then did the same with mine, taking us up to two 6s. I felt like his accomplice. The African Queen had none, as did Father Christmas. The silhouette needed three. He had two.

Everyone was still frozen, but he was the most gracious of losers. He gently placed one die in the centre of the table and rolled his dice for the next round. The others copied.

They all shook theirs randomly, but he always made five distinct shakes before placing the cup on the table. This time it was only four.

He bid, and it went round until the African Queen challenged me when she shouldn't have, trying to get the game back on course, and that took her down to two. Thirteen dice in the game. We rolled again.

'Two 2s,' she bid.

'Three 5s,' bid Father Christmas.

'Four 5s,' bid the silhouette.

The ex-pro dithered. Checked his dice. I needed to push him further. I let out a tiny, disparaging chuckle.

'Liar,' he mumbled, lifting his cup, and then mine, with no 5s or Aces under each.

The African Queen silently lifted hers, then Father Christmas lifted his, both revealing nothing that helped the silhouette.

Then he revealed his hand: two 5s, and two Aces. 'One, two, three, four.'

I couldn't help but laugh. It snorted out of me with a spray of saliva.

With his big left hand the ex-pro chopped me in the throat. My Adam's apple shot back against my larynx, choking me and stifling my laughter. The force tipped my chair backwards and I landed on my hand. I might have screamed, I can't be sure. I couldn't hear anything over the pain.

The first sound I did hear was the ex-pro: 'Who's laughing now?'

I started to retch.

'Pick him up before he chokes.'

He did as he was told and then I sat there, leant forward, spittle dribbling onto my front. I retched again.

Then he kicked his chair back and pulled out a cigarette.

'Where are you going?' the silhouette asked.

'For a walk.'

'He needs someone to roll for him.'

'Someone else can do it.'

'Sit. Down.'

He stood staring into the darkness for a moment, huffed, and then pulled his chair back in. He shook my dice far more calmly than he had before, and the others did the same.

Over the next rounds the African Queen lost all three of her dice challenging me, Father Christmas lost all but one of his, I managed to claim one from the silhouette, but he managed to peel one off me as well. That left him with three, me with two, and Father Christmas with one. Six dice.

With six dice it was pretty obvious what the odds were. It was also pretty obvious that they were in the silhouette's favour; he had half the dice. When the game started I had worked out that I needed a pretty even mix of skill and luck, neither of which I had. By this point, it would be a waste of skill anyway.

We all shook our dice. By which I mean the ex-pro shook mine. I watched the silhouette shake his. *Shake, shake, shake*, down.

In the first round Father Christmas challenged me and challenged me correctly; the next round he challenged me, and challenged me incorrectly. He was out. Four dice. Three of them were his. One of them was mine. We shook. I had a four. It was his turn to bid:

'Two 3s.'

Now, I could hope that one of them was an Ace and bid two 4s, but then he could bid one Ace. Or I could bid one Ace myself.

'Liar.' I wasn't even sure why I said it, but I had, so I revealed my four.

He revealed an Ace, a 5, and a 6. The African Queen, Father Christmas, and the reptile had stopped breathing. Bored, the reptile's cigarette smoked itself; he didn't notice it charring the velvet of his jacket.

We rolled again. *Shake, shake*, table. The ex-pro tilted my cup for me to see. It was his turn to bid again:

'One 5.'

I didn't have a choice: 'Two 5s.'

He paused for the first time. I thought it was a bad idea; any longer and the others would suffocate.

'Liar.'

He revealed a 5 and a 2. The ex-pro lifted my cup with desperate excitement. They all gasped at the die underneath, staring between me and the silhouette. Then he placed another die in the centre of the table.

We rolled for the last time. *Shake*, slam. And the ex-pro tilted my cup: one Ace. *Thank you, God!* Once again, it was his turn to bid:

'One 6.'

I could bid two 6s, but I knew for sure I couldn't trust him to have a 6. And if he did, he could bid one Ace next, and he would be right. No, it was obvious what I should do: 'One Ace.'

He paused again. All air had been sucked out of the room. All sound, all heat. We were a table in a vacuum.

'Two Aces.'

I couldn't believe it. It wasn't possible. But of course it was. I didn't even speak, I just moved my head at the ex-pro and he revealed my Ace. And with a swift flourish the silhouette revealed another. *Buggering, fucking, shit-sticks.* What were the odds?

'Take him outside.'

'Wait—'

Something hard hit me in the head. A shock of electric pain seared through me and everything span.

22

Get Me out of Here

I HAD MY THUMB in my mouth. No idea why. I think I was awake, but everything was dark, so how the hell was I supposed to know? After a while I could see a soft patch of light on the ground. Something was coming through those glass things on the patio. It had been Wednesday, one week since the disappearance. Then I had been chloroformed, then I had woken up in darkness, then slept again, and now there was light. I guessed that made it Thursday.

'Fuck,' I whispered to myself.

'Hello?' a voice replied from the darkness.

Shit. I'm hearing things again. 'Who's there this time?'

'My name's Joy.' It was a little girl's voice. A scared

little girl. My brain snapped to attention.

'Hello there, Joy. My name's Joe. Pleased to meet you.'

'Who are you?' Her voice was quivering.

'It's all right. I've been looking for you.'

'Did my parents send you?'

'No, no,' I reassured her.

'I want my mum.'

Oh god, I thought. *She doesn't know.* 'Don't worry, Joy, everything is going to be all right. I need to know if you're ok. Are you ok?'

'No, my shoulders hurt.'

'Your shoulders?'

'I can't move them.'

'Are you tied to something?'

'Yes, my hands are, they only untie me when they want me to eat or wash.'

'Who are *they*, Joy?'

'They're keeping me here. They bring food and clothes. I tried to run once but they grabbed me.'

I asked my questions gently. 'What do they look like?'

'They wear masks, and torches on their heads.'

'Do they speak at all?'

'No.'

'Other than keeping you down here, have they treated you ok?'

'I guess.'

'They've not hurt you or anything?'

'My shoulders hurt.'

I nodded to myself, listening for sounds of footsteps above. There weren't any. There were no sounds at all until my stomach gurgled.

'Pardon me.'

'Who are you?'

'Just Joe,' I replied.

'Why are you looking for me?'

'Everybody's looking for you.'

'But why you?'

'I'm a detective, do you know what that is?'

'Yes, you work for the police.'

'Not quite. I work for myself.'

'Who pays you?'

'People pay me. They pay me to find out things. Like where you are.'

'Then you work for them.'

'I guess you could put it that way.'

'My dad says you work for whoever pays you.'

'Your dad sounds very shrewd.'

She rustled slightly in the darkness. 'Did my parents pay you to find me?'

'Not yet.'

'I'll pay you.'

I smiled into the darkness. 'How much?'

'Mum and Dad give me one pound every week. I save most of them. I have fifty pounds.'

She was sweet. 'I guess that means I work for you.'

'Get me out of here.'

I nodded, not that she could see it.

She rustled again. 'Are you tied to something?'

'I'm tied to a pipe.' It felt to me like a cable tie on each hand. 'What about you?'

'A loop of metal, it's bolted to the wall.'

'What are you tied with?'

'It feels like plastic. It hurts if I turn my hands to feel it.'

'It's ok, leave it alone.'

I shuffled along the wall, trying to find where the pipe was fastened. I could hear her sniffling, sometimes a whimper.

'Talk to me, Joy, tell me what happened. How did you end up down here?'

Her voice was thick with tears. 'I just woke up down here.'

'When was that?'

'Eight days ago.'

'How do you know that?'

'The light.'

'You sound like a very clever girl.'

'I read books to myself now.'

'Really? That's very smart.'

'Mum used to read them to me, but now I read them to myself.' She sniffled a big wet sniff.

'Take me through a typical day down here; what

happens?'

'They wake me up with breakfast.'

'Sounds nice. Is it the same each day, or different?'

'Same: porridge.'

'It's very good for you, porridge.'

'Mum's always trying to get me to eat it, but I don't like it without mānuka.'

Mānuka. I smiled in disbelief, 'Then what?'

'They bring me some clean clothes and they untie me so I can change. Sometimes they wash me with a sponge. Later they bring me some bread and some kind of fruit. Normally a couple of pieces. A bit later they bring me some kind of stew or casserole thing, I don't really like it, I don't always eat all of it. Then one of them brushes my hair.'

'Every night?'

'Yeah. Just like Mum used to do when I was a baby. She would sing me…' the rest of the sentence was drowned in tears.

I tried to take things in a different direction. 'You said you read books. What's your favourite?'

'Pippi Longstocking. I've read all of them.'

'Wow, all of them?'

'Yeah.'

'Pippi's very brave, isn't she?'

'She's the bravest.'

'That's right. And she's really strong.'

'She can lift her horse.'

'Yes she can. Do you think you can be brave and strong?'

'I can't lift a horse.'

'I know, don't worry. In fact, tell you what, you be brave and I'll be strong, how does that sound?'

'Pippi wouldn't be tied up, she's too strong. She would just rip her hands from the wall.'

'I'm working on it.'

I kept fumbling. It was difficult to shift along the floor with my hands tied so low. The ties were starting to cut into my wrists.

'Am I dreaming?'

'No, Joy, I promise I'm really here.'

'I keep dreaming they've come to hurt me. Sometimes I think I've woken up, but I don't know if I've woken up or not because it's dark. Will they rape me?'

I stopped fumbling for the pipe. All I could hear was my heart. 'Do you know what that is?'

'Yes.'

My stomach chewed on itself. 'You're too young to know what that is.'

'My mum told me. She says I have to know, so I can stay safe. There are people who rape kids.'

I didn't say anything. I couldn't even think of the first word of the right sentence.

'Joe, are you there?'

'I'm here.'

'Did I say something wrong?'

'No, Joy. Not at all.' I took a long, damp breath. 'I used to have bad dreams too.'

'What about?'

'A girl, very much like you.'

'Why?'

'I let her down.'

'Do you still dream about her?'

'Not very often.'

'How come?'

'I did something worse. Now I dream about that.'

'I didn't do anything bad.'

'Absolutely.' I took another deep breath, purging and replacing all air in my body. 'Joy, I need to tell you something. And it's important, whatever happens, that you remember this. Remember this more than anything else. Do you understand?'

She didn't answer.

'No one else gets to define you. No matter what they did. It doesn't matter who they are. Only you get to define you. Only you.'

There was only silence.

'Joy?'

I could hear her sniffling. I slid along the wall until I could slide no further, I had found where the pipe was fastened to the wall. I gripped both hands round the copper, bent both legs up until my feet were flat to the wall. With every muscle fibre I pulled at the pipe and pushed at the wall. I screamed at the top of my voice, plastic cutting into my hands, now warm and wet; metal creaked, or maybe it was me, and I shot across the room like a cannonball, face-first into the dirt.

My hands were still intact, but I could taste blood on my wrists as I gnawed at the linked cable ties. Icy water was running into my shoes, the ruptured pipe spraying in the darkness.

'Joe!?'

'It's ok. I'm free.'

'How?'

'I ripped the pipe from the wall.'

'Just like Pippi would!'

'Keep talking,' I told her.

She was speaking but I couldn't make out the words over the water. Wrists now free, I felt my way toward the sounds until I came across her tiny frame.

'Joe?'

'Hello.'

I felt for her wrists, they were definitely cable tied to some kind of fixing. It was a flat metal plate with a loop, and it wasn't going to come out easily, I could feel four bolts into stone walls.

'I'm going to have to bite through the plastic, sorry if I dribble on you.'

'That's ok.'

I managed to get enough of a tie between my molars, then finally she was free.

'It's really wet!' she shouted. There was now about

an inch of water filling the basement.

'Let's get out of here,' I told her, and tried the metal door.

It was locked. I gave it a thump, but it was too well fitted and didn't even rattle. I gave it a drop kick, but it was no better and just got me wet. I had to jump to scrape the wooden board ceiling. It made a bit of a noise, not much. I did it again. No one came running. I stood on the pipe to feel around the glass tiles, but they were concreted in.

'Ok, ok, they'll have to come down at some point. We'll wait by the door.' I took her arm and moved her into the corner, the side with the hinges. I waited against the wall the other side.

'When the door opens, you stay hidden until I tell you to come out, ok?'

'Ok.'

The sound of the burst pipe had changed, no longer spraying onto dirt but splashing onto the surface of a pool.

'Joe?'

'I'm here. It's all right.'

'I lied about the fifty pounds.'

I smiled. 'Don't worry, you can owe me.'

After what seemed like ten minutes, it could have been longer, still no one had come down, and the water was now above my ankles. This was mildly distressing.

I put my hands in my jacket and was surprised to feel

something cold the size of a matchbox. It was my lighter, of course, I must have put it there after smoking that bitter cigarette. I prayed I hadn't got it wet. I tried it and it burst mercifully to life.

'Joe?'

I knelt down to her level and held the flame between us. Somewhere underneath all the dirt and grime was the sweet little girl I had seen in all the photographs. She was cute. She was cuteness personified.

'Nice to put a face to a voice.'

She smiled.

'We need to get them down here to unlock the door.'

She nodded.

I reached into my trousers, and with a yank, ripped out the thin lining of my pocket.

'Hold this, but only touch it with one hand.'

She did. Then I killed the flame, slid the lighter out of its metal case, opened the bottom, and dribbled what little was left of the fluid onto the cloth.

'Now I'm going to put you on my shoulders. Whatever you do, don't drop that cloth.'

I knelt down, she climbed on, and I stood up, wobbling toward the middle of the space.

'Wedge it as tightly as you can between the beams. Make sure it doesn't fall out.'

I could feel her fidgeting, but I couldn't see what she was doing. 'Joy?'

'Done.'

'Sure?'

'Yeah.'

'Ok, now take the lighter with the other hand, here it is…'

Her tiny fingers plucked it from my grasp. 'Got it.'

'Can you feel the rough bit on the top, feels a bit like a nail file.'

'Yeah.'

'Now, making sure you don't touch it with the other hand, put your thumb on that rough bit and push down and bring your thumb back as though you were rolling it towards you.'

'I know how it works.'

'Ok, good. Watch out, there might still be enough fuel in it to light.'

I heard the little *snick*-crackle of the flint. Then her voice: 'There's just sparks.'

'Keep them away from your other hand.'

'I know.'

'We need one of those sparks to hit the cloth, ok?'

'Ok.'

Snick. Nothing. *Snick-snick*. Again nothing.

'It's not working.'

'It'll work, just keep trying.'

Snick… snick-snick… snick… snick-snick…. snick-snick-snick, whoosh!

An orange glow reflected off the water: it had caught.

23

A Great Place to Die

THEY UNTIED ME from the chair to drag me outside, but my hands were still cable-tied behind my back. A few metres from the clubhouse they threw me down onto the damp grass, sending another wave of pain up my arms and through the rest of me. The silhouette was stood a few metres away, not quite imperceptible. I rolled onto my side, nose in the dirt, hot breath condensing back into my face. From this angle I could make out one strange, absurd fact: he was wearing slippers. Baby blue silk slippers.

From somewhere he produced a trench knife, the type with a knuckleduster, and handed it to the ex-pro. I scrambled to my feet, but he socked me hard in the liver with the brass. I crumpled.

'When you're finished he needs to fit inside your holdall,' he was informed.

'How am I going to do that?'

'Break his back and fold him over,' the reptile answered; the others hanging around like groupies.

'HELP!' I screamed.

I heard a little snigger from above me.

'HEEAAALP!'

'Shut up.' The ex-pro punched the knife through my side, into my lung.

It was less painful than you would think, but the sensation was more distressing than you can imagine.

The blade slid out of me. I tried to scream again, but I couldn't tell if I was making any sound. I was a side of beef.

'I'm not sure I'm comfortable with this,' Father Christmas piped up.

'Go inside,' the silhouette told him.

'Yeah, fuck off, Alan,' jeered the ex-pro.

'He's just a kid,' he pleaded.

'Be quiet.'

'Come on!' he begged, 'M—'

With a sudden jerk the silhouette jabbed him in the throat. He choked and spluttered.

'Don't *ever* say that name outside the group.'

'But M—'

He backslapped him this time and the old man fell to the floor. Then, with an elegant slippered foot, he pushed on his chubby neck. Father Christmas began to flail, squeaking and gurgling.

'You had to open your *fuckin'* mouth!' he crowed, his voice crude, shocking, nothing like the prim, clipped tones of before.

The old man's hands were clawing at the grass, pulling up clumps, his legs writhing, wriggling.

The others watched with cold shock. This was my only chance. Without a free arm I pushed up onto my knees, then unsteadily onto my legs, and still bent over, barrelled forwards into the mist.

From behind me came a muffled shout, but soon everything was wind and wet.

I ran and I ran until my heart felt like it was going to burst. My lungs were on fire. It could only have been a hundred metres, then my next step seemed to miss the ground and I landed with my face in sand. A bunker. I spat out a mouthful of it. Rustling footsteps passed not too far away. My head swam. Some light, from torches maybe, danced off the mist.

I shuffled on my knees and then I was up, and ran and ran again. I collapsed every few metres, pushing back up, going again. My legs were made of matchsticks. I threw my eyes in every direction, looking for people, something, anything, no idea where I was heading, or where I should be heading. The silver air was damp, thick, and impenetrable; the only clues I had were in the ground. It rose gradually under my feat, so

I was heading north, across the holes, away from the allotments; if I made it all the way over the hill I would end up back down into Coldean. But that was a long way. Too far.

I collapsed to my knees yet again, tried to catch my breath. I couldn't hear a sound. No footsteps. No shouting. The ground was too wet and the air too thick to carry a thing. I couldn't even hear my own heart. To my left there was a darker wisp of fog which became a figure jogging, searching, frantic, but not moving toward me. I could feel my heart again. I ran in the opposite direction, looking behind me, making sure the figure faded into the grey.

But it didn't, the figure was getting clearer and gaining on me. I ran faster, still looking behind. Beneath my feet the ground got steeper, then stonier, then I fell into a ditch. I landed on my lungs. They hurt. A lot. Footsteps scrabbled on the stone, stopped, started again, and passed.

I rolled onto my back, staring up at the mist, and at the stars that could just be made out so long as you weren't looking straight at them. What the hell was this ditch doing here? This couldn't be part of the golf course. It couldn't be a stream bed either because I was at the highest point in the city.

Don't argue with me. Some of you will argue the highest point is Ditchling Beacon; it is the highest point in East Sussex, but not in the city. Or you might say Devil's Dyke, which is technically correct, but honestly, are you going to argue that Devil's Dyke is *in* Brighton? The council might say so, but no humans. And don't tell me things changed in 2016; the top of Hollingbury Hill is still sixteen metres higher than the top of the i360.

I rolled onto my knees and shuffled along the ground until I reached a chalk path. Now I knew where I was: Hollingbury Camp. Or Hollingbury Castle Camp. Or Hollingbury Hillfort. Whatever, it's a sixth century BC fort.

I stumbled my way along one of the myriad paths, cutting through a maze of gorse. Finally, I came to rest on the trig point. It was as good a place as any to catch my breath. Just a quick rest. *I'll get up in a moment.*

The trig point is nothing but a concrete post, but it's one of the focal points of the universe. Or so it seemed. Trig points are just used to make Ordinance Survey maps, this one from 1947. But it was a geometric importance this place, an ancient place. This was the spindle used to turn the wheel of time. I felt a magnetic connection to the spot. People had trod these paths two and a half thousand years ago. They had looked around and seen only nature. And over time their descendants had moved further out, and started to build towns, and then the city, and then twenty-two years ago I had been born in it.

The mist was slightly thinner at this altitude, so I

could see about twenty metres in each direction. But anything beyond the fort didn't exist. I had slipped through a crack in the universe, back in time.

Leaning my head back, I looked up at the stars through a thin silver veil, the light that reached me from them was even older than the fort. I was slipping even further back in time, toward the birth of the universe.

My thoughts were rambling, uncompleted. The lung that had been burning was now ice cold. *This could be it*. There are still barrows here, I thought, burial mounds that is. It was the start of all civilisation, and now it was going to be the end of my life. I couldn't think of a better place to die.

I heard a panting to my left, like a dog. A flame-orange fox was sitting just two metres away. He had probably come to investigate who was messing up his home. There were probably babies curled up in the gorse. He closed his mouth, gazing out over the fog, listening for threats, before he looked at me. I stared into his amber eyes, he stared into mine. At least I wouldn't die alone.

Suddenly his face twitched, and his gaze shot over my shoulder. I followed it. To my right, a pair of fireflies were soaring in tandem through the fog. I watched their gentle arc. *Wait a minute*. They weren't fireflies. They were lights. But not torches. Headlights. Fog lights. *A road*. Ditchling Road. There was a chance I wouldn't die tonight. I looked back to thank the fox, but he had gone.

I pushed up against the trig point, my hands no longer hurting, but shaking. Shock. *Don't faint.* There was nothing for it but to run, and hope I could flag someone down.

I made a careful glance around me, I couldn't see torches, or shapes, or anything for that matter. The headlights had gone, I had lost the exact direction of the road now. But I knew it ran from south to north, I just had to head west. *Fuck it, let's go.*

I went for it. I ran down off the fort, almost falling over when I reached the ditch, but my momentum shot me up onto the path and I seemed to still be on my feet. I ran and I ran and I ran; I kept pounding the earth, convinced that everyone within a mile must be able to feel it. A treadmill of wet grass, bumps, and bunkers appeared as an obstacle course for me to tackle without toppling.

Then out of the mist a figure. A large figure. The ex-pro. In a split second his eyes filled with glee and a smile danced across his lips. He was wet with mist and sweat and his eyes had yellowed. He spread out his hands like a goalkeeper, or a rugby player ready to trap me. Maybe I should have stopped, maybe I should have changed direction, but I was going too fast, so I just ploughed straight into him. We both went down, him on his back and me rolling a few feet.

'You CUNT!' he screamed.

I was back on my feet and running and only God knows what he was doing but I could hear his footsteps.

'BASTARD! Come on then!'

My whole body was on fire, the little men inside me shovelling everything into the furnaces. I might explode.

The sound of his calls were getting quieter: 'He's here! HERE! HEEEEAAAARE!'

Another pair of lights swished ahead, nearer this time, I had to be really close.

At last, a steep slope. Thick grass. Bollards with reflectors, tarmac beneath my feet. A pair of bright lights came round a curve, blinding me. I would have raised my hands to stop them if I could. The light absorbed me. I didn't try to move, I just closed my eyes and prayed it wouldn't hurt too much.

24

Hero

THE WATER HAD reached our knees. The smoke had
filled the ceiling. We crouched in the narrow foot of air
between. Joy was where the open door would hide her.
I had broken off a piece of copper pipe to use as a club.
We were ready. We had been ready for twenty minutes.

I looked up through the haze at the blue puddle of
flame that had spread across the ceiling. They should
have come down by now. A horrifying thought flared
across my mind: *what if they're not in?*

'Joe…?' Her voice was feeble.

There was a splash. I ran and fished her from the
water. It was the smoke; I coughed, noticing how much
of the stuff I was breathing. It burned my lungs. Pushing wet hair out of her face I held my ear to her mouth.

She was still breathing. Just.

The water was spraying. Wood crackling. Plaster crashed onto the floor above. I could only imagine the scene. *This could be it.*

At last the creaking and cracking became a clattering, and footsteps rattled over the floorboards. I couldn't put Joy down, the water was too deep, so I transferred her to my left arm, like a baby, and held the pipe ready in my right.

The feet thundered down the steps and a key fumbled in the lock. A bolt was withdrawn. Then another key came out and another lock clicked. A padlock was thrown to the ground, and finally another bolt was drawn back.

The light of the opening door blinded me. The heat burnt. I swang the pipe with everything I had. It connected with something, and there was a large splash like a sandbag hitting the water. I pushed forward into the heat, only managing to squint for a few seconds before my eyes streamed.

Everything was a blur. A raging orange blur. I came up from the cellar to find the frame of the main stairs disintegrated. The cupboard was just a shell. The wall between the hall and the living room was collapsed and the floorboards charred.

There was a rumble like thunder and a shaking like an earthquake and then I watched the floor of the living room collapse into the cellar, followed by the wall between the living room and kitchen, crashing down into the watery abyss. The three photographs on the mantelpiece had blistered white until they melted black into their frames. The shelf of Joy's trophies clattered into the void.

I only had to make it to the door. The boards were black and creaked under my weight but I made it and wrenched it open to the bright world beyond.

As I transferred Joy back to a more secure grip and carried her down the front path, I couldn't see a thing. I wasn't conscious of the noise. Not the crumbling house. Not the scream of sirens, nor the shouts of the press. Just the fresh summer air.

It was all over. The fire brigade had arrived seconds after we emerged, the building now just a wet wooden shell. Men in uniforms and helmets paraded carefully around the outside, two others in full safety gear with bungee cord attached were tiptoeing through the carnage.

A paramedic had seen to my cuts and burns, and now I was sitting alone in the back of an ambulance, waiting whilst they tried to clear the street. They had connected me up to a saline drip for rehydration. I wanted the back doors open, the air smelt of cut grass, but they had shut them to keep out photographers.

Just as I was thinking about it, one of them creaked open. A warm smile poked its way in.

'Hey, dude.'

It was Andy Watson. I smiled back, I couldn't help myself.

'How are you doing?' He climbed in and sat next to my stretcher.

'You'd better close the door,' I told him.

'Nah, it's fine, they're all with Parker and Price at the moment.'

I nodded, but it disorientated me. I concentrated on the shaft of sunlight that was now streaming in, and the tops of trees I could glimpse.

'What coaxed you out of your basement?' I asked.

'They needed someone willing to speak to you.'

'Willing? Here I was thinking I'd solved the case.'

'Yeah, well… not the way they'd like.' His smile disappeared. 'Mr Tothova's body is down there. Was that you?'

'Am I under caution?'

'No, Joe. This is just me.'

'I take it I won't be getting a medal then.'

'Not from us, at least. At least, not yet. Everyone else? I think they'll treat you pretty fair.'

I looked through the doors toward police cars, Price was answering questions from reporters and looking quite flustered.

'She'll hang me if she gets enough rope.'

'She's too smart. Everybody just saw you carry the girl out of a burning building. Get a good headline tomorrow and they'll snuggle up as close to you as they can. It'll be a great triumph of police cooperation. If it turns out you did something you shouldn't have, they'll drop you twice as fast. You've been here before.'

His body language shifted, he turned to face me instead of the door.

'I need to tell you something else, before you find out some other way: Thalia was attacked last night.'

Vogeli. I seethed.

'She's ok, a few bruises. She pepper-sprayed the guy.'

An uncontrolled chuckle escaped from me.

'We brought him in on a routine assault charge, turns out there's a European Arrest Warrant out for him. You two do like to give us a headache.'

A desperate voice from outside cut through the air: 'Where's my daughter, where is she!?'

Both our heads snapped to attention. Then the ambulance doors were flung open by a wild-eyed and manic looking Maria Tothova.

Her eyes locked on mine, her lips pulled tight over her teeth. She hissed like a cat, and fearing that she might try and scratch my eyes out Andy quickly grabbed her arm and jumped down onto the tarmac. I could hear other footsteps rushing over to her. Then the sounds of a press gaggle.

Andy offered a raised eyebrow as he shut the door, leaving me alone. I could still hear though.

'Mrs Tothova!? Mrs Tothova!? Why did you fake the kidnapping?'

'People, please,' Watson begged. 'Please!'

'What my husband has done,' she started, 'is unimaginable.'

What my husband has done.

The ambulance purred to life, smothering the voices.

I laid my head back on the stretcher, and was soon rocked to sleep as the ambulance trundled its way down the clogged avenue.

Friday's headline was "JOY TO THE WORLD", stamped over a full page photo of me carrying her out of the burning house. The headshot of me from the barbecue was inset with the caption "HERO: Joe Grabarz". I did look mighty heroic, if I say so myself.

The paper was as sketchy as ever about how I had come to find her there. The article focused on the brief statements Price had made, the fact that Mr Tothova's body had been found at the scene, and the suspicions surrounding Mrs Tothova. Her lawyer had already spoken to Hacker. She was protesting innocence, saying that her husband was behind it all and she knew nothing about it. Once they spoke to Joy I was sure she would change her story. She would be an accomplice, but bullied into it by her oppressive husband. It might even work. She would have a great lawyer, I was sure. Until they find out she was bankrupt.

In a small item on page fourteen they reported a man found dead at his farm near Ditchling. He had hanged himself. They hadn't connected the dots.

I was enjoying the newspaper in my little office, with my feet on the desk, the sounds of the Lanes drifting in through the open windows, the heat still oppressive. Thalia was taking a few days off and I didn't have any clients booked. I had the place to myself. I had even locked the street door just in case. It was one week since I had heard of Joy Tothova. A hell of a week.

No one ever spoke to me about the van chase. The two children from the bungalow had completely recovered. Chris hadn't, he was dead before I regained consciousness. Still not a single officer had mentioned it to me. Not a soul. A man had died and I had been written out of it. Either that, or they really hadn't seen me. But how could that be? I decided not to wonder too much.

Mr Tothova had dumped my Honda somewhere. No one knew where. No one much cared either. I felt I should be able to sue someone for the cost of it, not that it was worth much in money. I was upset, but things go, things change. *C'est la vie.*

My phone had been found in the wreckage, ruined.

This morning I had been out and bought myself the cheapest one I could. It was smart. I was told they were all smart now. I was waiting for my provider to transfer my number to the Nano SIM I had just inserted. I remembered I had to call Clarence and gloat about our bet.

The new phone buzzed angrily with a text message: *"I'll tell you what…"*

That was it. And I didn't have any contacts yet. When I went to open the message to try and work out who it was it vibrated again:

"…be at mine in 15 minutes and I'll forgive you."

That made it pretty obvious. I went in and looked at the message. It was sent Wednesday night. I wondered if she read the papers. It buzzed a final time:

"That was your last chance. You won't be seeing me again."

That was that. She was too proud to go back on her word a second time, even if I had been chloroformed and trapped in a cellar. And to my great surprise, I was relieved.

I thought about Thalia and Vogeli, Monica, and the chase, and how everything had worked itself out in my twenty-four hours underground. Maybe I didn't keep the world spinning after all.

I got up and wandered through to the outer office, I was the only madman in this heatwave who had lit a fire. It was only a tiny fireplace, left from when this was someone's cottage. I hadn't fired it up since the winter, now it was throwing all sorts of unwelcome heat.

I looked at the heavy square envelope in my hand, weighing it for a moment. The fire crackled. Pockets of steam hissed as they escaped from the wood fibres. Outside, tourists scuttled through the alleyways, screaming and shouting and commenting on how beautiful and expensive everything was. The sound of buses drifted from North Street. Pigeons fluttered in the rafters, seagulls scurried on the roof. The smell of coffee and restaurants wafted in. And I stood frozen amongst it all, staring into my private hell.

I placed the envelope on the top log. The brown paper crinkled and crisped in seconds, spilling photographs and documents into the grate. In a few more seconds they were thin wafers of charcoal that danced in the air and crumbled into soot.

No one gets to define me.

Someone was banging on the street door.

'Hello?' they called. They kept hammering, I was worried they were going to chip the paint. 'Hello!?'

I headed out onto the landing, down to the door, and opened it. Standing there was a forty-something woman with hair all in her face. She pulled it apart, revealing bloodshot eyes. She sniffed some mucus down her throat.

'Are you the guy who found the little girl?' she asked through tears.

I studied her. She was wearing an uninteresting top and a pair of tight jeans. A leather handbag was hanging off her arm as though it didn't want to be there. She looked harmless.

I told her I was.

'I really need your help.'

I was supposed to be taking the day off, but she looked so desperate. And I always need work.

She followed me up the stairs and just as I led her into the reception area the phone rang.

'Take a seat in my office,' I told her.

She disappeared through my door and I picked up the receiver.

'Hello,' I answered matter-of-factly.

'Hello!?' came a startled, pompous, and frankly angry man's voice.

'Hello,' I said again, slightly more acidly.

'Is that Joe Grabarz?' he bellowed.

'This is Joe Grabarz.'

'Are you the man who found Joy Tothova?'

'Yes, I am.'

There was a pause, then a clearing of his throat. 'You're just the type of man I need.'

When I finally got back to my flat it was getting dark. It was cool at last. I leant on the living room window, looking out over the lights.

Brighton. The world's circus. Run away and join us. Gay or straight, black or white, everybody here is running away from something. Or running toward something. Some ideal. The city is a shining beacon to the desperate and the misunderstood.

It's nice that they think so. They never see what those born here see. But it's my job to maintain the illusion, in the hope that one day it might be true.

I moved to the bedroom window, looked over the flat rooves. A few lights were on. More were off. There was no baby seagull. He couldn't wait for parents any longer. His wings might not have been long enough, but it didn't matter. He had flown.

LAST CHAPTER

Nothing Is Solved

I WOKE IN a bright, white room. A sliver of vision was all I had, and everything beyond my fingers was a blur. I could move the fingers but not the arm. I didn't feel good. I felt like a bin bag full of broken crockery. Unable to move or talk, I lay there in desperate fear for what seemed like days. Every blurry figure entering the room was one of them coming to finish me, every injection swapped with poison, every dimming of the lights my death. But it never came.

'I told you so.'

'Told me what, exactly?'

'Too many things to list.'

We were on the pavement of a narrow road that cuts

between hospital towers. Me in a wheelchair, still not smoking, Daye leaning on a bollard, smoking his eightieth of the day. He had the cigarette in one hand and the cup from a flask of tea in the other. A few metres away a man and a woman were disinfecting the inside of an ambulance. There wasn't a green thing in sight, just tarmac and exhaust. Nothing about this place felt healthy.

In one of the supreme ironies of life, the vehicle that had hit me in the fog that night was an ambulance. It broke half the bones in my body, but the paramedics knew what to do. They didn't know my name, and I didn't have any ID on me, so I was admitted anonymously. Not that the Society knew my name either, they never thought they'd need to know. All of these things saved my life.

'The one you referred to as Father Christmas matches the description of Alan Douglas.'

The sound of someone drilling echoed off the concrete cliffs.

'Neighbours haven't seen him in two weeks. According to his bank statements he went to Australia to visit his grandchildren.'

'Who was he?'

'He was a bookmaker once, the type that would have your legs broken if you didn't pay up. Last ten years he was a book-cooker.'

'And the rest?'

'The ones you saw, nothing definite; but I've got some ideas.'

'And?'

'I've given them to my sergeant to work up.'

'Great,' I drawled.

'He's a good lad, you'd like him.'

'No thanks.' I took a deep, painful breath. 'And the one I didn't see?'

'You're asking me if I can identify a person you didn't see, by your description of his voice and a pair of slippers?'

I didn't answer that. 'What about the Jilanis?'

'They packed up, went back to Pakistan.'

'Anyone see them go?'

He blew out a thin stream of smoke. The air was so polluted it was hard to spot. 'No.' He threw the cigarette away.

I rubbed my ribs. One of the fractures had left a lump just below my left nipple. 'So what do I do now? When do I make a statement?'

'You don't.'

He stood up and threw the cold tea from his cup onto the ground, then screwed it back onto the top of the flask, burying it inside his coat, ready to leave.

'According to the file, the man who ran off the golf course that night never regained consciousness. He died a week ago.'

I couldn't understand him. He didn't seem the type

to lie in a casefile. Especially for me; this man who had tried to send me to prison six weeks ago.

He read my mind: 'Let's call it an administrative error. If I believe everything you've told me, which I do, then it might be a good idea for them to forget about you. As for what you do next, I'll leave that up to you. But you have a knack for trouble.'

I gave a mirthless laugh. 'Believe me, I'm never doing this again.'

I was out of hospital in a couple more weeks. With the Jilanis gone there was no point in speaking to Theresa. I went to Debra's to get my things out of the caravan but the caravan was gone. I couldn't bear ringing the doorbell so I just left. And like that I was back to the world. Back to the world of trying not to steal shit. Back to the world of trying to find a job, and trying to find somewhere to live. Using my newfound people skills I managed to get a job in The Reel and Razor, a film-themed cocktail bar. We did a lot of Vesper Martinis and White Russians. I even managed to rent a room above the place. Both the drinks and the rent were too cheap and I have no idea how they kept the place up. It isn't there anymore.

It had been around two months when I found myself in Gentjan Hajdari's favourite deli. I can't remember why I was in there. Maybe I recognised it and wandered in. Maybe I went there deliberately. Whilst I was tucking into a pretty excellent plate of falafel, pitta, humus, salad, and stuffed peppers the owner asked what made me try the place. I lied, said I was a friend of Hajdari's.

'Gentjan? Not seen him in weeks, how is he? Not been sick?'

'He's fine,' I mumbled.

'Really,' he frowned, 'just sick of us, I suppose.'

That was it, he went back to serving. *Not seen him in weeks?*

I found myself riding over to his bungalow in Coldean. The people living in it knew nothing about him, they had bought the house from a young man with a spider tattoo on his hand.

It had possessed me now. The only way to break free was to see it through. Then I would be done, then I would be finished. Against my wishes I had to speak to Sergeant Watson. I told him about Hajdari.

'Dude,' he said, 'I know.'

We were standing in a tiny basement, not too unlike Daye's office, also deep in the bowels of the station. It was dark, a couple of computer screens the only source of light. I'm pretty sure he did that so people wouldn't think he was in. So he could get away with working.

'You know what?' I asked.

'I know he was one of the drivers, and I know he's disappeared.'

'How exactly?'

'You told Daye that's how you ended up at the golf course, he told me, I looked into it.'

I frowned. It made sense. 'And?'

'And, what?'

'And what did you find?'

'Nothing, he's gone back to Albania. They didn't leave anything behind.'

He knew as well as I did that Hajdari hadn't gone back to Albania, but he didn't know I knew as well as he did.

'What about the phone data?' I asked.

SOCO had found Jilani's phone where I left it, and managed to pull the number from the burnt SIM. Daye had filed a warrant to get the data from the phone company. For every SMS this included the sender, time received, message contents, and the mobile mast the phone was connected to.

I already knew the phone did nothing but receive messages, and from one number at a time, which would change on the fourth of every month. They needed the data from these "sender" phones. They filed for it, and thanks to new anti-terrorism laws they got it.

'We can see from the data,' Watson explained, 'that they started with four drivers, growing to nine.'

Nine. I thought about nine desperate immigrants, nine families. And what might have happened to them now. Andy could tell what I was thinking and let me think it without saying anything.

Then he frowned, weighing something up, scratching his beard. Finally, he gave in to whatever it was: 'Take a look at this,' he said.

He flicked on the strip lights, revealing a large map that covered the wall from floor to ceiling. Looking closer, it had been stitched together from several OS maps, and covered from Shoreham on the bottom left to Peacehaven on the bottom right, and from Steyning on the top left to Lewes on the top right. Ditchling was at the centre top and Brighton at the centre bottom. The entire thing was marked with red and green pins.

'The red pins are the mobile masts,' he explained, 'to have signal a mobile phone has to be in communication with a mast. When an SMS is sent the phone sends it to the mast, it travels across the network, and is sent from another mast to the receiver. This mast data is all logged. It gives us a general idea of the location as the phone should connect to the nearest mast, depending on provider and network traffic.'

'And the green?'

'The pickups.'

There were hundreds of pins across central Brighton and Hove. Less in the suburbs. The odd one beyond the city limits. It was a thorough job. Far more thorough than I had ever been.

'We know they didn't send for their own pickups, because they only had one sender phone at a time, so the mast data is pretty useless. But where there is a cluster of green pins, like here,' he pointed to West Street, 'we know they frequented regularly.'

I looked at these clusters. There was one around Brighton Town Hall, Hove Town Hall, and other council buildings. Kings Road, The Chandler Club, and other places frequented by the rich and powerful. Hove Crown Court, and most strikingly the area containing Brighton County Court, the magistrates court, and the building we were standing in: John Street Police Station. The only cluster outside the city was in Lewes. It could be the Crown Court, but I took a wild guess it was Sussex Police Headquarters.

We exchanged a look that said too much. He had the same questions I did, there was no point voicing them.

'I've created a database on the computer, all the messages, dates, and numbers. So if you want to search by a specific driver, you can track every pickup they made and when. I can look up Hajdari if you want.'

'What if you wanted to search by dates?'

'Easy, what dates do you want?' He sat down in a swivel chair and rolled over to the computers.

'The day Mahnoor Jilani disappeared, to the day you saw your first corpse.'

I could feel his eyes boring into me. I was too busy looking at the map.

'Sure thing.' He started typing.

I was drawn to a solitary pair of pins. The only two in the top left of the map, north of Shoreham. One red, one green. The red pin, the mast, was in Steyning. The green one was a mile and a half south east, in the middle of nowhere, just outside a tiny village, nothing but four houses and a farm, called Botolphs. The green pin was in the OS symbol of a cross with a square base: church with a tower.

One red, one green.

'The red pins, are these all the masts?' I asked.

'Just the ones the sender connected to.' He was pre-occupied with his database.

'So this one in Steyning, for example, how many times was that connected to?'

'That's a one-off.'

A one-off. One message sent, one pickup requested. Was it enough to assume the sender himself wanted a pickup?

Watson read out the messages from the days in question: 'Edward Street/White Street, Ship Street/Prince Albert Street, Montpelier Place/Norfolk Terrace, Queen's Park Rise/Down Terrace, St James Street/Lavender Street, Osbourne Road/Lowther Road, Dyke Road/The Droveway, Orchard Road/Orchard Gardens, Rutland Road/Coleridge Street, Grand Avenue/Kingsway, Marine Parade/Royal Crescent, St Botolphs, Eastern Road/Upper Abbey Road, Kemp Town Place/Rock Grove. That's the lot. Any help?'

'No. Not at all.' I turned back to him and smiled. 'It was just a stab in the dark.'

I couldn't ride my moped on the bypass without feeling like a twat, it couldn't do more than about thirty-three, so I headed down Old Shoreham Road, all the way through Hove, Portslade, Southwick, over the Holmbush roundabout, onto Upper Shoreham Road, through Shoreham until I hit the Adur. I didn't fancy pushing it across the old wooden toll bridge, so I joined the Steyning Road and headed north, out of Shoreham, hoping to find another route across the river.

I rode under the swooping overhead spiral of the by-pass junction and onto the country road, then past the bus cemetery on the left and the abandoned cement works on the right, a set back row of houses, and then nothing but fields and pull-ins and the odd empty house. I was too far north already, but there was no-where to cross the river.

I kept going for another mile, came to a roundabout where I took the first on the left, and on this road finally crossed the river. Another mile, another roundabout. I took the first again, heading west along a single-track lane rowed with rotting trees that became rotting farms. And then a sharp left again, another small lane, closed in by steep banks of dead leaves, now finally heading south, on the right side of the Adur.

Every hundred metres or so a field or a farm would open up on one side. Then the "village" of Annington. Grain silos. A posh house with a tennis court. Fields. At last I rode through Botolphs, four houses and a farm was about right, until the "village" ended and there was nothing but fields on both sides, until a flint wall on my left, and behind it a graveyard, and beyond that a flint church appeared from behind a tree.

I pulled up by the wall, breathed in the country air. The road was empty. One side of the church there was a nice house, on the other a crap house, and nothing else but fields. From somewhere sheep baaed. The afternoon was ending a dim, windy, grey day. The shadows of clouds rolled down the hills into the valley. I pulled my jacket around me as I wandered ten metres from the road down a dirt path that skirted the graveyard toward a square flint tower, no more than three metres wide, and barely taller than a house. Behind that, the main church building was also flint, smaller than a barn, rectangular, and with a humble pitched roof. Part of the building dates from 950. A simple little church for simple little people living in simple times.

The door was unlocked. The inside was as modest as the outside. One space with a tiled floor, wooden pews, plastered stone walls, a meek altar, timbered roof, and a guest book that no one had signed. There was nothing here but the mournful air of forgotten history.

I stepped out and beyond the tree line, looking out down toward the murky river. Poking above another line of bare trees I could just see the chimney of the old cement works on the other side. It dominates the landscape, once a huge operation, it's quarry having carved an irreplaceable wound out of the chalk hill. The place is abandoned now. Between the church and the factory this entire valley is a graveyard.

I felt a scratching in my brain. A tingle. A tingle I would learn to trust. Possessed, I marched down the slope of the valley toward the Adur. As if upon request a footbridge appeared in front of me, part of the South Downs Way. If I had known it was there, I would have ridden my moped across it.

I crossed over to the Steyning Road, opposite that strange row of terraced houses in the middle of nowhere. I can only guess they were built for the cement workers. I crossed the road and drifted further until the titanic edifice was looming over me. The site might date from 1883, but the factory that is still standing was built after the war. It is nothing but concrete, steel, and broken glass now, still a gargantuan complex. A colossal monument to an industry that ripped up the land, the very Downs themselves, to forge the future.

It was dark now. I steeled myself and stepped into the shadows and the darkness within, swallowed by the skeleton of the beast.

Sparks crackled from my lighter. I knew the truth was here somewhere, in the darkness. Hidden amongst the broken windows, and the dirt, and the rats.

I crunched my way through the place, stepping over jagged steel, ducking through collapsed frames, up and down stairs, rusty bolts screaming in agony.

The feeble orange glow of the lighter gave me a dancing bubble of light, revealing straight steel, curved steel, bolts, glass, the word "DANGER" painted in black; details without context, until I was lost in darkness. But I was not alone.

In the middle of the void was a steel trapdoor. The chill wind played a tune across it. I tried to wrench it open but it wouldn't move.

Fumbling in the swaying light I could see a padlock. I grabbed one of the iron bars that were rusting away on the floor, making sure not to let iron splinters through my gloves, and swung as hard as I could. It pinged off without resistance and flew away into the darkness as though it wanted to give up its secrets. To be absolved of its sins. It was just an innocent padlock, it hadn't asked to be part of this.

It took everything I had left to lift the rusted door. The little flame flickered in the air that escaped. Or was it the breeze? Cold night rain was dripping through the obliterated roof, plummeting seven storeys down. All I could see in the flickering glow was bricks, and steel steps leading down into the crypt. My hand was shaking, but I convinced myself it was only the cold, and stepped down into the darkness.

I won't describe what the corpse of an eight-year-old girl looks like, left underground to die, except for the fact that the nail of her right index finger was worn down to a stump, clotted with blood, where she had scratched a word into the wall. Just one word:

JOE GRABARZ WILL RETURN

ABOUT THE AUTHOR

Tom Trott lives in Brighton, with his wife, and his wife's parents. He works in a Sixth Form College, and saves money by re-using shopping bags as bin liners. He sometimes uses leftover candle wax to make new candles. He likes gin. He rarely enjoys writing, but frequently enjoys having written. He reads less books than he should, eats more crisps than is healthy, and has been known to talk too much.

If you enjoyed this book, please tell anyone you can any way you can. And if you have actually read this page, please tweet me with the words #DeepSpaceNineIsEasilyTheBestTrek.

To purchase copies of this book and others, or to learn more, visit tomtrott.com

For news and updates, follow @tomtrottbooks on Facebook and @tjtrott on Twitter.